I SAW BRIGHT R
SETTING FIRE T THE DRY GRASS . . .

and then, for a brief moment, the creature that had caused all these horrors showed in the somber light of the rapidly spreading fire: a monstrous dragon prowling over the grassy plain like a chain of hills come to life. It was such an incredible sight that I stood there as if frozen—staring at the smoke that welled up from the flames—before realizing that the wind was driving the fire toward me. Then, at last, my legs obeyed me again, and I ran blindly for my life. . . .

THE BROKEN GODDESS

HANS BEMMANN has been a newspaper editor and lecturer and taught at Bonn University for twelve years. He published his first novels under a pseudonym. His bestselling *The Stone and the Flute* was the first novel published under his own name, followed by *Erwin's Bathroom* and *Star of the Brothers*.

THE
BROKEN
GODDESS

Hans Bemmann

Translated from the German by
ANTHEA BELL

A ROC BOOK

ROC
Published by the Penguin Group
Penguin Books USA Inc., 375 Hudson Street,
New York, New York 10014, U.S.A.
Penguin Books Ltd, 27 Wrights Lane, London W8 5TZ, England
Penguin Books Australia Ltd, Ringwood, Victoria, Australia
Penguin Books Canada Ltd, 10 Alcorn Avenue,
Toronto, Ontario, Canada M4V 3B2
Penguin Books (N.Z.) Ltd, 182–190 Wairau Road,
Auckland 10, New Zealand

Penguin Books Ltd, Registered Offices:
Harmondsworth, Middlesex, England

Published by Roc, an imprint of Dutton Signet, a division of
Penguin Books USA Inc. Previously published in Great Britain by
Penguin Books Ltd and in the United States in a Roc trade paperback
edition.

First Roc Mass Market Printing, December, 1995
10 9 8 7 6 5 4 3 2 1

PART
ONE

A T THE TIME, when the statue, caught suddenly in the beam of the headlights, practically leaped out at me from the dark bushes behind it, at the time I thought I knew what it meant. Of course, I was still possessed of what now strikes me as staggering self-confidence, the self-confidence that so irritated you at first and that I lost only during my quest for you, with all its metamorphoses and the many wrong paths I took.

I had taken a taxi at the station, giving the driver the name of the castle where the conference was being held. I would be addressing the authorities on folklore assembled there the next morning, setting out my theories on the contemporary relevance of those traditional texts of nebulous origin, often despised or misunderstood in periods claiming a climate of increased enlightenment, but now back in fashion again. I was so sure of myself at the time, so amazingly sure, that I blush to think of it today. Well, you know my occasional tendency to resort to cut-and-dried logical order as a refuge. I'd prepared my lecture carefully; a lot can depend on it when an ambitious young academic presents his views to a circle of recognized experts for the first time, as I was only too well aware. So I had a well-polished lecture in my briefcase,

I had copious quotations to back up my theories and I never dreamed for a moment that anything, let alone anyone, could throw me off course.

Feeling quite ridiculously pleased with myself, I sat back in the taxi, looked at the well-restored old houses of the town, which I'd never visited before, and appreciated the good job the architects had made of fitting shop windows, now brightly lit in the gathering dusk, into the newly cleaned façades with their stepped Renaissance gables. A sixteenth-century frieze of grotesques surrounded the shining double-glazed windows, plump *amoretti* tumbling through vine leaves. Was the frieze genuine? More likely a clever copy, or perhaps an existing remnant had been extended in the spirit of the original, for the old windows must have been much narrower. Still, I felt both appreciation and something like an affinity between the work of those creative restorers and my own ideas, which aimed to examine the fairy tales coming down to this century from the cultural primeval soup of archaic societies and make them relevant to the spirit of today.

My taxi had left the center of the old town now. We turned right off the main road, passed through a baroque gateway carved as if with surging stone waves, and drove into a large park. The headlights swept over bushes, catching tall groups of trees in their beam as they swung past, briefly illuminated the shining surface of a pond and, as the driver turned sharp left, that snow-white marble torso leaped into my field of vision, literally stepping into my path. My heart missed a beat.

"Stop!" I cried.

The driver stamped on the brake so hard that the car almost skidded. It came to halt at the side of the drive, quite close to the statue. The body was a woman's; you could still make that much out. The curve of her breasts was almost intact, her hips were rounded and the remains of a folded veil were held in front of her private parts by a hand whose gesture of concealment seemed final, for the arm it belonged to, like the other arm and the legs, had been hacked off. The shoulders ended in stumps merely hinting at their former grace, and where there should have been a face above them looking at me, I saw only the battered surface of a head tipped slightly to the left. I took all this in at a glance, staring for God knows how long, moved by the beauty of the body, which could still be guessed at, and horrified by its brutal mutilation.

The taxi driver was so startled that he sat there for a moment without moving, in silence. Then he turned around to me. "Something wrong?"

I shook my head, unable to take my eyes off the nocturnal apparition.

"Ah, I get it," he said, relieved. "You like that old classical stuff. Or is it just statues you fancy? Not in great shape, is she? But she's still got what a girl needs. Those museum people dug her up right here. She's meant to be a goddess of love or some such. Want to get out and take a closer look?"

No, I didn't want to get out, and, besides, I was beginning to feel foolish. How had I got into a situation that let this cabby speculate on my private desires? What did the thing amount to, anyway? Just a poorly preserved statue of Venus—indeed, a broken and badly damaged one—a fairly unremarkable piece of provincial Roman sculpture. It probably came from some local workshop of the third century A.D. Eventually I turned my eyes away from it, assumed an expression of indifference and said, "Drive on, will you?"

So that was the prologue to my arrival. I never mentioned it to you, either then or later—at first, I suppose, because my part in the little episode may have struck me as rather ridiculous, and later because of other, more deep-seated inhibitions that I didn't guess at then.

When it was all over, the whole story I'm about to try writing down here, you asked me how it began for us. Thinking that question over, I realized one thing: it all began with the statue. Not just the weathered stone, parts of it defaced beyond recognition, but all it once represented. Or put it like this: the image it still represents for me, though in a way that makes it harder and harder for me to grasp the full significance of that image.

Here you'll probably laugh and say, "But it's perfectly simple!" Well, you know how dense I can be faced with such things.

When did we actually see each other for the first time? I don't mean just the first casual glance—I mean when did we consciously become aware of each other? I can't give your side of the story, but I first really noticed you at supper with everyone else, and the first thing to attract my attention was one of those eloquent gestures you use to emphasize many of your remarks. It struck me as rather Mediterranean, and now that I was paying proper attention to you, I was almost surprised to hear you speak German, though I couldn't make out exactly what you said. The table where you and a couple of your colleagues were sitting was too far away. At one point you looked across at me—do you remember?—and I tried but failed to hold the glance of your dark eyes.

Soon afterward you pushed back your chair and rose to leave the room. You would be bound to walk straight past the table where I was sitting. I saw you come toward me—the vision of the broken marble statue briefly superimposed itself on the outline of your figure—and then you were gone. Only a scent lingered briefly in the air, a scent with which I'm very familiar now. I no longer have the faintest idea who was sharing my own table at the time or what we were discussing.

I may well have said nothing at all during the meal. I realize that I'm inclined to withdraw into my shell at such conferences until it's time for me to deliver my paper. That may be because once I get into conversation I always feel impelled to give away some of my ideas in advance, so that later, when I'm addressing my entire audience and I reach the point concerned, my performance loses a certain amount of conviction. I can't help feeling I've said it all once already. When that happens, I at least glance apologetically at the person I was talking to before, since I'm bound to be boring him by repeating myself. Or perhaps I'm proposing a theory he thinks he's already refuted during our conversation, but I can't leave it out now without endangering the whole logical structure of my lecture.

In fact, if you stop to think about it, that shows I'm afraid of losing my confidence if I even listen to arguments that might shake my own position. Ridiculous, isn't it? What kind of confidence is so easily demolished? Wouldn't it be better to abandon the whole deceptive make-believe from the start? If I didn't show I thought that all my ideas were gospel truth, then no one would be able to prove me wrong. But I'm getting a bit ahead of myself with all these "ifs" and "woulds," forgetting that I'm looking back at a time when I entertained no such notions.

After supper I went through one of the tall doors of the hall, which opened like French windows, and out into the darkness of the park to smoke a pipe. I kept away from the other conference members standing in small groups on the forecourt, which was lit by the chandeliers inside the hall. They were making the kind of small talk usual on the first evening. I went on out into the dark, guided by the faint pallor of the gravel on the path. Its crunch under my feet soon mingled with the croaking of frogs, luring me on until I reached a pond with waterlilies floating in the milky mist above its surface. By the light of the rising moon I could make out a small island in the middle of this oval pond. Ducks slept on the island, their feathers glimmering among the stones on its bank. Now and then their soft quacking could be heard along with the croaking of the frogs.

The path went all round this pond, so after I had stopped several times to look unsuccessfully for frogs I came back to my point of departure. I could still see a few of the conference members coming and going outside the lighted windows of the hall, but you weren't among them. Eventually I knocked out my pipe, went up to my room and went to bed.

I lay awake for some time, going through my paper in my

head to reassure myself yet again that my train of thought held water. I couldn't pick any holes in it, though I felt there was something bothering me. I tried and failed to work out what it was, and then at last I fell asleep. Sometime toward morning—it was still dark outside—I woke abruptly, with a dream so clearly before my mind's eye that I can still describe it in detail.

I'm looking for something very specific, something that matters to me enormously, and I am going about it in a manner with which I'm thoroughly familiar: I need the aid of a small animal for this purpose, a mouse perhaps, or maybe a frog. But anyway I'm certain that the creature would react to my tobacco pipe.

So I drop my pipe on the ground. At this point I realize I'm out of doors. It's cool and the sky is cloudy. It has obviously been raining recently; there are shallow puddles on the trodden earth of the path.

My pipe falls into one of these puddles. Water splashes up. I immediately hear a shrill squeak and see some small creature jump up. I look in the puddle for a wet mouse, but I see a very small, light-brown frog sitting in the bowl of my pipe. More frogs, even smaller, are swimming about in the puddle. Some of them still have tadpole tails between their hind legs.

When I bend down and hold out the palm of my hand, the frog jumps into it. It is cool and damp and feels very active. I tuck it carefully into my right-hand jacket pocket and I set off on my quest.

With this thought in my mind I woke up, but I had no idea what the object of the quest was supposed to be, or what use a small brown frog could be in my search for I didn't know what.

There's something about frogs. Frogs are figments of the subconscious mind. A mouse, now, would have been perfectly clear and straightforward. Mice are greedy, so where would a mouse lead you? To a piece of cheese or bacon, of course, the only point at issue being whether the cheese and bacon are on a plate or hanging on a hook that might move and close a trap. But in any case the alternatives are clear.

A frog, though . . . of course I remembered my walk that evening, the walk that took me round the pond where the frogs were croaking. We all know about dreams as the continuation of previous impressions. But such an explanation, plausible as it might be, did not satisfy me; it couldn't dispel my sense of being on shaky ground. I could still feel the frogs jumping round my ankles in the shallow water only too clearly; I could still feel tiny digits moving on the skin of my hand. You can guess what else occurred to me on the subject: the frog as symbol of fertility and sexuality—yes, that or something like it did hop through my dreams. I won't go into it any further just now. There'll be plenty of chances for me to return to the baffling activities of those slippery creatures, frogs.

I don't remember anything about breakfast, which is surprising for someone who believes in eating a good meal in the morning, as I do; indeed, I hardly feel able to get started without one. So it's very likely that I did have something for breakfast—my instinct for self-preservation seldom lets me down—but I don't remember whether it was tea or coffee, toast and marmalade or cold sausage, any more than I remember the company in which I presumably ate it.

The next thing I remember clearly is the moment when I stepped up on the platform, took my manuscript out and laid it on the desk in front of me. "Ladies and gentlemen, fellow students of the folktale and the fairy tale!" I began. Only then did I look at the top sheet. Greatly to my alarm, it was wholly illegible. I must have stared at the strange yet somehow familiar handwriting for quite some time before realizing that it was simply upside down.

A ridiculous mistake, of course, and easily remedied. I hastily put it right at once. But from then on I was obsessed by a notion that the upside-down letters were a sign that all they were supposed to say had gone wrong too, in some way I couldn't understand. As I forced the words out, I couldn't rid myself of the feeling that I was talking total nonsense. I clung to those words like a drowning man and, to begin with, I kept my eyes glued to my sheets of paper, which were handwritten as usual.

When I'm giving a paper of this sort, however, I always fix on some member of the audience, usually a woman, during the first few minutes, and go on as if I were addressing her personally, glancing at her at frequent intervals to see how she reacts to what I'm saying. My choice is generally an emotional one, made on the grounds of some spontaneous sense of sympathy, perhaps a look betraying close attention or intent interest, or a smile in response to some ironic aside of mine that encourages me to continue. In fact, that's probably why I do it: I want approval of my opinions and encouragement to keep going along the same lines. Maybe I combine a talent for entertainment with academic ambitions.

However that may be, I gradually fell into my usual lecturing routine, and by the time I reached the passage where I was going to put forward my own ideas on the motif of the animal bridegroom in the folktale, I was back in charge of myself sufficiently to decide that I would now raise my head and look around for someone to address directly. You may remember that I put this decision into practice at the point where I was suggesting that sexual partners who appear as frogs, lions, bears or terrible monsters of a less specific nature are shamanistic survivals of older ways of thinking that we, with our more sophisticated consciousness, abandoned long ago. It was just as I uttered these words that I looked up and into your eyes.

I don't know if it was simply chance or if my subconscious had already located your position in the room and made me look your way. But after that, in any case, I couldn't have looked around for another person to address, and I was thrown right off balance by the way you raised your eyebrows, together with the smile hovering so delightfully around your lips and suggesting doubt rather than anything else. I began stammering, and as soon as I'd pulled myself together to some extent I tried injecting retrospective ironic undertones into what I'd just said, an enterprise naturally doomed to failure. From then on my lecture veered off the course I'd so carefully set for it whenever I glanced at you, and it proved quite impossible for me *not* to glance at you. I'm afraid that by the time I finished none of my audience, and least of all I myself, could have said just what view of the relevance of the animal bridegroom motif to contemporary society I had meant to uphold.

It's difficult for me to describe the feelings that had me so confused at the time. I suppose the very first thing that attracted me to you so spontaneously was your physical beauty. But who can say whether the statue I'd just encountered still had such a hold over my imagination that I transferred the excitement it had aroused in me to you, or whether, conversely, the magic of your animated presence, your Mediterranean gestures, the figure I could guess at as you came toward me, the fragrance of your skin conjured up the image of the goddess of love, lurking in my mind and ready to spring? However, what do such questions of cause and effect have to do with a process where a figure of myth seems to merge with its incarnation in an individual?

Yet I now suspect there was already more than mere sexual attraction at work. The eloquent gestures of your hands that first attracted me surely conveyed something more than, and different from, the straightforward signals put out by a sexually active female and picked up by my own male hormones.

Or so I tell myself today, but at the time my mind was inundated and my brain blocked by their response to those signals, so I was more than annoyed, I was positively angry that you obviously disagreed with my ideas, even if you hadn't said so yet. I felt that way solely because your disagreement ran counter to my physical reactions and put an obstacle between us, one that might make it hard for us to come to an understanding—what kind of understanding, though?

The discussion that followed my paper led to such acrimonious argument about what I really meant between the supporters of the literary, historical and philological approach to fairy tales on one side, and the committed exponents of the social approach or sociology pure and simple on the other, all of them coming up with rival and increasingly farfetched interpretations of my theories, that no one seemed anxious to know what *I* thought, and I was able to retire from the fray. You didn't take any part in the argument yourself; you just glanced at me now and then in some surprise when I accepted some particularly wild version of my remarks silently and without protest.

Then, unexpectedly, we were seated side by side at lunch. It can hardly have been coincidence, although that's what it seemed at first. I was probably following my nose like a dog in heat. Or did you have something to do with it? Were you playing a game with me while I was intent on playing my own game with you?

I haven't even asked yet what *you* were thinking and feeling about all this. At the time my own emotions and fantasies had me in such a state that I never spared the question a thought.

You talked to the man sitting on your left first. He was a young man with a neatly trimmed black beard and rimless glasses; his name was Mikoleit, as far as I remember. I was beginning to fear he was attached to you in some way, but during the soup course I was able to work out, from some casual remarks you let drop, and much to my relief, that you and he couldn't have met before this conference. But I still felt something like jealousy. When Mikoleit or whatever his name is was busy for a moment opening a bottle of beer, I seized my chance and asked you straight out what you thought of my lecture. I said I thought I'd noticed you looking as if you disagreed or even disapproved, adding hopefully, "I may have been wrong, though?"

I waited eagerly for a "yes," but you shook your head, put your spoon down and looked thoughtfully at me for a while. Then you said, "Do you think fairy tales are really true?"

True, you said. I was baffled. That wasn't a word I or any of the participants in the discussion had used. The talk had all been of mythological characters, coded archetypal experiences, symbolic figures, narrative as interpretation. But *true?*

"Isn't that rather too naïve a question?" I said, realizing even as I spoke that I was admitting I could make nothing of such absolutes.

Your smile was entirely unabashed as you replied that since the word "naïve" literally means native or inborn and thus natural, you were perfectly happy with it.

"Then you think my lecture and the discussion afterwards were just hot air?" I asked, more aggressively than I really meant to. But you took no offense.

"I thought it was all very illuminating," you replied. "But I doubt if it got to the heart of the matter."

"So what do *you* think the heart of the matter is?"

"Life."

By now, if not before, I had a very strong sense that you weren't playing according to the usual rules in force at such seminars. How can I explain it? Did you and your friends ever play cowboys and Indians as children? It's possible—or is the metaphor too far from your female experience? Let me try it, anyway. Imagine you and a few other children are crouching quietly among the red currant bushes in the orchard, expecting a mock attack by your friends, and a horde of genuine Iroquois pours over the fence instead, yelling and waving tomahawks and out for your blood.

I felt much like that. Something I'd regarded as a genuine academic controversy was obviously just a game to you, and now you were trying to find out how seriously I took the actual subject—did it affect my life itself? I felt exposed before your brown eyes, which were still looking at me intently and with just a trace of irony. But at the same time that look, and the movement of your lips as they said, "Life," made me desire those lips and eyes.

I don't know if you realized that I was now on the verge of moving from arid theory to real life, or what I thought was real life at the time, but anyway, you ended our conversation by rising to leave the table. "Have I been pestering you?" you asked, as you left. "Well, I'm sorry. I'm going for a walk now."

Next moment I saw you go past outside the windows and disappear among the old trees in the park. But by now I was on my feet, ready to follow you. I was bold enough to take your last remark as a hint that I could find you out there in the grounds.

As I walked rapidly over the crunching gravel toward the shady entrance to the depths of the park I put my right hand into my jacket pocket, a habit of mine, and I felt something cool and damp moving there.

So there I stood on the path, still hearing the voices of people who had come out on the forecourt after lunch only a few dozen paces behind me, and I stared at the small brown frog crouching in the palm of my right hand, its lustrous golden eyes inspecting me with a somewhat superior expression. It may sound crazy to speak of such a tiny creature giving an impression that it felt superior, but that's how it struck me. Then the frog spoke, with a bit of a croak but articulating perfectly clearly. "If you're going to stand here much longer you'll lose the scent," it said.

"Which way should I go, then?" I asked. It was broad daylight, the sun was high in the blue sky, where a few clouds sailed, and, believe it or not, I was talking to a frog.

"Follow your nose," it said, "and meanwhile you can put me back in your pocket."

I did that. Then I set off, following my nose. At first I took these instructions to mean I was to keep walking straight ahead into the shade of the old trees that grew in the park. But there really was a faint scent to be detected, luring me on, a fragrance that was already beginning to seem familiar and that I pursued unhesitatingly, indeed eagerly, as I followed my nose.

I don't know how long I'd been walking like this before I realized I couldn't be on the same path as the evening before. There was no gravel underfoot now; instead, I was walking on damp, soft soil with roots running through it. I must have left the park without noticing, for dense woodland with a powerful smell of fungi stood to right and left of the winding path, which allowed me to see only a few paces ahead. Enormously tall beeches, straight as columns, grew profusely here, and there was luxuriant undergrowth between their silver-green trunks, with honeysuckle rambling through it, hanging down from the slenderer trunks like loose rigging.

I had no idea just where I was. I knew it would be sensible to turn and go back to the well-ordered world of the park and the conference, but I couldn't even slow down. Indeed, I was hurrying on even faster than before, perhaps because I thought I could still catch that scent in the air or perhaps because I was in the grip of an almost obsessive curiosity, a desire to find out what might be waiting for me in or beyond the wood.

After a while the ground ahead of me began to fall away and the path wound downhill, the trodden track becoming harder and harder to make out under the densely matted plants. Flowerheads of ground elder rose from smooth, dark-green foliage, and my feet brushed through wild balsam, its pods springing open at the touch of my trouser legs and sending the dark seeds hopping around me like tiny frogs. The undergrowth was lower here and there were alders among it. Around yet another bend in the path I suddenly saw a lake ahead. Its far bank was bordered by blue hills on the distant horizon.

I stood there for a while, looking out over the wide expanse of water, its surface glittering in the light of the sun, which was dipping lower in the sky. A few wild ducks flew up from the bushes ahead of me, beating their wings. Necks outstretched, they flew toward an island in the middle of the lake, quite a long way from the bank. It rose gently from the water. I could see meadows, bushes and the tiled red roofs of a village. There was a grass-grown hill in the middle of the island, with reddish rocks on it here and there, and the hill was crowned by a round towerlike structure, broad rather than tall, like the Castel Sant'Angelo in Rome.

As the faintly fishy smell of fresh water rose to me I felt a desire to dip my hands in the lake, and I ran the rest of the way down the grassy slope to the bank. Over to my right, behind a group of willows, stood a cottage with a trodden earth path leading to a landing stage. A broad rowboat with a pair of oars in it was moored to a stake there.

I walked slowly along the sandy bank toward the landing stage, so close to the water that the choppy little waves sometimes lapped over the toes of my shoes. At one point I stopped and dug a dark shell out of the damp sand, its inside coated with shimmering bluish mother-of-pearl. I remembered finding such a shell once before, when I was a child, on the banks of a river that flowed slowly through open countryside. I hoarded it among my secret treasures for a long time, until it broke one day and was thrown away. I walked on with my find in my hand, sat down on the landing stage and watched the play of colors passing over the silky smooth hollow of the shell every time I moved it.

"No pearl in it?" asked a voice behind me—a curiously hoarse voice.

I turned and saw a short, rather thin-legged man dressed in dull green wool right behind me, looking at me with protuberant, yellowish eyes. I hadn't heard him coming. His broad face, beardless and rather flat-nosed, looked friendly and good-tempered; he didn't seem to be laughing at me.

"No," I said. "Do they ever have pearls inside?"

"Depends on the way you look for them," he said. "You want to be taken across?" And he jerked his head in the direction of the village on the island.

So he was a ferryman. I hadn't thought of it before, but once he suggested the idea it seemed almost inevitable that I would let the man row me over, particularly as I thought that I could just catch a faint trace of the fragrance that had lured me as far as this on the landing stage.

"Have you rowed anyone else across today?" I asked. "A girl, maybe? A young woman?"

"Chasing a girl, eh?" The ferryman grinned. "I might have known it! Jump in, and I'll take you over."

I didn't care for the way this total stranger made it so clear that he took the point of my question. Among the people I usually mix with you may be able to work out from what someone says more than he actually wanted to give away, but it isn't done to show it. There are certain rules whereby, for instance, you ensure that the person whose strategy you've seen through doesn't lose face, even if you've then had to carry on the conversation in such a way as to foil him. I had some skill in those little games, which often determine the course of academic debate, so I wasn't best pleased to have this rustic character deny me the chance of using it.

One way or another, all this should have deterred me from getting into the boat that rocked lazily on the gently moving water, but one foot was already on the damp boards between the seats before I had time to think that far, and then I felt even less inclined to withdraw it and listen to further comments on my intentions. So I brought my other foot into the boat to join it, and sat down on the seat in the prow while the ferryman untied the painter, pushed the boat off from the landing stage and moved nimbly past me in the swaying craft to fit the oars into the rowlocks. Then he sat down too and started to row, digging the oars deep into the water.

As I climbed in, I had put the shell in my pocket, and I noticed that the little brown frog must have slipped out. I thought perhaps the smell of the water had attracted it as it attracted me, or else it felt that now it had put me on the right track it had done enough.

Dangling my hand over the side and trailing my fingers through the cool water, I looked at the island we were slowly approaching and wondered what kind of track I intended to follow when I got there. My memory refused to provide a visual image of you. All I could dredge up was a vague recollection of the sway of your hips as you walked rapidly away and disappeared from view among the trees in the park.

And yet I was sure that I would find whatever I had come for on the island. I never doubted for a moment that it was *your* track I was on, and it never occurred to me to wonder why you had left the conference and gone for such a long walk. Indeed, at this point the conference itself had entirely vanished from my mind. I was interested only in the woman I had seen walking through the trees of the park, going this way. What did she want in the village? Who was she looking for there? Or had she climbed the hill to the tower?

"What's that tower?" I asked the ferryman, pointing to the island. However, he didn't even turn his head; he just went on staring back at his cottage over my shoulder, and he grunted, "We don't go there."

For some time we rowed on across the lake in silence, the ferryman looking back at the bank and moving rhythmically back and forth in time with the oars, while I looked ahead of us at the tower where "they didn't go." Where who didn't go? The ferryman's family? The villagers? I had no idea.

A dark dot detached itself from the top of the tower, came closer and became recognizable as a bird, rather a large bird flying toward us on the wide span of its beating wings, its beaked head thrust forward on a long neck.

"A stork!" I said. It struck me as something worth remarking on: I hadn't seen a stork for years. But my comment seemed to alarm the ferryman. He bent even lower over his oars, rowing faster as if to escape some danger. As he pulled on the oars he glanced briefly up at the bird now circling overhead, and ducked down again next moment. I thought I saw fear in his eyes.

"Don't you like storks?" I asked, and tried to make a joke of it by adding, "They bring babies, after all!"

"Bring them?" he repeated between two rapid strokes of the oars. "Take them, more like! Not just babies, either."

I didn't know what he meant yet, but his manner showed clearly enough that the stork struck panic into him. My strange ferryman didn't calm down until the bird flew away toward the bank, which was far behind us by now.

What kind of people were these? Where was I? I was getting a very strong feeling that every stroke of the oars was taking this boat back into some archaic time, into another reality, one I didn't understand.

We were a good deal closer to the island now. The ferryman wasn't making straight for it anymore, but steering the boat over to the right, toward the village. As we rounded a promontory I saw a small harbor that it protected like a breakwater. A few fishing boats were tied up to the quay and above it rocky ground rose steeply to the village, some three masts' height above, with the mighty tower looming darkly over it in the steel-blue sky.

The sun had sunk behind a blazing bank of red and purple cloud on the horizon, a rather dramatic sight which told me I would have to stay on the island, at least for tonight. As the ferryman made his boat fast to the quay, I asked him if there was any way I could spend the night in the village.

"More than one," he said, winking as if we'd come to some agreement long ago, except that I wasn't sure what it was. It was almost as if the man were pimping, though in a very roundabout way. As I got out of the boat I asked what I owed him for the crossing. I expected him to name quite a high figure for almost an hour's rowing.

"Give me the shell," he said.

When I took my find out of my pocket and looked at the inside of it, iridescent in the rosy evening light, I was troubled by a passing notion that I ought not to let that shell out of my hands for anything in the world. But then I saw how ridiculous such an idea was—I had no reason whatever for thinking so—and I gave the man what he asked, feeling pleased to have got off so lightly and eager to be wherever he was taking me at last.

We were standing on the quayside as we struck our bargain. Apart from the two of us there was not a soul in sight, just a few ducks swimming among the fishing boats in the calm waters of the harbor.

The ferryman took a linen bag out of the boat, put the shell carefully away in it, and then jerked his head to indicate that I should follow him. Steps had been cut in the steep limestone cliff, fitting the formation of the rock and leading up to the village in an irregular zigzag. The lower part of the cliff already lay in gray shadow, and only at the top did a sharply contrasting strip of rock still reflect the reddish light of the setting sun.

The farther up the steps we went, the more intense did the color of that bank of cloud in the west appear, and I hoped to see at least one last gleam of sunlight that evening, but I was disappointed. Even when we reached the top of the steps, no dazzling light met my eyes. I stood there for a moment or so watching the distant horizon finally darken.

Night was falling fast as we walked along the village streets. Now and then they went steeply uphill or downhill, or were linked by steps. The cube-shaped houses, gray with age, seemed to have been built on the uneven cliff top to no particular plan, with paved streets added later to make them more easily accessible.

We met few of the villagers, and they all seemed to be

THE BROKEN GODDESS 21

making for the same place as we were—an inn, as it soon turned out, where the whole village obviously gathered in the evening. Even before I could make out the building in the rapidly falling dusk, I heard the confused sound of voices growing louder as we came closer: a regular sound rising to the night sky as if it came from a single multiple organism, almost magically attracting everyone who hadn't joined the chorus yet. Then I saw the villagers seated on benches at long tables under the trees of the inn garden, in the flickering light of hurricane lamps. They were short, flat-faced people, and they chattered away in their broad, rather hoarse dialect without moderating the volume of their voices in the slightest.

My companion steered me purposefully between the benches to a table at the far end of the garden. The benches down its long sides looked full, but the ferryman said a few words and people moved to make room for us. They obviously did so at a particular place and not at random, although I didn't realize it until I sat down and saw the girl beside me. At that moment she turned her face toward me, and the sight of it was a shock: she was you, yet not you. She was clearly one of these people whose continuous chatter rose through the leaves of the trees and high into the night sky, but in some indefinable way she had your features.

Had the ferryman known who was waiting for me here? When I turned to ask him, he was openly relishing my surprise. He winked at me again in a manner that made any questions superfluous and raised his glass of beer to drink my health.

Only then did I notice that a glass had been put in front of me too, but I was looking at the girl again when I drank the first sip of the cool, rather sour beer it contained. Or was I looking at you? I'm still not sure. All I know is that we were sitting so close on the rough wooden bench that I could feel the warm, living flesh of her thigh beside mine, and that feeling of physical closeness was immensely exciting.

"What's your name?" I asked, looking into her dark brown eyes. They really did look like your eyes now.

"Rana," said the girl. "Didn't you know?"

I can see what she meant now, but at the time I still hadn't noticed anything, and I was further confused by the fact that I hadn't yet found out your first name. And Rana's face changed from minute to minute in the flickering light, now looking identical with yours, then as strange as the faces of those other people sitting at the table and making the mild evening air vibrate with their chatter until my ears hummed.

The ferryman had joined the chorus himself now and took no more notice of me. The sound of the villagers' voices, rising and falling like the swell of the sea, drowned out any reasonable or indeed unreasonable ideas in my head, and I felt that I too would soon become a helpless participant in this clamorous evening ritual if I didn't get away.

However, I didn't want to leave entirely on my own. I leaned over to Rana and whispered to her: did we have to spend the whole evening here? As I put my mouth close to her ear to make myself heard, I became aware of her scent again, so intensely aware of it at such close quarters that I breathed it in greedily like an intoxicating drug.

Rana shook her head, smiling, and instead of replying she pointed to the bushes surrounding the garden a little way from where we sat. Next moment she had slipped off the bench and disappeared through the dark foliage. I didn't for a moment hesitate to follow her.

And then we were off on a breathtaking chase! I heard Rana ahead of me, breaking through the branches like a startled deer, and I pursued so fast that twigs, springing back, whipped around my ears. I ran blindly after her for a while, guided by the rustling and cracking in the undergrowth, led on by the fragrance that lingered where she had passed. The chase went uphill now. After a while the undergrowth became thinner, I felt grass underfoot and the next moment I was out in the open under the starry sky, running straight into the arms of Rana, who had stopped to wait for me.

We stood there in the dark for a moment. I could see only the outline of Rana's head, but I felt the living reality of her fast-breathing body all the more keenly, and I thought I was already at the end of my quest. I was much mistaken, not just about the events of that night but in a much more fundamental sense.

Before I knew it, Rana had freed herself from my embrace. Keeping hold only of my hand, she drew me farther up the slope. "Come on! There isn't much time left."

A little later we had reached the wall. It was made of stones quarried from the rock of the island itself and was not particularly high; you could reach up and touch the top with your hand. Above it, black and massive against the night sky, loomed the shape of the tower. The center of the island seemed within reach. I had no idea how immensely far from it I really was.

"Here?" I asked.

"Here and now!" she said. "Come on, let's climb the wall, quick!"

That wasn't exactly what I'd expected. I had something else in mind. Then she added, "I suppose you have the shell?"

"What shell?" I had no idea what she meant, but then I remembered the fee I'd paid for the crossing. "You mean the one I picked up on the bank? I gave it to the ferryman."

I sensed her alarm when she heard that. "Then we might have spared ourselves coming all the way up here," she said. "Why in the world did you give it to him?"

"He wanted it for rowing me over," I said. "I did have a kind of feeling at first that I oughtn't to let it go at any price, but then I thought that was just childish. I mean, look at it sensibly and it was a bargain!"

"Bargain!" The way she flung the word back at me showed me she was angry. "You'd have done better to trust your feeling than look for bargains. Did this journey mean so little to you?"

"I never thought of that," I said. "I just got into that boat on impulse because I thought I was following a scent."

"What kind of a scent?" she asked, intently.

"A real scent, actually—of perfume. It may have been yours. I'm not certain now."

"Well, you'd never have got over this wall anyway with so much uncertainty weighing you down," she said.

I wasn't taking that. "Like me to show you how quickly I can get over it?"

"I wouldn't if I were you," she said. "Have you any idea what's waiting for you over there? You wouldn't stand a chance, not without the shell."

"Then let's stay here," I said, and tried to take her in my arms. But she pushed me away, shaking her head.

"Not here," she said. "If you must be a frog, then I'll stay a frog for your sake. Come on!"

As she said that, I felt, once more, as though you were speaking to me, though I couldn't make any sense of her words. She gave me no time to try working things out either, but turned left and hurried along the foot of the wall, so that I had to follow her if I didn't want to get lost in the dark—and in no circumstances did I want that, for her "not here" sounded like consent as well as refusal.

After we had gone about a quarter of the way around the hill where the tower stood, Rana stopped and waited for me to catch up. She leaned against the wall, which was still giving off the warmth it had soaked up during the sunny day, and looked at me. I could see her face clearly in the starlight.

"Look at me again," she said. "Then perhaps your memory won't fail you entirely when we're down there on the bank."

I was more than willing to do as she asked, and as she had stopped running away and was standing there perfectly still I took her in my arms. This time she let me kiss her. I looked into her eyes as I did so, and once again I was almost sure it was you I held in my arms.

But there was no certainty to be had that night, if indeed any kind of certainty *could* have been had, which I now doubt. Before I knew it, Rana had slipped between me and the wall and was off again, leaving me with nothing in my hands but the feel of the rough stone. "Come on down!" she called. "Down and down until we reach the water!" And she ran downhill away from the wall.

Everything happened fast that night, and I felt a growing restlessness in myself, impelling me onward as I ran or almost hopped downhill following Rana's scent, for although the land near the bank didn't end in a rocky cliff, the slope became steeper and steeper, and there were rocks on the grass of that slope, scattered among the few low bushes that grew there, so that I kept having to leap blindly into the dark.

In this way I went down and down until I was within earshot of a regular sound rising up to me from below, increasing in strength and intensity with every leap I took. I couldn't make out how the volume of the islanders' voices could be the same on this side of the island, some way from the village itself, but there was no doubt about it: this was the identical hoarse and, to me, entirely incomprehensible chatter that had made the inn garden almost intolerable. Now it was rising up the slope again to suck me into its noisy vortex. I couldn't withstand the pull of it any longer.

As I hopped from stone to stone, down into the dark, I made out the faintly shimmering surface of the lake below, but although the sound of their voices filled my ears, I couldn't see any people there: no people at all, only a frog hopping ahead of me over the rocks and down to the bank, and I made haste not to lose track of her, for I was a frog too, taking a last great leap from land into the shallow water to find my mate among countless other frogs, whose croaking rose to the night sky in a resonant, all-pervasive chord.

As soon as I was crouching in the water myself I joined the chorus of my fellow frogs, becoming part of a multiple yet uniformly reacting organism. It consisted of innumerable bodies all driven by the natural cycle to act in the same way. The frog now croaking in the shallows had found his mate, like all the others who had arrived before him, was squatting on top of her in a twitching embrace, and both flowed away in an endless orgasm, while the water around frothed with the fertilized spawn of countless coupling frogs, the hour of their corporate mating mercilessly dictated to them by their hormones, a single pulsating, fertile mass, predestined to keep the growth and decay of the natural process going, generating more frogs to prey on insects and be eaten themselves by larger, stronger creatures in the food chain.

However, the frog I now was didn't come close to that last experience until it was nearly morning and getting light. Then the storks came sailing down from the gray sky and landed in the shallow water, flapping their wings. They thrust their long, pointed beaks into the water in search of frogs, decimating the enfeebled couples who had just ensured that they would produce the necessary offspring and were weak now morning had come. The frogs felt vague alarm as the shapes of birds passed overhead in the sky, and later on as the storks' beaks snapped, seizing their prey.

I came partly back to my old self only when I was seized myself and abruptly saw death facing me. The stork had me firmly clamped between the upper and lower halves of his beak, but he wasn't hurting me too much. He waded to land and spat me out on the grass.

"I don't like the taste of you," he said. "What are you, exactly? You don't smell of frog either, not a bit."

What could I say? I scarcely knew what I was myself now that I had this frog's-eye view of things. Finally I said, "You have an excellent palate, which is lucky for me. As a matter of fact I'm supposed to be a philologist and an authority on fairy tales. Or I would be if I hadn't turned into a frog."

The stork didn't seem in the least surprised. "Oh, an enchanted frog," he said, as if he met them every day. "That sort of thing used to happen to kings' sons mostly, but of course they're thin on the ground these days, and the few still around generally make idiots of themselves. Well, at least you seem to be knowledgeable about these unfortunate accidents, which makes me wonder how such a thing could happen to you of all people."

"I've no idea either," I said. "And this story isn't running quite true to form. The way it's supposed to go, the prince gets changed into a frog by a wicked witch, and he doesn't meet the young princess who breaks the spell until later."

The stork didn't seem convinced by my line of argument. "You mustn't be so pedantic about it," he said. "Anyway, you're not a prince, are you? You're an authority on fairy tales."

I felt that this stork didn't take me entirely seriously, but at least he went on trying to work out what had really happened. He asked who had cast the spell on me.

"Rana," I said, without a moment's hesitation.

"I think I know the name," said the stork. "Sounds like zoological terminology, right? Who is this Rana?"

"I'm not perfectly sure myself," I said. "At first I thought she was a girl from the fishing village, but I had my doubts from the start, because the more I got to know her, the more she seemed to resemble a young woman I met fairly recently."

"All the same, by your account of it she sounds to me very much like an enchantress," said the stork. "In which case your story is working out as usual after all. All you have to do now is look for a princess."

I didn't feel in the least inclined to go along with this suggestion, and anyway it didn't seem much practical use. "What would a philologist do with a princess?" I inquired. "Anyway, to be honest, I'm after the young woman I just mentioned, and I'm almost certain she was the same person as that girl Rana. Rana ended up turning herself into a frog too."

"Goodness me!" said the stork. "*Two* enchanted frogs! Now there's an entirely new variant, I'll give you that. My word, I hope I didn't have her for breakfast."

"I shouldn't think so," I said. "I still had her in my arms when you snapped me up. And you probably wouldn't have liked the taste of her either."

The corners of the stork's beak twisted in disgust, no doubt as he recalled my unpleasant flavor. "You may be right," he said. "We tend to notice the taste of your sort instantly, which is just as well. Think how risky it would be getting turned into a frog otherwise! Not many of you would have survived at all, considering the proportion of frogs that generally get eaten by storks, and as for breaking the spell, which you're all so keen to do, well, there'd be no further point in it, would there? There's just one thing I don't understand: if she cast the spell turning *you* into a frog, then who cast the spell on *her*?"

This question set me thinking, and I began to doubt if matters were as simple as the stork believed. After a while I answered him with another question. "She said if I must be a frog, then she'd stay a frog for my sake. What do you make of that?"

The stork looked thoughtfully at the sky and said, "Let's look at this thing logically. For a start, when she made that remark, she was actually saying two things: first, about you, that you couldn't help being a frog—you were naturally disposed to be a frog, as it were, and didn't need any outside influence. And second, about herself: that in the given circumstances she would stay a frog, and it was something she'd do for your sake. Now that in its own turn means three things: one, she loves you, a fact liable to overrule all else; two, at that point in time at least she was already a frog or she was still a frog, or she couldn't have said she would *stay* a frog; and three, given a different set of circumstances she might have seen a chance of breaking the frog spell on herself and very likely you too. In what circumstances did she actually make these remarks?"

Situated as I was, I found it very reassuring to be talking to a bird with such a command of logic, and I told him as briefly as possible what had happened up by the foot of the wall, and how Rana reacted when she found out I didn't have the shell anymore.

"Well, naturally!" said the stork. "That explains everything. The shell could have helped the pair of you on your way. But you paid that puffed-up frog of a ferryman with it, thinking you were getting a good bargain!"

"He wanted it," I said, but that cut no ice with the stork either.

"He wanted it!" said the bird, quite put out. "Do you always give everyone what they want? If so, there soon won't be much of you left at all!"

I still didn't see what was supposed to be so special about my find. "You all make as much fuss about that shell as if it were made of solid gold and worth heaven knows what. I just picked it up in passing. What good would a shell have been to me climbing the wall or hopping down among the frogs?"

"Don't you understand yet?" said the stork. "We're not talking about just any old shell. We're talking about this particular shell, the one you picked up and put in your pocket. Why would you pick up something like that? Because you liked it, and what you like says something about you. Never mind exactly what the object is. It could have been a stone or a bit of driftwood. Once you'd picked it up, that shell was a part of you—and you go using a thing of that nature to pay the first person who asks for it, instead of keeping it until giving away something that belongs to you really matters."

"Are you saying I could have broken the frog spell with it?" I asked.

"Perhaps," said the stork. "But anyway, you needn't think you're going to get what you want in a hurry now. Now you've bungled everything so badly at the start, it's going to be a lengthy quest, and if you're an authority on the fairy tale you ought to know what *that* means."

I was certainly entirely familiar with the concept, but I would have never dreamed of applying it to myself in waking life. "In the fairy tales I know it's the woman who sets out on the quest," I said.

"That's a question of the narrative perspective," said the stork severely. "About time the man did some of the work for a change, if you ask me."

"I won't get very far as a frog," I said, thinking less of my powerful frog legs than the dangers to which my present shape exposed me. I couldn't expect every stork to be as affable as this one.

He seemed to guess what I was thinking, for he said, "You've been acting so like a frog here that if you set out on your quest from this island, it would have to be *as* a frog. That could be dangerous, but on the other hand you'd pick up the scent again more easily here. Back on the other bank you'd be an authority on the fairy tale again as soon as your foot touched the ground. However, you'd be more likely to take the wrong path there, The choice is yours."

So what should I have decided? Would we be closer to each other now if I'd stayed put? I've no idea. In any case, I chose the more familiar existence of a philologist. I'd had quite enough of hopping through the grass as a greenish-brown frog, and I remembered all too clearly the sensation of struggling helplessly in a stork's beak. I didn't want to go through that again.

However, that was exactly what happened as soon as I told the stork my decision. I feared this really was the end when he picked me up again and began running across the grass in order to take off, holding me in his beak. Then he rose on his broad wings and carried me back to the opposite bank, very much faster than the ferryman had rowed me over. My situation was so uncomfortable that I scarcely had a chance to enjoy my aerial view of the island and the glittering lake. Once the stork reached the bank, flying low through the bushes, he simply dropped me in the grass, and there I lay, a full-grown authority on the fairy tale, watching the bird gain height and fly back to the island.

If I were to write now that at that moment I felt as if I'd woken up where I found myself, and had merely dreamed of being a frog on the island, I'd be giving an entirely erroneous idea of my feelings. It wasn't like that: I couldn't shake off the notion that I'd returned from a very concrete kind of reality to a world that seemed very much paler and less real than my experiences on the island. Here, in the castle with its carefully cultivated grounds where the conference was being held, things that had actually happened to me on the island were just a subject of academic and theoretical discussion. I still heard the noisy croaking of the frogs in my ears, and up under the clouds I could still see the stork that had carried me across the lake with so little ceremony, spitting me out on the well-tended turf like an indigestible morsel of food.

Still rather dazed, I stood up and tried to get my bearings. It was early afternoon. The sun was still high in the sky and reflected in water. For a moment I thought I was looking down on the lake with the island and the tower at its center, seeing it from the aerial perspective of my flight in the stork's beak. Then I realized that I was standing on the edge of the pond round which I'd walked on the evening of my arrival. The small island in the middle of it scarcely had room for a dozen ducks.

On the other side of the pond, where the path led to the old castle where we were now discussing folk and fairy tales, I saw a number of people walking up and down in front of the tall windows: conference members taking advantage of the fine weather for conversations out of doors. I remembered leaving the building in similar circumstances and at about the same time of day, which confused me. Had a whole day passed since I walked through the park and the woods and down to the lake? Or had I slipped out of ordinary chronology and returned at the same time as I left the castle?

That question was still bothering me as I crossed the short turf of the lawn to the drive leading to the castle from the main gateway, and as I rounded a group of shrubs I found myself facing the broken statue.

This time I could see it in broad daylight, which showed the sensuality of its body unshadowed and revealed the damage it had suffered even more brutally. And now I thought I knew what the savage destruction of its face meant. Whatever the features were like, they must surely have shown a human face shaped by the sculptor's desires into the ideal image of a lover whose gaze, bent on the observer, promised the fulfillment embodied in the mythical figure of the goddess. And then someone had come and battered the face, unable to bear the sight of it any longer. It was the only explanation for such wanton destruction. Perhaps the perpetrator had fallen among the frogs himself and felt betrayed by the face; perhaps he believed that the heart-stirring expression of the features was only a lie, suggesting that emotional communication or some such sentimental nonsense existed where there was really nothing but the dictates of the hormones, insisting on copulation for the procreation of the species: a compulsive process leaving everyone still fettered to the loneliness of his own desire.

I stared at the battered stone of the head that made the violated goddess an unperson. What had my taxi driver said? "She's still got what a girl needs." All a woman needs to satisfy a man's desires. A face would just have been a distraction. What was the point in exhibiting the torso, robbed of its original meaning, to the visitors to these grounds? Was it to remind them how far humanity had come since a Roman sculptor tried to express his concept of love in this statue? Or was the torso meant to show that those aspects of our bodies generally thought to show the nobility of human nature are just unnecessary ornament, encouraging illusion? I found the sight of the damaged stone intolerable; I wished they hadn't put it there.

As I stood in front of the statue deep in such thoughts, wondering whether the emotional turmoil into which my meeting with you had plunged me had no cause or aim but to arouse biochemical reactions and release the drives thus set off in my stock of hormones—and as I was beginning to take a violent dislike to this idea—you came along the path out of the grounds toward me. For a moment I contemplated disappearing into the shrubbery, because in my present state of mind I simply didn't feel up to meeting you, but then I realized you'd already seen me. I wondered whether to go a few steps toward you, to avoid an encounter right in front of the statue, but in the end I stayed where I was, looking at you challengingly (as I thought) and thus facing whatever was coming toward me head-on, so to speak.

Understandably enough, you entirely misinterpreted the expression on my face, which probably just looked half-baked. You stopped when you reached me and asked if I'd taken offense at what you said at lunch just now.

I shook my head in silence. Well, at least I now knew one thing: the whole episode of Rana and the stork must indeed have taken place in a different dimension of time, because it was obviously less than half an hour since I left the dining room. As I looked at you I was forcibly struck by the similarity between you and the frog-girl, and it occurred to me that you might have been in the place I'd just returned from too, in the shape of Rana. I almost asked you. I wonder what you would have said. I'd still like to know. At the time, however, I was afraid you might think me mad, and that kept me from putting the question. In the end I just said well, you *had* irritated me quite a lot, but not in any way I could possibly take amiss.

As I spoke, you looked away for a few seconds, your gaze lingering on the statue where you had found me standing, and I wondered if you were showing that you fully understood the deeper reasons for my ruffled temper. But you may just have been looking for a way to change the subject, because next moment you asked me if the statue was really as old as it looked.

I don't know if you remember our conversation in such detail as I do. Perhaps it didn't matter as much to you. To me, however, there was something equivocal about it. I felt as if I were on shaky ground that might give way any moment and plunge me into a bottomless pit.

"It's old enough for there to be a chance that the sculptor still believed in what his work was meant to embody," I said.

You were looking at the statue now, not me, and you

asked if I meant he still believed in the power of the classical gods.

"Well, yes, more or less," I said, adding that I'd taken archaeology as a subsidiary subject in my degree course and studied the sculptures of the late Imperial period.

"What do you mean, *more or less?*" you asked, ignoring the little excursus about my academic training.

"You asked about the date of the statue," I said, "but I'm wondering what the goddess really may have meant to the artist at the time."

"You think this statue could have meant one thing for him and something different to us today?"

Us, you said, and the word went straight to my heart. Were you already referring to the two of us as a couple, you and me? Or was it just a manner of speaking? I could hardly inquire into the exact significance of your question, of course, so finally I said, "Perhaps the artist was luckier than we late-born rationalists. Wouldn't it be more inspiring to believe in a goddess who moves the heart than in the chemistry of hormones, which just gives us an illusion of such noble emotions?"

When I said that, you shook your head almost indignantly, looking at me as if I must be deranged, which confused my feelings more than ever. Even the way you show displeasure is so lovable that it's hard to react appropriately, and at this point my inability to do so made me aggressive. I said, quite violently, "Well, anyway, someone came along some time or other, couldn't stand the sight of the face any more and smashed it in."

"That may well be so," you said, "but there could be all sorts of reasons for it, not all of them the goddess's fault. And can anything be said for a person who smashes faces and tries to destroy beauty?"

I was still feeling the effects of my experience among the frogs; I felt it in my bones, or perhaps as an ache of foreboding in the pit of my stomach. Anyway, I suggested that people's ideas of beauty might differ. "Perhaps," I went on, "whoever damaged the statue thought the goddess's face too beautiful a falsehood, which would also be an illustration of the dubious nature of aesthetic categories."

When I said that, you looked straight into my eyes with the glance of a surgeon about to apply the knife. "Someone must have treated you badly if you can talk like that," you said.

That went home. I was about to ask what business it was of yours, and, anyway, I wasn't ready to allow such memories to surface in my conscious mind—not yet. I felt a moment's sheer panic before I thought I had recovered sufficient control of my voice to reply. "Perhaps I'm after more pleasant experiences," I said in as dry a tone as I could manage.

I saw at once that I'd gone too far. Your eyes were opaque as dark stone. "Then you'd better not get on the wrong side of the goddess, had you?" you said with cool sarcasm, turning and moving away as you spoke.

We didn't exchange another word at that conference. I do remember that our eyes met from time to time, and I felt—or hoped?—you were sorry to have been so brusque with me. But neither of us was able to take the first step toward the other. When I came down to breakfast on the last morning, you'd already left.

PART
TWO

PART TWO

I SHOULD HAVE TOLD MYSELF, sensibly, that the episode—if it warranted such a description—was now at an end, all over before it ever really began. On the way home I tried persuading myself that the significance I'd read into our meeting was based on nothing but my own greatly exaggerated interpretation of a few unimportant events and conversations. Just what had happened, after all? It was a flecting encounter, charged with no more intensity or meaning than dozens of others at such conferences.

And what reason had I for supposing I might have made an impression on you? I didn't feel I'd cut a very good figure at the conference, although later, much to my surprise, the paper I had given was instrumental in getting me a new academic appointment; an influential professor who'd been present recommended me. I still don't know what induced him to do it. Perhaps it was the ambivalence and surface impartiality of the ideas I proposed rather hesitantly, affected as I was by my disquiet at the time—such things are sometimes seen as the hallmark of a particularly scrupulous and scholarly approach. Look at it that way and I have you to thank for my job, or at least the unsettling effect of the look in your brown eyes. I've only just thought of that. A happy discovery.

Though it doesn't alter the fact that I'm well aware of the inadequacy of my remarks at the conference, not just in my paper but in my conversations with you. Remembering it today, I can see, to my own amusement, that I made a fool of myself in quite a number of ways.

The hopeless confusion in which I found myself—not without some help from you—can hardly have been any secret to you. Did it amuse you to observe my chaotic state of mind? I had that impression now and then, but otherwise I have no idea what you may have been thinking. And that's the crucial point: did I just persuade myself—or more precisely, did my physical reactions to you as an attractive woman just delude me—into a belief that more had happened in those few hours than a brief meeting, and some conversation at cross purposes? Or am I right in thinking, as I can't help thinking for all my skeptical self-examination, that, to use your own words, it began for us there? Which amounts to asking, among other things, whether you were with me on the island of frogs.

For a time I felt convinced you were. But how could I be sure of anything about those slippery characters? Remembering my headlong chase through darkness vibrating with the croaking of the frogs, I began to fear that although everything had seemed to be going my way at first, I'd been well and truly fooled on that island.

All the same, I couldn't shake off the idea that you really were there, though I could dredge up no actual evidence from my memory—at the very outside, a vague feeling that could have been aroused by the scent drifting into my nostrils on the landing stage, which persuaded me to set foot on the damp planks at the bottom of the boat.

But over on the island, where were you, if you weren't among the frog villagers? Perhaps you were prowling through the darkness farther uphill on the other side of the wall, a lioness, unaffected by my designs on you, merely stopping now and then and freezing, one forepaw raised, when the distant croaking of the frogs rose from below to disturb the silence of your domain.

If that sounds an extravagant flight of fancy, I didn't hit on it by chance. However, I must go rather farther back to explain where I got it from—supposing you don't know already, that is. What I've been writing so far in this second part of my story mainly goes to show how increasingly uncertain I felt when I tried to think about our first meeting: uncertain of my own feelings, even less certain what you might have been feeling and thinking during those few days.

But there was one certainty to which I did cling: having met you, I not only knew of your existence, I also recognized, in an unaccountable way, how very important you are to me. Not that I realized that until you were gone, and then I knew it from the nature of the loss I felt. It was physical, as if something vital had been torn from my heart. Anyway, I knew I mustn't lose sight of you, although, for conscious or unconscious reasons, you didn't make it very easy for me to stick to my purpose.

We had really had so little conversation that all I knew about you was your surname, not even the place where you lived, let alone your address. Unfortunately, your name wasn't on the list of conference members (perhaps you'd registered too late) and when I asked in the office, they wouldn't tell me what I wanted to know at first, because, said the secretary, it wasn't usual to allow people access to such information. She didn't relent until I made out I'd promised to send you a copy of an article of mine on the subject of the quest in folktale, but I'd forgotten to get your address. Then she said she supposed she could make an exception under the circumstances, since I'd given a paper at the conference.

So I learned that you're an art historian, you live in Munich and you work in a museum there. Now I thought I knew where to find you, but I soon discovered my mistake: without knowing it, I had just set out on my own quest, and quests, as my studies of the subject show only too clearly, are usually littered with obstacles and other inconveniences. Although, of course, many of the people I met later on my long journey would say I had only myself to blame.

For the moment, however, I thought I had a precise goal: a certain street in Munich. I still had some time left before the academic term began (time I'd really meant to use preparing a course for my students), so when I got back from the conference I didn't put my bag away but simply repacked it, bought myself a ticket and caught the next train to Munich.

It was only on the way to Munich that I began to see how hastily I'd made my decision. I had packed a few books, with the idea of not neglecting my duties entirely, and I'd meant to do some work in the train on the subject of my course, which I'd airily announced as "Masculine Aspects in the Animal Bridegroom Tale-Type." However, I soon found myself reading the same sentence for the third time running, and still hadn't the faintest idea what it was about.

My thoughts drifted away at a tangent from the critical work I was reading, losing themselves in the crowded streets of the Munich suburb I'd looked up on a map of the city before I left home, to find out where your flat was. Only when I'd reached the point of picturing the place (a building in the old Munich style, four floors of rented flats, windows surrounded by lavish and historically interesting stucco work, an exterior once painted a cheerful yellow, the color still just visible under its patina of dusty gray), only as I breathed a sigh of relief on coming in out of the summer heat-haze shimmering between the walls of the buildings and entering the cool, dim stairway, only as I slowly climbed the worn flights of steps (up to the second floor, I guessed)—well, only then did I realize I could give no reason for my visit, and I certainly couldn't justify it. If only you had really asked me for the article I used as an excuse to discover your address, I would at least have something in my hands now. I would have been very glad to give you a copy, too! But you hadn't really asked for it at all.

And then, all of a sudden, I actually was holding it, a slim leaflet bound in stiff brown card like wrapping paper, and handing it to you as you opened the door of your flat. I had no recollection whatever of climbing the steps or ringing the bell, but it was all a part of the dream into which I smoothly slipped.

In this dream I am standing on a landing facing two front doors in a wooden frame that is painted dark brown and occupies the entire width of the landing; you still see them sometimes in old blocks of flats. I'm facing the left-hand door. You have just opened it, but you don't take the little leaflet I offer you. Instead, you come out of the hall of your flat and accompany me down the stone steps, which are marbled with pink. Meanwhile I can hear a dog barking down in the echoing stairwell. We meet it at the back door of the building: an enormous black dog like a giant schnauzer. It ignores us, but pushes through the narrow doorway and out into the open air with us.

We immediately find ourselves in green meadowland resembling a park, with a few tall trees standing on the slightly undulating turf. Their trunks are straight and slender, with broad crowns of dark green foliage very high up. It is early in the morning; the sun is still quite low in the pale-blue sky.

As I walk over the close-mown grass with you, I see all manner of small creatures moving around: birds of various kinds, large and small, dogs—even a monkey running on all fours crosses our path. You tell me the monkey belongs to an old lady who lets it out here.

As we approach a wide waterway I see where we are: we're coming to the Nymphenburg Canal, but ahead of us it ends at the foot of a gentle, grassy slope, as if cut off short. I see a group of children playing with a big, tawny golden animal down on the bank. At first I take it for a dog: I'm about to point it out to you, but you've gone.

I go on down the slope alone. When the animal lifts its head and looks at me, I see it is really a lioness. I feel uneasy facing this powerful predator roaming free, yet she is a handsome sight standing there surrounded by three or four children.

Then, although I don't remember taking the last few steps, I am beside the lioness and resting my hand on her neck. I feel the warmth of her body and the play of her muscles under the short, thick coat; I am alarmed by my own daring in touching her, but I don't take my hand away. I want this pleasant sensation to last.

At that moment I was woken by the sound of my book closing before it dropped from my left hand and fell to the floor. But I could still feel that vibrant power under the palm of my right hand. It was resting on the velour-upholstered arm of my seat, but the exciting proximity of the lioness was still so present to my mind that I was readier to trust my feelings than my eyes. I stared long and hard at the narrow arm of the seat, covered in cinnamon velour, as if it must surely change into a live lioness before my eyes. But then I became aware of the sound of the train moving; I sensed, rather than saw, the landscape passing by on the other side of the carriage window, dark forests of evergreens and then rolling countryside. There was a large brown animal in the distance, standing in grass near the railway line. My heart raced to meet it as it came rapidly closer, but it was only a cow grazing in a meadow. The cow looked up as I was carried past, flicking her tail lazily, as if to say: Be careful what you do.

I retrieved my book from the floor, watched with an indulgent smile by an elderly lady sitting opposite. I didn't even try to go on reading. The farmhouses of the Dachau Moor were already rushing past outside, and I saw a village church with an onion dome. By the time I had done up my bag and put my jacket on, the train was already rattling past suburban houses and over the points, and a little later it came into Munich Central Station.

I lost no time in hailing a taxi and giving the driver your address. I may have been in such a hurry because I feared my courage might desert me if I stopped to wonder—over a beer and liver pâté, for instance—just how I was to explain my arrival to you.

In fact, I was in such a state that the taxi journey, which must have been quite a long one, has completely vanished from my mind. My memories don't begin again until I was standing outside the block of flats, finding it hard to believe you could live there, since it wasn't at all what I'd expected. No tall nineteenth-century façade, but a plain, modern building only a few years old and two stories high. It was one of the last buildings in a street that curved and rose uphill slightly, with front gardens making it look almost rural. I found the card with your name by the door and pressed the bell at once, before I could change my mind.

The automatic opener hummed, I pushed the door open, climbed rapidly to the second floor, found the front door of your flat and rang that bell too. Next moment I heard footsteps coming, I felt my heart beat faster and harder, and I was expecting to see you. But another woman opened the door.

I forget what I said in my confusion. I expect I gave my name and stammered something or other—asked if I could speak to you, perhaps, or something of that nature. I could see the woman recognized my name when she heard it; she'd seemed rather cool at first, but now her face showed immediate interest. Something in it reminded me of you, although she was fair, with eyes much lighter than yours—greenish, if I remember correctly.

"I'm afraid you've missed her," she said. "My sister's on holiday—she left only a few hours after she got back from the conference."

My face must have shown my disappointment only too clearly, for she added, after a moment, "You didn't come to Munich just to see her, did you?" When I still couldn't utter a word, she opened the door a little wider and said, "I can't let you go just like that. Can I give you a cup of coffee?"

I felt she was curious about me. What had you told her? I'd very much have liked to know.

She didn't tell me, of course, although she began talking about you as soon as we were seated opposite each other at the low table in your living room. "Actually, you were lucky to find me here," she said. "I've only come in to water the plants, and I wouldn't have been here long."

"Lucky only in the short term, then," I said, and was surprised to see how like you she looked when she laughed.

"I didn't mean it that way," she said, "and you didn't come to see me, anyway."

Even for the sake of politeness, I could hardly deny that. I asked her straight out where you had gone for your holiday. But at this point my luck did seem to have run out.

"I don't think my sister would want me to tell anyone where she is," was the reply.

Anyone, she said; that was some comfort. If you'd really left such instructions, they were obviously of a general nature, not confined just to me. But your sister's secret smile made me suspect she had ideas of her own. At any rate, whatever she'd heard you say about me didn't seem to make her any less discreet.

All this reminded me of what the stork had said. "A quest after all, then," I murmured under my breath, and when your sister looked inquiringly at me I explained: the quest was classified as a motif in the study of folklore. "You never find out exactly where to find the person you're looking for in the old folktales, but you do meet people along your way who give you various gifts to help you with the quest."

"So you're going on, then?" asked your sister. "Where to?"

The question bothered me. Is your sister really one of those people who never set off anywhere until they know just where they're going? Perhaps I'm doing her an injustice, but it rubbed me the wrong way at the time. There may have been a suggestion of mockery in her voice, too; I can't be sure now. "Anywhere," I said. "Do you think I could just go home now and sit there studying the fairy tales that got me into this?"

She looked at me in surprise, probably more startled by my tone than my words and by my refusal to let her branch off into light conversation. She thought for a moment, and finally said, "Then I suppose I'd better do what's expected of the people you meet along your way."

As she spoke she rose to her feet and left the room. No sooner had she closed the door behind her than I began looking round your living room for any clues. There was a bookcase crammed with books on the wall directly opposite me and I began deciphering the titles on their spines, as if they might hold a secret, coded message for me. The top shelves contained collections of folktales and fairy tales, all of them familiar to me, and my eye passed rapidly over them until it lit on a slim, small-format book I didn't know. *Metamorphoses,* said the title on the spine, which had a pattern of colored tendrils. My heart missed a beat, struck by the message—not that it got me any further.

Just below the folktales was a row of art books, their backs neatly aligned with the edge of the shelf to present a smoothly undulating surface: *Renaissance Architecture, Leonardo, The Villas of Palladio, Piranesi, Turner's Watercolours, De Chirico,* and then a large volume that stuck out a little beyond the rest, as if it had been consulted recently and put back on the shelf in a hurry. *Frescoes in the South Tyrol.* A clue?

There was nothing equally eye-catching about the rest of the titles, but a profusely illustrated book lay open on the little desk under the window, as if someone—your sister?—had just been leafing through it. Next moment I was beside the desk and looking down at the book. I immediately recognized a color photograph of the cathedral square in Bressanone. Then I noticed a piece of paper stuck in the volume like a bookmark a few pages back. A few words were visible in handwriting—yours? I hadn't seen it yet. "The Lioness, Bressanone" was the address on the note, but before I could take it out of the book I heard your sister on her way back. Like a child misbehaving, I hurried back to the table, and I was sitting there drinking my coffee when she opened the door.

She gave me a small plastic bag; I could feel a few rounded objects inside it. "These may come in handy," she said, and then—oddly, I thought—she glanced at the desk where the open book of photographs and the note inside it lay. Had she left the room on purpose to give me my chance? I was still wondering about that when I was outside your flat again. Perhaps she'd just put a few items into the bag at random and was listening at the door to discover what I made of them? But her gifts seemed to me far from random when I took them out one by one: a rosy apple that lay cool and slightly rough-skinned in my hand, a walnut and a sweet chestnut. Such things grow and ripen as far north as Munich, of course, but they are typical fruits of the country near the Adige and Isarco rivers, and I took it that all three of them together confirmed my theory. I put the three gifts away in the bag I carried slung over my shoulder, went to the railway station and bought myself a ticket to Bressanone.

That journey by night across two national borders lingers in my memory like a confused dream. The train was not very full; at least, I'd found an empty compartment, entrenched myself in it behind drawn curtains, switched off the ceiling light, leaned back in the corner seat by the window and tried to sleep. I was not very successful, for here, in this narrow, moving space, lit sporadically by the bright lights slipping past outside, I stopped to work out the point of my enterprise for the first time since I'd left home in such a tearing hurry.

What did I really expect? I tormented myself by imagining the various embarrassing situations that might result from my entirely unexpected arrival—indeed, my invasion of your privacy. Perhaps you hadn't gone on holiday alone; perhaps you were meeting some man in Bressanone, or you'd met him when you set off, a lover who held you in his arms at night after spending the day with you looking at North Italian art. I saw myself materializing at the breakfast table where the two of you were sitting; I felt your cool glance transfix me while your companion, smiling sarcastically, asked what I wanted and then, as I muttered something disjointed, waved me away from the table as if I were a mongrel pestering people for scraps.

Or perhaps you were with a party touring the area, a bunch of talkative culture vultures pointing flashing cameras at all points of the compass, with a guide shepherding them through historic old streets, churches, painted cloisters. Such a body of guards, always busy, avid for art, would make it impossible for me to get near you. I could almost see a pair of fading schoolmistresses putting their heads together, whispering, drawing conclusions about us, the kind of conclusions that would surely keep you from so much as exchanging a word with me.

All this, and a good deal more like it, unreeled in my brain like a bad B movie, but it seemed there was no way I could avoid these nightmare experiences, for I stayed put in my corner seat and made no move at all to leave the train at the next station and travel back. I never for a moment thought of interrupting my journey; I accepted the risk of making a truly appalling fool of myself—I was eager to look into your eyes and see in them what you thought of me.

That was probably the main thing that had set me on this course since I last met your gaze, back in the park beside the statue with its broken face—your surgical gaze, which had begun cutting open the ulcer embedded in my subconscious mind and which I hid even from myself. But I wasn't letting my memory make its way into that secret place. I stood up, switched on the light, and found the book I'd attempted to read on my way to Munich.

At some point I'd slipped an old ticket in it as a bookmark at a passage dealing with quests. Whatever interest had made

me mark that passage in the book at the time now seemed
superseded, indeed invalidated, by the circumstances in
which I returned to the text. I now read it with the interest
of someone personally involved.

One sentence in particular caught my attention. It ran: "Although quests are almost always undertaken by the female
protagonist as she follows the trail of her lover, having driven
him away herself by recognizing him too soon, the motif
implies a kind of reverse quest, undertaken by the lover himself. He is obviously not ready to be recognized yet, and he
takes flight instead." I wasn't happy with this notion. It
seemed to suggest that some previously unrecognized error
must be brought to light. I felt I was under personal attack,
and was positively relieved when the Austrian customs officer
opened the door of my compartment to check my passport
and ask if I had anything to declare.

When he had gone again, I put out the light, took off my
shoes and lay down to see if I could get some sleep after
all. The sound of the rolling wheels never faded from my
consciousness, but I dozed until the Italian border official
roused me again after a couple of hours or so, asking to see
my papers. I spent the rest of the journey looking out of the
window of the dark compartment at the mountainous nocturnal landscape through which the train was rushing toward
the valley, on its way to the place where I hoped to meet
you and see myself reflected in your eyes.

It was about midnight when I got out of the taxi outside the
hotel where I thought you'd be staying; you know the one I
mean. Of course the place was in darkness, the door locked,
and I had to ring for the night porter, who kept me waiting
a long time before he opened the door. He blinked at me as
if I were some strange apparition unexpectedly interrupting
his first deep sleep of the night, and didn't seem to come
gradually awake until I'd asked him for the third time if there

was a room vacant. He asked, unnecessarily, if I'd booked, and when I said no, he shuffled off and vanished into a dark and cavernous passage. "Hasn't booked," I heard him muttering as he worked it out. "Hasn't booked, wants a room, funny sort of guests we get these days!" Seeing me about to follow, he turned abruptly and snapped, "You stop there! I have to go and look, don't I?"

I took the porter's behavior to be another of the obstacles I must expect to encounter on my unplanned journey, and was glad to see him reappear some considerable time later and usher me in. I followed him, making my way along the dark passage to the reception desk, which was dimly lit by a weak electric light. He wordlessly handed me a key with a number tag and jerked his thumb toward the stairs. When I asked if you were staying in the hotel, he ignored my question entirely and withdrew, muttering, into a room behind the reception desk.

Not until I was in bed in the room allotted to me did it occur to me that a large tip might have broken the unfriendly porter's silence, but by then I couldn't bring myself to get out of bed again, get some clothes on and drag the gruff Cerberus from his slumbers once more. Then again, if he was more loquacious by day, he might mention my inquiry, at least to the other staff, and if you happened to learn of it— well, I could already see you shrinking like a mimosa, closing up your fragile petals against the unexpected downpour of my attempt to approach you.

No, I thought, it wasn't worth going to those lengths for information that could do me no practical good just now; I'd find out easily enough next morning anyway. But probably I was just too tired.

Next morning ... yes. Nothing turned out as I'd expected next morning. When I entered the breakfast room I immediately found myself face to face with you, and the look in your eyes made me feel as if you'd been eagerly awaiting me and was glad I'd finally arrived. This impression left my mind in turmoil and instantly cut the ground from under all the elaborate reasons for my appearance I'd been preparing while I shaved. As I stood there in the doorway, not sure how to react, you beckoned me over to your table. You were obviously in good spirits. So there I sat opposite you, barely able to tell the waitress whether I wanted tea or coffee, and feeling the choice between orange juice or an egg quite beyond me.

Had you known I'd be there? Did your sister telephone or had the night porter tipped you off? Or had you actually been hoping I'd turn up, against all reasonable expectations? You've never told me, simply answering my questions with a smile, as if I must know already or must at least find out for myself. But I realize I'm offering only my own interpretation of your behavior here, and giving away my own state of mind at the time.

You, at least, seemed quite unperturbed by any such doubts or questions. When you told me you were planning to drive to Verona that day and asked if I'd like to come too, it was like a sudden gust of wind catching the sail of my desires, and caused me to gulp my breakfast down with unaccustomed haste. I could hardly wait to be in your rented car driving south beside you. But I hurried up to my room to fetch my bag. I wanted to have your sister's three gifts at hand.

As you drove the little Fiat along the road to Bolzano, I tried to entertain you with an account, culled from my student days and several later visits, of everything of interest I knew about the history and culture of the area (and some things of lesser interest too). I now suspect that by the time we reached Klausen I may have been getting on your nerves with my extensive comments on the early settlement of the citadel and monastery of Sabiona, later known as Säben. Even then I feared, momentarily, that I saw a certain displeasure in the lift of your brows as I plunged into a description of the archaeological excavation of the place's sizeable burial ground, which was in uninterrupted use from the late fourth century to the second half of the seventh century. Some of the first Bavarian invaders of what was originally a Romanic region were buried there. Yes, well . . . as you can see, the moment I start on that subject my interest in it carries me away and I get all entangled in details again. However, at the time the pleasure of showing my knowledge off to you carried me happily over any shoals, and I didn't hesitate to add precise facts and figures concerning the funerary customs of the period and the clothing and jewelry with which its people buried their dead.

But perhaps you were just amused by the peculiar form of masculine display behavior that made me spread my academic plumage before you. Anyway, your good humor seemed unimpaired. You even showed a certain interest in my remarks, asking me whether Bavarian men and Romanic women lay side by side in any of these later graves. As you asked, you took your right hand off the steering wheel in an eloquent gesture, giving me such an odd, sidelong glance that I wondered in all seriousness how I was supposed to take the question. Your Mediterranean manner suggested the most hopeful of interpretations to my mind.

However, I couldn't answer it. The only burials I knew about were individual tombs, containing grave goods that provided information about the provenance of the dead. I thought it unlikely that the new Bavarian masters would *not* have fallen for the charms of the dark-eyed Romanic women, but there was no saying now who slept with whom in life, whether it was done by force or tenderly, or, indeed, whether the Bavarians and the local women remained strangers until death.

You confused me. I thought I knew you as a rather reserved woman, withdrawing quickly from any attempt at intimacy, yet now you seemed strangely different. I was fascinated by the way you drove, too—with verve, though not aggressively—by your quick reactions as you negotiated the heavy traffic and your angry exclamations when a car suddenly cut in on you. I even felt that the farther south we drove, the more southern your own manner became. You were in a hurry to leave the lowering porphyry ravines of the Isarco Valley behind, and you seemed to breathe more freely when the view ahead of us opened out on the landscape of the Bolzano basin.

Once the city was behind us you weren't in any more haste. "We're making a little detour. I want to show you something," you said, turning off the main road and toward the wine-growing villages of the upper Adige. You seemed suddenly to have all the time in the world, dawdling along in your little car past the vine-clad slopes and the chestnut groves, stopping now and then to point out an old shooting lodge, gray with age and buttressed by oriels, but when I looked inquiringly at you, you always said, "No, we're not there yet. Wait and see," thus heightening my curiosity.

At one point you stopped the car in a little parking place among chestnut trees. When I asked why, you said, "Look, the first sweet chestnuts are ripe!" and pointed to the spiny cases lying on the ground. Many of them had split, shedding their shiny brown fruits.

I watched, fascinated, as you shelled the sweet chestnuts with a little penknife you obviously kept in your handbag for such purposes, peeled off the bitter, brown inner skin, put the pale kernels into your mouth raw, with barely concealed greed, and munched. You politely offered me some, but you seemed relieved when I said I preferred my chestnuts roasted.

I don't think I'd ever seen anyone eat anything with such frank enjoyment, which was all the more surprising because I'd thought of you as so reserved and self-controlled. "I've had a passion for raw chestnuts since I was a child," you said, munching the hard kernels. So that was what your sister had in mind when she gave me the chestnut. (Do you always keep a stock of them at home?) When you couldn't find any more ripe chestnuts, I was tempted to offer you her gift, but I remembered just in time that people in fairy tales do that sort of thing only in the direst emergency, and we certainly weren't in a dire emergency now. You were still finishing the last kernel as we drove on.

The lake lying in a great dip in the ground to the left of the road beyond Kaltern obviously wasn't what you wanted to show me either. The sight of it reminded me of another lake, but there was no island here. When the scent of water came in through the open car window, I thought of frogs, but this was noon, not the right time for them to strike up their croaking chorus, and anyway the noise of the engine would probably have drowned it out.

Soon afterwards Tramin church tower rose ahead: "There's a good café there," you said, but it turned out that the café wasn't the object of our detour either, although the lunch we ate there was indeed excellent. You didn't tell me what we had come to see until, at your suggestion, we were going for a walk to help us digest our lunch, climbing a steep slope between vineyards to a church dominated by its massive Romanesque tower. We walked so fast that I had heartburn by the time we reached the top of the hill, but I forgot all about that the moment we went through the door on the south side of the church and I saw the colors of the frescoes flare in the dim light, their pictured stories covering the walls of the Gothic nave all the way up to the spandrel of the ribbed vault.

Before I could go closer and look at the details, however, you took my hand and drew me into another, parallel and older nave, even darker under its flat ceiling. You didn't let go of my hand until we were looking at the paintings in the round Romanesque apse.

Then at last I saw what you wanted to show me. The frescoes depicted strange creatures, half human, half animal, fighting each other with grim ferocity. No noble simplicity and quiet grandeur here, but distorted, angry faces above naked bodies, human from the waist up, beast below. The hybrid being trying vainly to leap to its right was no philosophical centaur but a wild man with the body of a powerful fighting dog. He was attempting to tear off one of the muscular birdlike legs of the monster strangling a snake beside him, who, in his own turn, was holding the centaur's tangled hair and wrenching his head backward. Meanwhile, however, the bird-legged creature presented a clear target to a fish-tailed archer who was aiming an arrow at him. A broad frieze of such monsters rioted all over the wall. Farther right was a creature with a bestial head sprouting directly from its broad buttocks, which had a tail between them. There was a web-footed being with a dog's head taming a serpent. There was a mermaid with two tails: she had folded them defensively over each other while she peered through the gap between them.

To left and right of the apse, enclosed in its walls, stood two ugly statues seeming to bear it up, Atlas-like: a bearded man on the left, a fat, shapeless woman on the right. Their teeth were bared in malevolent grins. Both appeared to be on the point of collapsing under the weight of the upper part of the apse, which was painted with scenes from the Christian tradition. The extraordinary contrast between the apostles conversing serenely up above and the deformed creatures of a hellish underworld that seemed to lurk around the saints took my breath away, and the longer I stood there staring at the frescoes, the more I felt as if those monsters might suddenly leap off the wall and drag me into their savage dance.

"Why did you bring me here?" I asked at last; only after I'd spoken did I realize I had used the familiar "you." I couldn't keep to formalities in the face of the terrifying vision before me.

"To show you this," you said, using the informal pronoun too, and after a moment you added, "They remind me of that statue in the park, the broken one. There's a theory that these frescoes, too, are distorted versions of the classical gods and goddesses, remembered in the Dark Ages as demonic hybrids incarnating human lusts and passions. And Heaven's up there above their merciless power—you can see it as either an unattainable region or a burden weighing us down with its demands, like that distorted human couple. Some people think they're supposed to be Adam and Eve, standing on earth with their legs bent and hardly able to bear the weight of Heaven. I wondered if the barbarian who smashed the face of that statue of Venus couldn't just have been trying to make the inaccessible, perfect goddess into the likeness of his own imperfect humanity?"

That last remark surprised me, and as I thought about the idea, I realized again how little I knew about you—very little about your tastes and wishes, nothing whatsoever about any hurts *you* might have suffered. "Come on," I said, "let's get out into the fresh air," and you looked at me as if wondering where that might be. Outside the door I took you in my arms, reminding you that we'd begun using the familiar pronoun to each other in the church, an event that had to be celebrated. And so it was, as you know.

Indeed, I've only been writing down this part of the story to show you how *I* experienced it, and because I can't know what parts of it seemed to *you* significant enough to be remembered. It's always hard to know what the other person is seeing and feeling at such moments—and it's only too easy to project one's own feelings. How do I know who you really are? Though that question was much farther from my mind then than it is now, when I do at least ask it.

After Mezzolombardo you joined the motorway; you said you wanted to get to the vicinity of Verona, and once there you'd see your way clear to what you were after. There was just the suggestion of a double meaning about that, enough to launch me on some bold speculations. I had held you in my arms at last, which was more than I'd hoped for. The longer I thought about it, the more the experience, which still hadn't fully sunk in, showed me your hasty departure from the conference in quite a new light. I eagerly made the most of that light's apparent brightness, seeing myself reflected in your behavior. It flattered me to think I'd made such an impression on you that you obviously felt you had to save yourself by rapid flight—in vain, as it now turned out.

I don't know if you can guess how very ready I was to immerse myself in such speculations as we drove along the motorway, past the bleak mountains of the Trentino. I thought the landscape here rugged and unwelcoming, its almost unbroken rocky slopes, covered with low brushwood as if by the coat of an animal, looming to right and left of the valley and gradually decreasing in height. It was an oppressive place, one to be driven through quickly until we reached the point where the Adige emerges from the mountains just before Verona, its broad stream flowing out into fairly flat countryside, with only a few hills and rises in the ground to break the monotony.

We took the turnoff from the motorway for Verona, but to my surprise you didn't drive on into the city (I was already imagining a visit to the Capulets' house, with an opportunity for me to play Romeo). Instead, after a quick glance at the road map, you turned into a narrow road winding its way through orchards and vines draped over pergolas, sometimes passing through hamlets with flat-roofed, tumbledown cottages and little baroque churches in poor repair, although the crumbling stucco did not impair the dignity of their architecture.

Now and then the road forked, and I noticed that where the negotiable roads allowed it, you always tried to steer a course southwest. Eventually, however, we got lost among a maze of minor roads and you had to ask a farmer the way. Your Italian sounded as if you had spent a good deal of time in the country, and your gestures were very much like those of the farmer himself as he described the various turnings you ought to take, with many an eloquent wave of the hand.

We drove on along a cart track. Grass and weeds had shot up so tall between the wheel ruts that we could hear them brushing along the underside of the car. A bitter scent of mugwort and wormwood drifted in through the window. We drove halfway around a gently rising, shallow cone of a hill and reached a village on the far side. The name on the battered, peeling sign could hardly be deciphered, but the legible parts that remained seemed to be enough for you. "We're nearly there," you said.

Leaving the car outside the village inn, we walked past the last houses, along the foot of the hill and through vineyards. We came to a stretch of open country like a park, with a few tall, slim cypresses towering up. You kept a couple of paces ahead of me, as if you could hardly wait to get where you were going. Eventually we turned into an avenue of ancient poplars, their trunks hollow, some of them split, barely clinging to life with the aid of a few leafy shoots springing from the furrowed bark. Ahead of us, between the two lines of trees, was the classical façade of a villa, the regularity of its design and the classical, pillared pediment betraying the hand of Palladio.

As we came closer, the dilapidation of this architectural gem gradually became visible, with the plaster of the walls cracked and sometimes crumbling, panes of glass broken, window frames missing. A kind of trattoria had obviously been opened on the ground floor years ago in a last attempt to keep the villa alive: I could still make out advertisements for San Pellegrino and Campari near the main entrance. They were faded now and beginning to merge with the weathered façade. In the last resort, however, none of this could impair the wonderful harmony of the building as it was fully revealed when we finally reached it. Or that was my impression, for in spite of all the damage and the flaws, I found I could picture the villa as it was originally conceived—I could see something that wasn't there anymore.

I tried to share this thought with you in a few very inadequate words, and wondered aloud what effect daily exposure to the laws of such symmetry had on the people who used to live there. "What can they have been like?"

I meant that as an exclamation, or a rhetorical question at the outside, but you picked it up at once and asked if I really wanted to know. When I didn't reply at once, you said,

"Come on, I'll show you what lies behind this handsome façade," and you went on ahead of me, turning right along the front of the villa and then on for a little way, following the wall round the grounds to a place where it had fallen or been demolished, leaving a gap about a meter wide. We had to clamber over the tumbled stones in this gap, and came out on waste ground where tall thistles and mugwort grew.

Without a moment's hesitation, you plunged into this wilderness. Whippy shoots tore at your clothes, catching at them with countless hooks and thorns, but you went on as if possessed, your eyes eager to see the secrets of this garden. To this day I don't know just what came over you, but I had the impression that nothing on earth would hold you back. I broke off a stout branch from the wild tangle of brushwood all around us and used it as a machete, slashing you a way through the forests of stinging nettles and brambles and round to the back of the villa.

There we came upon the remains of a terrace, paved with slabs of marble and with four or five steps leading up to it. Weeds sprouted only from the cracks of the paving here, unable to make quite so much growth. Standing on the terrace, slightly raised above ground level, we could see something of the nearer part of what had once been the park. If you looked hard, you could make out a pattern of paths bordered by hedges, like a palimpsest under the rank growth of vegetation, which was less luxuriant on the trodden gravel. But now the hedges were almost as tall as trees.

None of this would have seemed particularly remarkable—just the grounds of a villa run to seed—but for the marble statues whose limbs emerged everywhere in the untamed undergrowth, reaching out of the jungle of tangled brambles, traveler's joy and rosebushes gone wild. Here there was a slender female arm, the fingers seeming to stretch out playfully for a spray of honeysuckle, there the shaggy head of a mighty ox thrusting its way through dark green clouds of box hedge. Wherever I looked in this wilderness I saw statues or barely identifiable parts of statues—a stag's branching antlers, the gaping jaws of a snake, the wingspan of a great bird taking flight.

When I asked you if you'd been here before, you shook your head and said you'd been told about the place; you'd come here on purpose to see the villa for yourself—especially its garden.

"It's chaotic," I said. I meant its present neglected state, but you corrected me at once.

"Of course," you said. "Chaotic—but it always was. There's planned chaos behind Palladio's regular classical façade. I'm going in there now. Are you coming, or is it a bit too much for you?"

Our expedition reminded me of a film I once saw about exploring ruined Maya cities in the Ecuadorian jungle. We often had to free the statues from tangled leafy branches and climbing creepers before we could make out what they were meant to be, and all the figures we laid bare were the grotesque products of an imagination running wild. Some were a satirical counterpoint to mythological themes, but some were simply carved from the snowy marble without any such points of reference, like the strange elephant which was the first statue we found. Its trunk ended in a snake's head with venomous fangs inside the gaping jaws. Only when we had pulled the ivy off the unwieldy creature's back did we see the figure of a naked woman lying there. The snaky trunk threatened to descend on her, while she looked up at it with an expression of desire, even lust.

Before you could offer any views on this strange composition I had an instant interpretation of my own ready: there had been a count, I said, the master of this house, who chose the elephant as his emblem—for its great strength or perhaps its enormous physique—and commissioned a sculptor to depict the lascivious games he played with women, frankly and openly. I thought this up in a hurry, less to get to the heart of the sculpture's meaning than to see your face show what you thought of my flight of fancy and read your reactions there.

I don't know what you really made of it; it certainly wasn't meant to be taken seriously, but you decided to play the game too and asked, laughing, how I knew all these details. Or was I drawing on my own experience?

By now we'd made our way farther into the jungle, where we found more monstrosities on which to exercise our fancy: for instance, a pair of figures springing from a single scaly fish tail in the broken basin of a fountain. Inextricably joined by the tail, they were engaged in a violent struggle. Both leaned back as far as possible from their shared extremity to give themselves room to wield their weapons: the male, a bearded merman, held a trident in his raised hand and was aiming it at the naked breast of his female opponent and twin, who, in her turn, was trying to run a curved knife into the shoulder he had exposed. They were staring into one another's eyes, and their faces, distorted by hatred, made it clear that the struggle was a mortal one, never mind which of them struck first, for then they would both die.

I felt cold horror rise from the depths of my subconscious mind at the sight of that deadly fusion, but I forced it back down to the silent underground place where it belonged, and commented on the fact that both torsos grew from a lower body that seemed to be sexless. I added something facetious to the effect that if one couldn't feel desire, the result was obviously hatred. Remembering your laughter now, I think it was forced, but at the time I either didn't or didn't want to notice.

From then on, however, I couldn't shake off that sense of danger lurking below the surface, although we both pretended to find nothing but entertainment in freeing the monstrous statues from their coverings to look at them, bestial and naked as they were. There was a poet crowned with the antlers of a twelve-point stag, for instance, reciting verses from an open book in praise of a female figure, who replied to his homage with a vain or indeed lecherous simper, for just behind her, almost fused with her, stood a wide-mouthed monster whose webbed fingers she was allowing to caress her.

We saw human beings imprisoned in turtle shells, unable to touch one another. We freed a group showing the rape of Leda from its tangle of plants, only to find it in a much worse erotic tangle. In this version of the story the lord of the gods had only partially succeeded in turning into a swan: the bearded head of Zeus still rose above the body of a bird with great pinions, and his muscular legs, their toes like claws, were braced on the ground beside the swan's feathered tail. However, he had obviously changed too far into a bird to carry out his plan, ready though Leda seemed to receive him, her yearning arms outstretched. The distorted face of the impotent lover showed his despair clearly enough—the comedy of the situation made us laugh again, but I felt the smile freeze on my lips as I turned aside and made my way on into the bushes. I wanted to be rid of the sight.

Darkness was beginning to fall when I suddenly saw the head of the lioness. Her body was caught in a tangle of wild vines from which a few bunches of grapes hung, already turning color. As I stripped the leafy tendrils from the lioness's shoulders, the palm of my hand could almost feel the powerful play of muscles under the short fur of her coat, and my heart missed a beat as I saw a man lying underneath the beautiful creature in the matted, overgrown grass. My eyes may have deceived me in the dwindling light, but I thought he resembled me like a twin brother. He lay stretched beneath the lioness. She stood over him looking into his eyes, her jaws half open, and you couldn't tell if she was going to lick his face or bite his throat. Even the man on the ground didn't seem to know; I couldn't tell if his features showed terror, or joy at the presence of the beloved.

I stood there for some time, looking down at my likeness. Then I heard twigs crack as footsteps approached through the bushes, and I felt what the man like me seemed to be feeling: alarm mingled with stirrings of joy at the sound. The next moment you were beside me.

Without stopping to think twice, I embraced you so violently that it must have alarmed you. For a moment you stood rigid as wood in my arms. But then I suppose you realized I was seeking refuge from my own fears. You must remember how we kissed there among the vines, beside the lioness and the man who looked like me. It wasn't the same kind of kiss as up in the church, when we kissed to mark an occasion, or at least, to be honest, that was my excuse. This one was quite different, more like a flight into your arms from the monsters and horrors of this rampant garden—a flight from my fears, suppressed by my desire to feel your lips and your body.

It was almost completely dark when we let go of each other. Black nightmare shapes crouched all around us in the shadows, reaching out for us with thorns and snares as we tried to make our way out into the open. We returned in silence to the inn where you had left the car.

"Let's stay here," I said, not very hopefully, as you opened the car door. You looked at me for a long moment and then closed it again. I have only a vague memory of what happened next, as if I'd experienced it all in a kind of trance: the smoky room where three or four men sat drinking red wine from small, sturdy glasses, talking loudly as if some violent argument were about to break out; the landlady in her stained overalls, who gave me a long key and jerked her head toward the stairs; the room on the first floor with its old-fashioned double bed and the cheap picture of a saint on the wall above it, as if heaven must be present here too. I do know that I turned off the ceiling light, and I'd just switched on a small lamp on the bedside table—it gave a very dim light—when you said at once and very firmly, almost severely, "No light, please!" Then, in pitch darkness, came the rustle of clothes being shed, the sighing of the feather mattress, a sense of plunging into your perfume and, at last, that indescribable feeling of my body against yours, which lapped round me like flames blazing up.

Much, much later that night I lay awake and heard you breathing peacefully beside me. You had fallen asleep on the side of the bed where I had first been lying. If I put out my hand, I could touch your body, and if I wanted, I could reach over it to the lamp on the bedside table.

Why did I want to look at you, in spite of your request? Even now I still can't say exactly. Perhaps I was afraid it wasn't really you at all breathing there beside me, but some nightmare or monster from the wild garden. Perhaps my eyes simply wanted the same satisfaction as my other senses. I remember thinking that I must see you at any price, however high. So I finally reached out to the bedside table, found the switch and pressed it.

As I said, the light was a dim one, but for a moment I saw you fully naked beside me, indeed almost under me as I leaned over you, and your beauty made my heart tremble. Then the moment was gone. You opened your eyes and looked at me like a stranger who had intruded into your slumbers uninvited. They were not your eyes, though, but the narrow eyes of the lioness who slipped off the bed without haste, reached the door in one supple movement, opened it with a blow of her paw, and then was gone into the darkness.

I can write it down on paper calmly now. But at the time I was frozen with horror, incapable of any rational thought, let alone any movement, and my heart trembled for fear the lioness might come back and stand over me, her jaws open to bite.

I lay there like that until day began to dawn outside. As the light grew brighter, the terrors of the night seemed to me less and less plausible, and yet you'd gone, there was no doubt about that. If I'd thought the night before that my quest was at an end, I now knew it had only just begun, and with an almost classic episode at that. Your clothes and your bag were still there in the room, and your perfume rose from the pillows, increasing my grief at your desertion of me.

The sense of smell is a curious thing. Scents stimulate my powers of memory with extraordinary precision, bringing back very remote childhood experiences: for instance, the flavor of a leaf from some weed I chewed in the garden as a child, but have never tasted since, makes me remember exactly what it was like to be in that garden. Or I pick up a shell that still holds the scent of the sea, something I haven't smelled since I went to the seaside at the age of seven, and at once I can feel the fine sand between my toes and see the surf spreading over the beach as it runs out. A drop of tincture of arnica brings the image of a summertime Alpine meadow before my eyes. In the same way I couldn't stop thinking of you in that room, with your fragrance still clinging to me, lingering around me. The sense of smell plays merciless games with our brain cells.

So I was impelled to leave the inn when daylight pitilessly revealed the shabby room and your absence. I pressed rather more than I owed her into the landlady's hand—she entered the bar, her hair untidy, as I came down—and then, without stopping for breakfast, I fled from her mocking smile and out of the room, which smelled of stale cigarette smoke and spilled wine.

Your car was still outside the door, so in the vague hope of finding you, whatever shape you might be in, I retraced our steps to the dilapidated, beautiful villa with that harmoniously regular Palladian façade hiding the prodigies of a wild imagination. I clambered through the gap in the wall again, bracing myself for the sight of the grotesque statues, and as I looked into their unblinking eyes and became engrossed in their frozen gestures of horror or lust, they seemed to me reflections of my own internal world, a world that I'd tried to hide from myself and that was now exposed to the bright light of the morning sun.

Though very likely that's just how I see it today; then, such realizations were at the most only beginning to form in my mind, and I hastily tried to find some sort of distraction to suppress them along with the morning's frustrations in general. For I didn't find you in the garden either, and I felt my loneliness all the more keenly among those statues watching me, marble-eyed. I found my distraction in a discovery I made only that morning: the brambles trailing over all the bushes, some of them clambering to twice the height of a man, were

covered with ripe, purple berries, and I began stuffing hand-
fuls of fruit into my mouth. When I couldn't reach any more
blackberries, I began working my way into the jungle, ignoring the sharp thorns that scratched my bare hands. They tore
the skin of my chest and thighs right through my clothes.
Bleeding, I ate my way on into the thicket of thorns, trying
to tread down last year's growth, dry now and therefore even
pricklier, so as to reach the berries beckoning to me a little
farther on, hanging in clusters among the dark green leaves
armed with their sharp thorns. I stamped down a place for
myself in the tangled brambles so that I could bend the fruit-
bearing shoots down and strip off the berries with my mouth.
The juice ran over my chin.

Driven on by insatiable hunger for the sweetness, I went
crashing through the thorny, prickly brambles, devouring berries as I went, and I don't know how much longer I would
have gone on like that if I hadn't suddenly come out, surrounded by angry wasps, on a grassy slope that fell gently
away to a wide expanse of water merging with the morning
mist not far out from its bank.

I went down to the bank, dipped my scratched hands in the
cool water and washed the purple juice off my fingers. As I
did so, my thumb felt the edge of something sharp, and I
dug a shell out of the sand. It was like the one I'd given the
ferryman as his fee. Like but not identical, for when I turned
it over to look at the shimmering interior, I found a bulge in
the mother-of-pearl, a partly formed pearl gleaming in the
milky morning light.

In view of this find I wondered for the first time just what
kind of place I had reached on the other side of the tangle
of thorny brambles through which I'd forced my way, like
the Sleeping Beauty's prince. Instinctively, I glanced along
the bank, and, sure enough, there was a landing stage with
a rowboat made fast to it, and a cottage a little farther up

the slope, although it didn't look the same as the cottage I remembered, the one where my ferryman lived. Nonetheless, I was almost sure I must have emerged from that wilderness garden of strange desires on the banks of the lake where I met the frogs.

This time I knew the value of the shell, and I didn't intend to lose it again. I therefore decided to try dispensing with the ferryman's services and simply borrow the boat. As I looked out over the lake, the mist began to lift, rising in an opaline haze toward the sun and giving a clear view over the broad expanse of water. The island with the tower rose from the mists in the middle of the lake, vague at first but soon clearly visible, although its contours seemed different, as if I were standing at a different place on the bank this time.

Keeping in the cover of some bushy willows, I crept through the shallow water near the bank toward the landing stage, took a couple of leaps over the last part of the shore, which was in the open, untied the boat, got in and pushed off. I had only just fitted the oars into the oarlocks when I saw the owner of the boat run out of his house. Sure enough, he wasn't the ferryman who had rowed me over before. Swearing angrily in the hoarse island dialect, he raced down to the landing stage, but before he reached it I had the boat under way and was a dozen lengths out onto the lake. However, the man wasn't giving up yet. He took a great bound, dived full length into the water with a mighty splash, and swam powerfully after me like an outsize frog.

I rowed for all I was worth, but the grimly distorted face of the swimmer following in the wake of my boat didn't recede, and as he reared up, pulling his arms through the choppy water, I saw that he was holding a long fisherman's knife between his teeth. The sight gave me strength to row a little faster, but I still couldn't shake off my pursuer. Indeed, I had a feeling that he was gaining on me slowly but surely; one reason could be that I'm not much of a rowing man. After about half an hour's hard work the oars felt heavy as lead when I bent forward and tried to lift them from the water, and the palms of my hands were burning. Now and then I turned my head to look the way I was going and see how much farther I still had to row.

When I had the boat level with the promontory that acted as a breakwater and was moving toward the harbor entrance, I looked back at my wake again and saw the swimmer's hands grasp the side of the boat. The next moment he had heaved himself in and was straddling the stern seat, his knife in his right hand. It was opened and pointing aggressively at me. He used his left hand to make signals, like a pilot showing a steersman the course to take, and he kept his round eyes fixed on me the whole time, unblinking and implacable. You see, he seemed to be thinking, you can't get away from me! But he said not a word as long as I was rowing the boat.

When it scraped against the wooden planks of the quayside, he rose and had jumped ashore before I could ship the oars. He stood there, legs apart, his long, sharp knife in his hand. "Pay before you come ashore," he said. And when I asked what he was charging, he growled, "You know very well what I want."

So I had to hand my shell over after all—though I wonder now if I really had no alternative. I was certainly afraid of the man's long, gleaming knife, but it was my fear that delivered me into his hands. He might not have used the knife at all if I'd taken no notice and simply walked off. You can never tell with these characters if they're in earnest or just testing you. But I wasn't prepared to take such a risk.

In fact, I'm almost sure, now, that he did mean to test me, because as soon as I'd given way he became quite friendly in an oily way. He pocketed his knife and said I could look around the village until evening, when we'd meet in the garden of the inn. There was a finality in his tone that suggested he had not the slightest doubt I'd be there. Obviously he thought me unable to resist the compulsion of the great nocturnal croaking party, and the way he showed it as he walked off and up the steps to the village without another word made me so angry that I instantly decided to prove him wrong. "Don't be so sure!" I called after him, but he clearly thought that was an empty threat, and didn't even turn to look back at me.

As soon as he was out of sight I followed him, but I did not linger in the village. Instead, I found a path that led up the slope away from the houses and toward the center of the island. I climbed rapidly on over stony ground overgrown with dry grass and fragrant cushions of thyme, and after making my way through some belts of low scrub, I saw the wall rise ahead of me again and the broad, round tower beyond it.

I sat down in the sun at the foot of the wall for a while. Leaning against the warm stones, I looked out over the wide expanse of the lake and wondered what to do next. Judging by Rana's remarks when I reached this frontier before, climbing the wall without something like the shell to protect me must be risky. But I was not sure now whether to believe the frog-woman. Heaven knows what ulterior motives she might have had to say so; or, then again, she too might have been testing me in her own way. Anyway, it was time I made up my own mind instead of going along with what other people said. As soon as my train of thought reached this point, I rose to my feet, set my hands on the top of the wall, vaulted up and jumped down on the other side.

I had jumped without looking to see where I would land, and it wasn't until I let go of the wall that I realized the drop was more than twice as far on this side as the other. Luckily the ground on the shady side of the wall was soft, not stony, and thickly overgrown with grass and weeds, or I might have broken my legs. Even so, I jarred myself quite painfully as I landed, catlike, on all fours, and I lay there for a moment before scrambling up. The first thing I realized was that I couldn't get back the way I had come. From this side, even a jump wouldn't take me to the top of the wall.

My next discovery alarmed me considerably more: all of a sudden the tower I had thought quite close when I was still on the other side of the wall was a long way off, shrunk to the size of a tiny cube on the horizon, where the ground rose gently to a low hill. Between me and the castle the ground was like undulating savannah, with a few isolated stands of tall trees and bushes. When I was pursuing Rana, I had gone almost a quarter of the way round the wall in a relatively short time; now the same wall enclosed the land on both sides of me as far as the eye could see, its curve barely perceptible, and there was no view of the area I had just left.

I don't know if I can make you understand the change of perspective that occurred in that split second when I jumped down, so far as it's possible to convey such tricks of human perception at all. That instant, extraordinary enlargement of the landscape rather resembled those moments when, looking at the causes and possible effects of some apparently trivial and ordinary event, you have a sudden revelation that drastically shifts all your horizons. Or it's like seeing a curtain pulled back: up till then you thought its pattern represented the whole world, but there's a view of almost limitless reality beyond. It's an alarming experience!

I stood there at the foot of the wall for some time, staring at that empty landscape. A few birds circled above it, high in the sky, and I was afraid to come out of the shadow of the wall under their eyes and walk defenseless into the emptiness, for at first I thought that, apart from the birds, I was the only living creature on this walled, yet almost boundless grassy plain.

Then I saw the centaur.

I should have realized by now that once again I was in the kind of place where things happen that you wouldn't think possible—even after scholarly academic study of folktales and mythology. All the same, the sight shook me badly. The hybrid creature had a human torso growing from shoulders that would normally have ended in an animal's head. He had emerged from a grove of trees about three hundred meters away, and was looking at me. The centaur had seen me, there was no doubt about that. Next moment he began to move, galloping toward me and brandishing a stout cudgel in one hand. In spite of my danger, I noticed that as he raced in my direction he moved more like an outsize dog than a horse. My first reaction was to run for it, but the next moment I realized it would be useless trying to escape this four-legged monster.

I leaned back against the solid wall as if for protection, and I remembered what the frog-woman had thought of my proposing to climb the wall and come down on this side of it—the side where I now was—without any helpful object. Something like this half-human creature might obviously have been expected, but he really was an alarming and truly unnatural sight as he galloped toward me through the tall grass bleached with sun and drought. It's difficult to form an idea of him if you know such fabulous creatures only from paintings and classical or neoclassical statues. Actually seeing such a creature in the flesh, and moreover in an aggressive mood, just didn't seem possible.

We're used to thinking of mythological figures as imaginary, fictional creations, at most, endowed with a certain symbolic or metaphorical significance when we mention them today. But I don't suppose it was always so. At some period there must have been people who thought of them as real beings who actually existed but whom—unfortunately, or perhaps fortunately—they hadn't yet seen for themselves. Perhaps they sometimes really were seen by those who were prepared to see them. What can we know of the minds of people in an age when such myths came into being and were believed true?

However, these are ideas that occur to me today. At the time I'd evidently dropped into some such archaic era myself, and I was terrified as this mythological fossil—he was only too living a fossil—came toward me.

The doglike centaur slowed down as he approached and asked, in distinctly unfriendly tones, what I was doing here. Don't ask me how I could understand him; he spoke a strange, barking language, but all the same I knew what he was saying.

"I had to give the shell away again," I said, as if the hybrid creature must know I had been here before, though on the other side of the wall.

He snorted contemptuously through his wide nostrils. "What would I do with a shell? Women's foolishness! Are you alone?" When I nodded, his expression became more malevolent than ever. "That's bad," he said. "I think I'll throw you back over the wall. Or do you have something for me?"

How was I to know what he wanted? Even as he galloped up he'd struck me as familiar, and now I realized I actually had seen him before: painted on the wall of the apse in the church above Tramin. Don't get me wrong: I don't mean he was a creature of the same kind—he was unmistakably the very *same* dog-footed creature, his face coarse and distorted by anger and passion under tangled, bushy hair. As I stared at him, I searched my pockets frantically and found the bag containing the three things your sister had given me for my journey.

"Would you like an apple?" I asked.

"What's that?" He'd obviously never encountered fruit before.

That gave me a glimmer of hope. I took the apple out of the bag and held it under the centaur's bulbous nose. He snatched it with unexpected rapidity, smelled it, and asked what you did with it.

"You eat it," I said.

"Eat it?" He clearly didn't trust me. Sniffing the fruit again, he held it out to me and said, "You first!"

So I became taster to a dog-footed centaur. Once I'd chewed and swallowed a mouthful myself, he snatched the bitten apple back, sank his teeth into it and ate it, stalk, core and all. He seemed to enjoy it. When he had finished he wiped his hands on his shaggy hips and said, "Well, you're a clever fellow. Now I can't throw you back over the wall."

When I asked why not, he replied, "We've eaten together,"

and looked at me suspiciously, as if the question showed I wasn't so clever after all. However, it seemed that once we'd eaten together nothing could be done about it, for my new friend shrugged his shoulders, said, "Come along, we'll go and see the Old One," and then trotted along beside me through the tall grass, docile as an oversized but well-trained dog.

So we set off in search of the Old One, whoever that might be. When I automatically began making for the distant tower, my companion shook his head disapprovingly, as if I had something most unseemly in mind. So we turned away from the object of my desires (though why I should have felt that way about it I could hardly have said at the time), leaving it on our left, and went toward a grove of trees that was very much closer. I thought at first that I saw brown, dried clumps of brushwood between their trunks, but as we came closer they turned out to be the roofs of a few log cabins, thatched with grass and twigs. When I finally stepped into the shade of the trees I could see how dilapidated the log cabins were. Their roofs, patched and patched again with turf and branches, would hardly have kept out a heavy shower of rain. The ancient gray tree trunks that formed the walls had green moss growing between them, and there were moldly, rotting places under the splitting rafters.

My companion led me to one of these log cabins. The doorway was flanked by two tree trunks like pillars and surmounted by a triangular pediment of weathered boards fastened to the wall with rusty nails, as if once, a long time ago, someone had tried to make the building look like a temple and failed dismally.

As we approached this hut, I had the impression that the dog-legged centaur was becoming increasingly uneasy. He approached the roughly framed doorway rather like a boy coming home from school with bad marks, anticipating a paternal thunderstorm.

Such a storm duly broke over him next minute. The door was thrust open, and out came another equally familiar figure, the bird-legged creature with the spiral cap whom the medieval church painter had depicted already at odds with my centaur. Russet feathers bristled around his hips; he was brandishing an empty snakeskin in his right hand like a leather whip, and he bellowed, "Who's this you're bringing back, you brainless dog? May lightning strike you! I want nothing to do with these human creatures who've left us to rot! Why didn't you throw him straight back over the wall into what he calls reality?"

The dog-footed centaur hung his shaggy head and stammered, "I—I've eaten with him."

At this the bird-legged creature cracked the snakeskin about his ears, shouting, "You greedy monster! See what you've done to us now!"

I could make nothing at all of this; I merely registered the fact that I was obviously far from welcome. The dog-footed centaur had now retreated out of range of the Old One, taking refuge behind the log cabin. Thereupon the Old One's anger seemed to have blown itself out; the rudimentary wings growing at his hips smoothed themselves down and, as he turned to inspect me, he tried to assume a certain threadbare dignity.

That gave me time to look at him more closely myself. His wrinkled face, distorted by passions, appeared ageless, especially as I couldn't see his hair under the close-fitting cap which ended in a spiral coiling forward. Or had he used some kind of pomade to stiffen and shape his own hair into this weird style? I never found out. His headgear reminded me of the scroll on the capital of an Ionic pillar. His naked torso was muscular, and his right hand, now hanging down, still held the limp snakeskin as if they had grown together. From the hips down, his body was covered with russet feathers to the place where his thighs bent back as if the knees were back to front, and beyond that there were bare bird's legs ending in claws. He looked as if the medieval painter had been here and painted him from life.

"So you've eaten with that stupid cynopod," he said after a while. "What was it you ate?"

"An apple," I said.

My reply seemed to cheer him. He brightened. "You don't have another on you, do you?" he asked, looking at me hopefully.

When I shook my head apologetically, he looked resigned. "I should have known," he said. "They're always snatching the fruit away from under our noses. My wife had a garden once where golden apples grew, but thieves came and stole them. I think we were going down in the world even then, though at least we looked as if we had a say in things. But they stole our apples."

As he spoke, I remembered all you'd said about the hybrid creatures on the fresco in the old church, and though I had found it hard at the time to see how the noble image of the Father of the Gods in ancient Greek mythology could have changed into this bird-legged monster, I now had confirmation that it was so. Behind his complaints—which related only superficially, I felt sure, to a lack of vitamin-rich fruit in his diet—I felt a much deeper sense of loss, going far back to mythological sources and not to be cured by an apple alone. Indeed, he immediately said I could spare him my pity, and asked what I was doing here anyway.

I was not sure what to say. Your name would hardly have meant much to him. I stammered something about a lioness who had escaped me.

That seemed to revive his interest in me. "A lioness?" he inquired, as if to make sure of my meaning.

"Yes, a lioness," I said. "She ran away from my bed."

"Your bed?" Abruptly, he roared with laughter, clapping me on the shoulder so powerfully that I abandoned any doubts I might have entertained of his ability to hurl thunderbolts. "So you're that kind!" he cried, when he had finished laughing. "Come indoors! You must tell me more about it."

Seated opposite me with his spindly bird's legs under the rickety wooden table, he didn't seem quite so unnervingly abnormal, although the slack snakeskin still dangled from his wrist as he poured pale yellow wine from a clay jug into the double-handled drinking cup he had pushed my way. Then he served himself, raised his cup and said, *"Kaire!"*

Not wishing to appear ill-mannered, I returned his classical greeting before the sour wine puckered my mouth.

"Nectar and ambrosia," said this down-and-out Father of the Gods sarcastically as he pushed a piece of dry, flat bread toward me over the cracked tabletop. Then he leaned back on the settle by the wall and made me tell him every detail of the events that had sent me on my rash journey.

It was a weird situation: I could see his face reflecting his interest in the vicissitudes of my story—and yours. At first he smiled, like an expert amused by the stumbling efforts of a novice, but then the smile began to freeze at the corners of his mouth, as if the distance between himself and my tale was fast diminishing and then entirely gone, replaced by the greed for life my words had clearly aroused in him.

I hope you'll forgive me for telling my story so frankly to the bird-legged being; at the time, his extraordinary appearance made me feel I was committing no indiscretion. He seemed like some kind of nonhuman authority in whom I could confide without reserve—a superhuman authority, perhaps, even though he'd so obviously come down in the world.

Finally, I tried to describe the panic-terror that seized me when the lioness rose beneath me, leaped off the bed and left the bedroom—a terror that still had me in its grip. When he had heard my halting tale, my host shook his head in astonishment. It just went to show times had changed, he said. Clearly we had reached a point where women changed shape to escape their lovers' arms! Long ago, in his heyday, *he* used to change shape to get access to his mistresses. "You seem to be an educated person. I suppose you know those old stories," he said, with a slight query in his tone, and when I nodded, he went on:

"The trouble began with people misinterpreting my adventures from the start. Humans always measure everything by their own standards, so they failed to understand their sig-

nificance. I was playing my part as the progenitor of all life
when, in the shape of a bull, I made fair Europa my mistress,
and as a swan made love to the beautiful Leda, and impreg-
nated Danaë as a shower of gold. But later they said I
changed shape just for fear of my wife's jealousy. The tales
they told were more like some small-town marital farce than
the mythical shape-changing of gods. A disrespectful lot, you
humans!"

He looked gloomily into his cup, took a sip and swallowed
the acid wine in a great gulp lest it should rise to burn his
throat again. Then he leaned his heavy torso forward over
the table, staring into my face with red-veined eyes. "You've
all become so clever and knowing!" he said savagely. "You
want to know all about everything; you've lost the faculty of
wonder. Back in the ancient days, when you'd only just
learned to throw stones and everyone feared daily for his life,
you felt awe when I hurled my bolts of lightning and my
thunder crashed overhead. All eyes were averted in fear and
trembling from the living flames I lit. Until that bold adven-
turer came and stole my fire to cook his food. I was revenged,
but what good was that? Once you humans have stolen a
thing, you never let it out of your greedy hands again. And
ever since you've never ceased to ridicule me, lumbering me
with a miserable set of relations to whom you ascribe every
mean action of which you're capable yourselves."

This was said in rising anger, and I felt as if I were shoul-
dering the blame for all the deposed deity's grievances against
mankind. In fact, he may have had a point, now that I think
of my critical and academic approach to the old mythological
legends. At any rate, I felt compelled to defend myself, and
I asked what difference it could make to a god if we projected
our own human ideas on him.

"Don't call me that," he said, almost as if afraid. "I am only
an image made by men, with their limited powers of thought,
out of something too great for them to comprehend. Perhaps
I was once meant to be something like a god, but now I'm
only the distortion of a mythological figure. The worst of it

is that we're dependent on the idea you humans have of us. After your storytellers had credited me with all those amorous adventures, along came a pious monk, very keen on chastity, who saw me as such an incarnation of lechery that he painted a picture of me in a book with this wretched snake in my hand, symbolizing the cunning and secrecy he thought I used to worm my way into the heart of any girl I fancied and deflower her. He left me my eagle, the eagle that once fed on the liver of Prometheus, who stole my fire, but in the monk's picture I hold the proud bird by the throat like a goose to be crammed. It hangs in front of my belly, its claws on my feet. That little picture in Hrabanus Maurus's encyclopedia must have been so worn with much turning of the pages that a good deal later someone else, taking it as the model for a church fresco, couldn't make out the details clearly and gave me these bird's legs. They make me look as if I'd only half succeeded in turning into a swan. I've been deformed by ideas influencing other ideas and removing me so far from my original nature that I'm left to lead a wretched existence in this half-world of fabulous monsters."

Sitting opposite him, listening to his lament and drinking his sour wine, I couldn't help being overcome by a great sense of sadness, caused not just by the acidity of the wine in my stomach but by a different process going on inside me. I felt, as if it were all immensely speeded up, a sense of the idea mankind must originally have had of the unimaginable power that brought into being this world and all the life in it; I saw how we had gradually dragged that idea down to our own level and refashioned it in our own image, stripping it of all its dignity, never resting until we could feel superior to the deformed creature our destructive words and thoughts had made of it, until it was mere material for art historians and anthropologists to play with, disappearing so entirely from general knowledge that such mythological figures as my companion don't even feature now in the advertising of consumer goods.

I must have uttered that last thought aloud, and I added,

remembering the statue I'd encountered at the beginning of my journey, "Well, except for one of them."

"Ah, yes," said my melancholy companion. "You mean my foam-born daughter. Everyone still speaks of *her*—or perhaps I should say every man does. But when he does, he reduces her to something more like the patron saint of madams."

"You may be right there," I said, and I wasn't just thinking of my taxi driver.

Before I could go on, my host swept the palm of his hand over the tabletop, as if brushing aside all this gloomy talk, and said he had wandered from the point, for we were really talking about the lioness who had escaped me. But if I was looking for her here, he said, I'd come to the wrong place.

So I told him what Rana had said to me (or did you tell me, in the shape of Rana?) before we joined the company of frogs. This story seemed to cheer him up at last. "Frogs, eh?" he said, with a distinctly malicious grin. "Well, you seem to have had quite a bit of experience already! Your lioness may well have come over the wall, but you won't find her here among us outworn figures of myth, vegetating in the shade of sacred groves run wild. She'll be on the other side of the river, roaming the grassland beneath the tower. Can you swim?"

The question came as a shock. I suppose I'd been thinking of a quest as a kind of inward exploration, demanding intellectual effort at the most of its protagonist. The lioness hunt in which I was engaged, however, suddenly seemed to have shifted to the plane of athletic ability. Could I swim across a river? I supposed that depended on how broad it was and how strong its current. There could be treacherous eddies that would engulf a poor swimmer without warning and drag him down to the bottom. I'd never tried to swim a river before, as I told the former Father of the Gods, but he pointed out that when you're on a quest there are quite a number of things you must do for the first time.

"And the current is the least of your worries," he said. "There's an evil-tempered Triton lurking in the river. He can't bear anyone to trespass on his preserve."

"Can't you order him to carry me over?" I asked.

"Carry you over?" The bird-legged being shook his head in such astonishment that the spiral curl at the end of his cap came loose. "You can think yourself lucky if he doesn't shoot you down like a defenseless coot! He's handy with a bow and arrows. And if you think I can *order* him to do anything, you're very much mistaken. Even the old disorder of Olympus doesn't prevail here these days; it's pure anarchy. But why am I telling you that? You must know just how much power over the forces of nature I'm still believed to have!"

"What about the dog-footed centaur out there?" I asked. "He obeys you, doesn't he?"

"Sometimes," he said. "And he's only a dog who can talk a bit. He'll stay with me as long as I feed him."

After that, he couldn't be prevailed upon to give me any more information. Instead, he asked if I knew any games to help him pass the time. I taught him the guessing game of Scissors, Paper, Stone—you know the one I mean—and I gave him a tiny pack of cards I found in my trouser pocket and taught him to play two-handed patience until he had more or less got the hang of it. "That lazy dog out there wants to wheedle my last bit of magic out of me—I'll fool him nicely with this," said he, with satisfaction. "He has just enough brain to learn the rules, but he'll never understand the little refinements and the tricks."

What with all this, I did at least get him to promise to show me where I had the best chance of swimming across the river unharmed in the morning.

When darkness fell, the dog-footed centaur came in, settled in a corner and was given his food, some kind of gray porridge made of coarse grain, oats and buckwheat and a great many weed seeds. It had a bitter taste. I know, because my host set the same porridge before me and had nothing better himself: "Somewhere in a godless world there are still a few farmers who put a little of their meager harvest outside the door at night as an offering," he said.

He didn't tell me how the grain got into his larder, and I

tried to imagine him going from door to door by night to collect it. But then I remembered who he was, and considered the paranormal possibility that everything offered to a supernatural being—if he actually *was* supernatural—comes of its own accord to the being for whom it was intended, in ways beyond the grasp of human reason. At any rate, I didn't notice him leaving the log cabin in the night, and I could hardly have missed it, for he had offered me the wooden settle in the living room as a bed and would have had to pass through the room to get outside. He gave me a coarse, musty-smelling woolen blanket to cover myself.

Next morning we set off for the river. The bird-legged being whistled up his doglike centaur, who had gone back on sentry duty at first light. "We may need him," said my host, "though most likely he'll only make trouble for us."

Later, after we had made our way through waist-high grass and damp, low-lying woodland for about two hours, we came to the bank of the river. It was not as wide as I had feared, but its black waters rushed past, foaming, still driven by the force of their fall from the slopes of the mountain range that loomed in the blue distance. So vast was the landscape that I had entirely forgotten landing on a rather small island the day before. But the tower, a little closer now on the other side of the river, and outlined more clearly against the backdrop of the mountains, had a magical fascination for me, and I would have flung myself straight into the river without more ado had the bird-legged being not prevented me. He drew me into the cover of a willow bush and asked if I wanted to go drifting downstream to Hades with an arrow in my neck. Furthermore, he advised, I'd better take my shoes and socks off so that I could swim better.

"The Triton misses nothing," he said, "so I'm going to attract his attention. I and this half-witted dog here will start a quarrel and, meanwhile, you must keep behind the bushes and wait for your chance."

On hearing this the centaur started trembling and growled hoarsely that he wasn't going to stand there presenting the angry Triton with an easy target when he surfaced with his bow. However, he was actually beginning the quarrel he wanted to avoid, for his master—if that was the way to describe the bird-legged being—seized him by his curly hair and dragged him out of the shelter of the bush onto the open bank, announcing his intention of holding him tight to stop him from running away.

At that moment the Triton made his presence known with a horribly discordant interval blown on a conch shell (it was a diminished fifth; I worked that out later experimenting on the piano). Blowing the conch for all he was worth, he made straight across the current, lashing the water violently with his fishtail. As soon as he saw the wrestling gods, or demigods or whatever they were, he dropped his spiral, pearly shell into the water, snatched the bow from his back and put an arrow to the string. The doglike centaur howled with fear and grabbed one of his adversary's strong bird's legs to drag him into cover. The pair of them were engaged in a kind of dance—two steps forward, three steps back—so that the Triton couldn't take proper aim.

Seeing my chance, I slipped into the water as quietly as possible, dived under and went rapidly downstream with the current. When I came up to the surface for the first time and looked back, I saw the Triton rising out of the water, his tail lashing violently. He shot an arrow that passed the centaur's head, still forcibly bent backward, and buried itself in the bird-legged being's shoulder. At the next moment the bushes hid the scene as they rushed by, and I had to work hard to avoid being washed up on the same bank again myself.

The image of which I lost sight at that point, as you'll have noticed, was identical with part of the fresco in the little church. Don't ask me how it could be so. I can't tell you just where I was at that moment. Everything that happened to me seemed very real—but what kind of reality was it? Was the whole scene destined to be played out there because a thirteenth-century church painter had portrayed it on the wall of the apse, thus predetermining it, or at least envisaging its possibility? Sometimes I suspect (or hope?) you know the answer to such questions, because I did, in fact, meet the lioness on the opposite bank of the river.

But that wasn't until later. At first I had my work cut out for me swimming, and I was driven a long way from the place where I had gone into the water. For a while I was tempted to let myself drift with the current, but I felt an irrational fear that somewhere ahead the river might tip its dark waters over the very edge of the world, down into a bottomless abyss, and that fear made me go on fighting the strong current until at last I felt solid ground under my feet again, first gravel, then fine sand welling up between my toes. I waded over the sand through shallow water and came out on the bank.

As soon as I had climbed the shallow slope, overgrown with short, coarse grass, I looked for the tower. Once again, it was so far away that at first I couldn't see it at all. Then I made out its dark outline, barely visible against the shadowy blue background of the mountains. Before setting off toward it, I hung my clothes and shoes over the branches of an alder to dry, sat down in the grass and let the sun shine on my back.

Or was there any sun shining there at all? I began asking myself that question as I wrote down the last sentence but one. Very well: I was wet from diving into the river and swimming, and I undressed to dry my clothes. Those are all concrete actions and I remember them perfectly. And it must have been warm or I'd have felt cold, and after a while both I and my clothes were indeed dry. But I can't remember now whether there actually was a sun in the sky. I may have written the sentence down simply because it's the kind of thing you'd expect in the circumstances.

I shall have to check my memories more carefully if I want to make sure nothing creeps into this account that might have been expected in the circumstances but didn't happen in reality, so far as my memory can grasp and retain any kind of reality at all. For now I come to think of it, there was something oddly two-dimensional about the landscape where all this took place too, as if it had no depth of structure. I remember a steppelike plain overgrown with harsh, gray-green grass, stretching away to the undulating, dark-blue shape on the horizon, which I visualize as a mountain range, with that vague and rather darker shape that I took for the tower in front of it, but merging into the blue of the distance.

At first my interest was focused entirely on the distant tower. It told me which way to go. As soon as my clothes were nearly dry I dressed and began making for my scarcely discernible goal, taking a diagonal path away from the river into the shimmering, gray-green plain above which I cannot actually visualize a sun that provided the dull light around me, a light that cast no shadows. Here and there my steps disturbed an animal; the grass rustled, something with a furry coat scurried through the stiff stems, and then there was silence again. But these were only little creatures, shrews or hamsters, perhaps; no lioness could have hidden in the grass, which barely reached my knees, and I was not really sorry. Even though I was in search of the lioness, my heart trembled at the thought of coming too close to her. Sometimes a flock of little brown birds flew up, whirring in its low flight close above the ripening ears of grass, and then settled again.

It may be that my sense of time had also gone awry in the

plain on this side of the river, or perhaps time itself followed different laws: anyway, my memory tells me I walked for hours and hours toward the distant tower before it looked any clearer against the blurred background of the mountains. For a very long time, indeed, it seemed not to alter at all, but there came a point at which I seemed to see more and more little creatures scurrying away from my feet in the steppelike plain, and now I saw many flocks of birds flying over the grass too.

I went on like this for a while, until the nature of the terrain began to change: the grass became green and juicy, and the ground sloped gently down to a hollow, where a narrow expanse of water shone. The sloping grassland was dotted with bushes, and there were a few trees for the eye to rest on, so that the impression someone like myself walking toward the place had was of a landscaped park.

I was surprised at first not to have noticed the trees as I approached, for they were relatively tall, but then I realized that to anyone crossing the plain even their tops would lie below the horizon, in this dip in the ground. As I gazed at the view that had suddenly opened out ahead of me, I realized I was familiar with the sight, in that *déjà-vu* manner that admits of no doubt: at first you may not be able to think when and where you saw such a scene before, but gradually forgotten dream pictures surface from the memory. It was like now. Then I saw the monkey. His back was bent, he rested the backs of his hands on the ground now and then, but he moved almost like a man as he emerged from the bushes above the narrow lake, coming over the grassland toward me at a slow trot.

I was not best pleased to meet a monkey when I was looking for a lioness. The encounter struck me as undignified, as if I were not being taken seriously in this place, which was clearly inhabited only by animals, or as if someone were mocking my serious intentions. Goodness knows my familiarity with Indian folktales and legends should have enabled me to see the monkey as a perfectly dignified receptionist, but I suppose I was too much influenced by Western prejudice to get over a feeling of contempt for his kind.

Anyway, I tried to ignore the monkey and walk past him as if he wasn't there at all. However, that turned out impracticable. The monkey wasn't as small as he had looked at first, and he was remarkably muscular. When he stationed himself in front of me, his wrinkled forehead came up to my throat, and he asked me politely, but very firmly, to provide immediate proof of my right to enter this place.

I never thought of questioning his own right to make such a demand; I asked what kind of proof he expected me to give.

"Well, a shell, for instance," he said drily, ignoring the ironic tone in which I had spoken. "A shell with a pearl growing in it, maybe." He seemed to know exactly what kind of a shell I'd found this time.

So there I was once more, empty-handed, and it was obvious that if I had to show this monkey some kind of entrance ticket I'd forfeited my chance yet again. I was irritated by the impudent way he stared at me when I couldn't produce what he asked.

"Out of my way!" I said, furious with myself for my own mistake, and I stepped forward, intending to push the monkey aside. I had expected resistance and was surprised to find that this ridiculous representative of officialdom just let me walk past. But the next moment he gave a shrill whistle and the peaceful, idyllic scene instantly changed. At his signal, the birds who had followed me here in little flocks flew up all over the grassland, the air whirring with their beating wings, and dived toward me from all sides. Seconds later there was a whirling cloud of feathers all around me and shrill cries rang in my ears. I put my arms over my face to protect my eyes, for I could already feel sharp beaks pecking at me. The ground at my feet was alive with scurrying little furry creatures too, climbing up inside my trouser legs and sinking their sharp teeth into my calves.

"No!" I cried. "No!" And when that did no good, I cried, "Let me talk to you, monkey!"

At that all the fluttering birds and scurrying furry animals left me, and next moment they were scattered far and wide around the meadow, as if that violent attack had never taken place at all. I was face-to-face again with the monkey, who looked up at me alertly, or perhaps expectantly.

His expression might have been thought friendly, perhaps deferential or even foolish, but the experience I had just had showed me something in the depths of his golden-brown eyes that I find hard to describe; it was more like a barely perceptible quivering than anything else, as if the depths of his eyes were under almost uncontrollable tension, or as if, just for a split second, I could see the immensely fast vibration of light waves. Nothing had ever before given me so alarming an impression of danger as what seemed to be hidden behind the monkey's calm gaze.

"Talking's always a good idea," he said. "Perhaps you have something to offer me after all? I don't absolutely insist on a shell, especially as it may be that someone's waiting for you here."

"Who?" But I never got round to asking about the lioness—or you, which comes to the same thing—for the monkey raised a hand so firmly that the words stuck in my throat.

"What are you offering?" he asked.

He'd have made a good businessman, I thought. "What for?" I asked back.

"For your life in the first place," he said, and I did not doubt for a moment that he meant it. Indeed, your sister probably saved my life, because it was the little bag containing her gifts that I finally brought out of my pocket. I opened it, took out the walnut and offered it to the monkey.

"A walnut!" he said, taking it from my hand with pointed fingers. "Not bad. That may do, so far as your life's concerned."

Placing the nut between his strong teeth, he bit it with care, breaking it into its two halves. He gave me one and extracted the kernel from his own half of the shell. As I looked hesitantly down at the half walnut in my hand, he shook his head disapprovingly. "What are you waiting for?" he asked. "Eat it! You must eat with me or it's no good."

So I ate the half kernel, though I had little appetite for it. The monkey was satisfied, and at last he asked what I wanted here. When he heard I was looking for a lioness who had run away from me, he shook his head thoughtfully and asked if I knew what I was letting myself in for. "The walnut won't get you very far with her," he said.

By this time I was feeling better, and I was disinclined to listen to any more good advice from this monkey. "I suppose I can go on now," I said. It was a statement rather than a question.

"Go where you like," said the monkey, baring his yellow teeth in an impudent grin, as if to add: But you won't get far. However, I thought I'd show him I didn't need his good-will, and I marched angrily past him, down the slope toward the water.

I wonder now what I was really after when I went down to the water under that monkey's ancient eyes, feeling his mocking glance at the nape of my neck, not looking back and almost certain I was taking a fatal step in the wrong direction. But I couldn't change the way I felt. I know now that I was actually going in the right direction; it was the way I felt that was wrong.

So what *was* I after? Was I looking for you in the shape of the lioness? Or was it simply that I couldn't bear the thought of your leaving me in that shape? Was I simply anxious to salve my pride, which had abandoned me when you did? I could scarcely wait to see myself reflected in your eyes and read in them your acknowledgment of my success in staying close on your heels. Something of all that drove me on, as if my journey into the unknown were simply a childish game of hide-and-seek. Why did I never ask, then, who you really were and what you wanted of me?

Nothing was further from my mind than such questions as

I walked along the bank of the lake that lay at the bottom of the grassy valley. Here again flocks of birds flew up out of the bushes as I passed by, rose in the air, wheeled and circled, their feathers gleaming brightly, and settled again in the ripening grass beside my path.

When I had passed a stand of trees and had a better view of the bank, I saw some children farther ahead of me, close to the water's edge. Oddly enough, I felt alarm at coming upon human beings here, even children—or perhaps that was *why* I felt alarm. I suppose I'd imagined I was the only human creature to have entered a world inhabited by animals, and thus a world I could subject to my will. Or my fears may have risen from my subconscious, where the dream I'd suppressed again lurked, my dream of meeting the lioness surrounded by a troop of children on the banks of water. And as I came closer I did indeed see the gleam of tawny fur among the small figures. Before my alarm could slow me down, the ring of children opened out and the lioness came to meet me. She stood there on the grass in all her fierce beauty, looking at me.

So now I had reached the goal I'd set myself, and only now did I realize that I had formed scarcely any idea of what would happen next. Had I hoped the lioness would turn straight back into you as soon as she caught sight of me? I don't know if I'd entertained such hopes at the time, at least subconsciously. It's possible, for I was at the center of everything I undertook to do at first, and I scarcely noticed anything but my own interests.

At any rate, the lioness didn't turn into you. She went on gazing into my eyes in a way that made my heart tremble. Only when I noticed how the children trusted her, putting an arm round her neck or stroking her coat, did I pluck up the courage to venture closer.

At the time, spellbound by the sight of the lioness, *my* lioness, I took no more notice of the children, but now I'm trying to remember what they were like, those children standing there playing with the strong, beautiful animal. If I try to picture them in my mind, all I get is a blurred impression. I can't even remember how many there were: there may have been some six or seven girls about nine years old.

Seven girls? Writing it down, I think of the Pleiades, the daughters of Pleione, set in the sky as a constellation of stars to save them from the hunter Orion, who follows on their heels for all eternity. Where, then, had my quest taken me?

And it's no good trying to remember what they were wearing. They weren't naked, I do know that. Otherwise, however, I have only a vague impression of uniform and entirely unremarkable garments of an indeterminate color. In a way that's difficult to describe, those girls were unlike children as I know them. I can still hear their speech in my ears like the distant twittering of birds, clear and melodious, but entirely incomprehensible. Their movements were gentle and graceful. They took hardly any notice of me as I stepped past them and, as if in a dream, laid my hand on the lioness's neck.

Then I felt it again at last, the power vibrating under the shorthaired coat, a sensation that both excited and alarmed me, although the lioness rubbed her head trustingly against my hip, and the glance of her eyes, remarkably dark for such an animal, passed gently over my face.

As the monkey had spoken to me, I was prepared to find that the lioness too would speak a language I could understand, but that didn't seem to be so. Rubbing her head against me, she uttered soft growling, purring sounds like a domestic cat, and she even seemed to expect that I would understand this feline means of expression. However, that was too much to expect of someone who had an academic training but wasn't very familiar with such creatures and their behavior. In fact, it was her pushing and butting, rather than the sounds she made, that finally made me think she was trying to get me to go in a certain direction. When I tried the experiment of letting her guide me, she immediately showed her satisfaction and trotted along through the knee-high grass at my side. She obviously meant me to accompany her to the distant mountain range that lay like blue clouds on the horizon, and as I sought some landmark by which to take my bearings, I realized we were heading straight for the tower.

So the tower was obviously our goal, just as it had been my own from the start. Hours of walking over the plain, now overgrown with rough steppe grass again, offered little variety, for the green valley with its trees and bushes and its lake was soon out of sight behind us. I might have become bored with our way through the monotonous landscape—for at first the mountain chain swimming in a distant haze scarcely seemed to get any closer at all—but for the tension between me and the lioness I sensed at every step I took. The beautiful creature sometimes padded so close to me on her silent paws that my hand brushed her warm coat, and then she moved a little away from me and walked on through the tall grass, half hidden by its waving stems. The lioness seemed as familiar as if she had prowled through my dreams forever, and yet at the same time she was strange to me, and strange in an alarming way.

At some point it began to get dark, but the twilight was not the kind I knew. When the sun has been standing in the sky all day, or was behind clouds but perceptibly present, and then gradually loses strength as it sinks until its bloodred globe dips into the hazy horizon, you know night is coming. You can estimate the length of that night; its limits are set by the course of the heavenly body that will rise again at a precisely determinable point in the east. But in this sunless world the coming of darkness had something final and indeterminate about it. As the light dwindled, so my fear that it might never return again grew.

The behavior of the lioness changed too. She kept close to my side, pressing so firmly against me that I was in danger of losing track of our way now that the distant mountain chain had already merged with the darkening sky. Finally I stopped, because I had a strong notion I had been walking round in circles. This seemed to be what the lioness had been waiting for. She suddenly drove her head so hard into the back of my knees that I fell on the grass, and then she was standing over me, growling and purring, but the sound soon ceased to be a gentle purr and became a throaty snarl rising angrily from the depths of her chest and ringing in my ears in a very hostile way.

My fears, suppressed with difficulty, surged up again and flooded my brain, if that's the right way to describe the sort of panic where your thoughts chase back and forth like excited ants, and your heart stops for a terrifyingly long moment before beginning to beat a wild tattoo in your rib cage.

The monkey had warned me that the walnut we shared might suffice only to keep the peace between him and me. What could I offer this fierce lioness? I quickly took the bag from my pocket and tipped your sister's last gift, the chestnut, out on my hand. Now we'd find out if the lioness remembered enough of her former existence to be overcome by greed for the sweet kernel, just as you'd been overcome by it under the chestnut trees. If she was all lioness, she wouldn't like it much. But fortunately that was not the case. No sooner had she seen what I held in my hand in the fading light than she began acting like a mad thing, nuzzling the shiny brown chestnut with her soft nose as if urging me to extract the delicious kernel from its brittle shell.

By now I was familiar with the ritual of sharing a meal. So I broke open the thin shell, took out the kernel, which was already rather desiccated, and divided it into two equal parts. I offered one of them to the lioness, who picked it up carefully from the flat of my hand with her teeth as if in a pair of tweezers. I was about to put my own piece in my mouth when it struck me that by doing so I was depriving myself of the last thing that might help me in this strange, dangerous world. So I merely pretended to put something in my mouth and chew it hard, while I put the half chestnut and the empty bag back in my pocket.

The lioness was deceived. She stretched out beside me, purring contentedly, and so we fell asleep in the rough grass of the steppes under the dark, starless sky.

When I woke it was still pitch dark. There was such a total absence of light that I seriously wondered if I had gone blind overnight. Trying to make out my immediate surroundings by touch, I discovered that the lioness was no longer beside me. Wherever I reached, I could feel no warm, living body, only the rough, coarse grass, flattened and now cold on the ground where the lioness had lain down in the evening. Nor was there any sound to be heard, far or near, except for the soft rustle of the wind as it blew through the grass, rising and falling again.

Left alone, unable to make use of my eyes, I was seized by such panic that I couldn't move a muscle. For a while no kind of reasoning could dispel the notion that was forcing itself upon me, that I was lying on a narrow ridge and might fall into a chasm if I made the slightest movement. You have no idea what horrors the imagination can conjure up in such a situation. I still don't know if I lay like that in the dark for minutes, hours or even days—as I said before, our usual concept of time didn't seem to apply in that place.

Then, with strange abruptness, light returned to the steppes. In the twinkling of an eye the darkness divided into a sky that was still dark but was shading into gray twilight, and the rough black plain of the grassland. As the sharply drawn line of the horizon reappeared, I recovered my awareness of lying on firm, level ground in a world where an above and a below existed. I sat up, enjoying my ability to follow that line with my eyes and feeling sheltered at the very center of this world of grass and sky.

And then I saw you coming toward me in the dim half-light that proceeded from no particular spot in the gray sky, as if you had suddenly emerged from the motionless grass in a place where, a moment before, there had been nothing. At first, I could hardly believe I was to get you back so unexpectedly, without further effort, and I dared not trust my eyes, which were only too ready to be deceived. But the closer you came, the more clearly I saw your face, and I set my doubts aside, though you were dressed in a way that startled me. In this place, however, was it really so surprising to see you in the kind of grand robe worn by a princess in a fairy-tale film?

Dressed up in this costume, you stopped in front of me and said, "Get up off that dry grass and come with me!"

I was more than willing, but all the same I said, "I really ought to wait for the lioness. She left me here. Or isn't there any lioness now?"

As I said that, I saw a stubborn set to your mouth that I'd never noticed before. You didn't answer my question, but said, "Never mind the lioness! Don't you know she was only making up to you? She means you harm. Come on, quick, before she gets back!"

You beckoned, and two horses were suddenly standing beside you, magnificently saddled and bridled. I helped you into the elegant sidesaddle of one horse, swung myself up on my own restlessly prancing mount, and we galloped away over the steppes, which flowed past beneath our horses' hooves.

Ah, the pleasure of riding in that carefree way! You were always in front of me by a head, and I tried to bring my own horse up beside you. Now and then you turned, laughing, your hair floating loose around your face, and by now I didn't mind about anything so long as I could ride with you, though the tower had long since disappeared from my field of vision. But what did I care for the tower now?

We were riding toward the mountain range that had seemed so far away. I hardly even felt surprised to find how quickly we left the grassy plain and entered a valley. Green meadows and ploughed fields lay between rising chains of hills, the foothills of the mountain range itself.

You turned your horse into a bridle-way leading to a village. On a hill above the cottages stood the most perfect example of a fairy-tale castle I have ever seen. I knew this must be our journey's end even before you raised your hand, pointed to it and called back to me, laughing, that this would be our future home.

By now I was entirely caught up in this story, which seemed to be bringing my quest to a sudden happy ending. We were soon riding through the village, but I hardly noticed it, so enchanted was I by your company. On the path leading uphill to the castle, however, the shrill chirping of a bird brought me out of my dreams. We were riding uphill through vineyards covered with fine netting to protect the ripening grapes. One of the little brown birds that had attacked me earlier, on the monkey's orders, was caught in the mesh of some netting right beside the path. It was struggling, beating its wings frantically and calling—yes, it really did seem to be calling for help. I reined in my horse, bent down and carefully disentangled the bird's delicate claws from the snarled threads. One of its ventral feathers, bearing a streaked pattern, was left in my fingers.

"I won't forget this," said the bird, twittering, once it was free and sitting on my hand. "Call me if you need help. You only have to blow that feather into the air."

I wondered what help such a tiny bird could give me, but when it looked at me with its little black pin-sized eyes, I suddenly felt it might be able to do all manner of things.

"I'll remember," I said.

It chirped once again, as if confirming its offer of help, rose from my hand and flew away, keeping low above the nets.

I was slightly surprised to see that you had obviously noticed none of this. You had ridden on, and you didn't rein in your horse and look round for me until the bird had flown away.

"Aren't you coming?" you asked, an almost reproachful note in your voice, and as you spoke, a small, deep frown appeared on your forehead. I'd never noticed that before either.

I made haste to urge my horse on and rode along the

bridle-way beside you until we passed through the great gate, which was wide open, and entered the courtyard. We dismounted there. A groom stood ready to take the horses away and tend them.

The courtyard itself struck me as strangely empty. There was no one in sight but for a few servants going about their business. You led me up a spiral staircase into a kind of medieval bower, a lady's room with a fireplace in it, obviously your own private retreat. Under the window, which was carved into the thickness of the wall, stood a small desk with a pretty stool. There were also two armchairs on the woolen carpet, and a four-poster bed stood in the corner by the interior wall, with its brocade curtains drawn.

"Do you live here alone with the servants?" I asked you. I'd already forgotten that I first met you in another world, though I was aware that we were familiar with each other.

You said something evasive about the lord of the castle, who seldom put in an appearance. "You'll understand in due course how our life is to be ordered here."

Ordered, you said; in the circumstances, I thought the word strange. But when I asked what you meant, that frown reappeared on your forehead. And when you said I must show a little patience, it sounded like a reprimand. "When the time is ripe, you'll find out what your position is. Now, come with me! Let's go to the hall for dinner."

You led me down the spiral staircase to the ground floor. As we walked along a corridor paved like a chessboard with red and white tiles we met a manservant. It struck me that he scarcely took any notice of you, let alone greeted you, and as he passed, he gave me a rather disdainful glance, as if wondering what business I had in the castle. Then I remembered that the groom had given us no greeting either, behaving as if his sole concern was to take the horses from us and lead them to the stables.

So I already felt I was on shaky ground when we entered the dining hall, where my misgivings were in no way dispelled. A few men and women sat close together at the lower end of a long table; they were rather better dressed than the servants, but did not look like lords and ladies. They might have been senior functionaries in the management of the castle and its lands. I never did find out exactly what they all did, but they had one thing in common: they were very hostile to me from the first, as if they would have liked to see me thrown straight out.

You showed me where to sit, a little way from these people, about halfway down the long side of the table, and you sat down beside me. The head of the table, where a beautifully carved armchair almost like a throne stood, remained empty, although it was richly laid with golden plates and dishes, as if the lord of the castle might enter at any moment.

The servant girl banged a soup bowl down in front of me so hard that the contents slopped over. The rest of the company grinned as they watched, spluttering with suppressed laughter. The girl didn't serve you in quite so offhand a manner, but the way she marched away from the table without a word to us couldn't have been called friendly. The soup was nothing special either: lumpy and oversalted, and there was nothing else to eat.

We were the first to rise from the table. I felt as if we were running a particularly painful gauntlet in passing our companions. Their glances were ironic or surly, following us until I closed the door. I had hoped you would take me to your room with you, but I'd been deluding myself. You stopped outside a plain little door on the ground floor where the dining hall was situated and told me I was to sleep here for the time being. Your words did suggest that this state of things might change, but considering the size of your curtained four-poster, I found it disappointing to have to stay down here.

The room into which you led me was a disappointment too. Little light fell on the bare stone walls through the slit of a window, which was really just a loophole. A very narrow bed stood by the right-hand wall. Even at first glance it looked as hard as it later proved, and it was the only item of furniture.

As I looked around me, rather taken aback, you finally seemed to notice that my surroundings depressed me. Gazing at me beseechingly, you said I must be patient for a while, until one thing and another could be arranged. I was at a loss to know what "things" you meant. With those words you suddenly and surprisingly flung your arms round me and kissed me, and then you were out of the door before I could reconcile any of this with my own feelings.

I sat there for a while on the hard bed, baffled, mulling over my strangely unfriendly reception in what looked so magnificent a castle from the outside. As twilight gradually fell, I rose to take a closer look at my room before it got really dark. The only things I found apart from the bed were a wrought-iron candlestick with a thick wax candle in it and an old-fashioned tinderbox. The tinderbox was quite a test of my skill, but I eventually managed to light the wick of the candle, using the stone, the steel and the tinder.

I was very relieved to have some light in the place, wholly unfamiliar as it was to me, and I felt better as soon as the candle was burning with a steady flame, casting its light on the rough-hewn, gray-brown squared stones of the walls. I made up my mind that once night had fallen, I would look round this large building, whose occupants showed me such undisguised hostility.

The door creaked on its hinges as I opened it, and I waited for a moment to see if I could hear anyone out in the corridor. But all was quiet. So I picked up my candlestick and began exploring the castle.

First I went along the corridor I knew already, to the foot of the spiral staircase down which I had come with you. At this point the corridor turned sharply left and I followed it past four or five closed doors to a flight of stairs leading to the cellars. Hoping that I might find a door there providing me with a way to leave the building unobserved if need be, I went down the stairs. Cool air rose to meet me.

The stairs ended in a low, vaulted passage where I could only just stand upright. After I had taken a few steps, I heard soft squealing and mewing, and then, a little way ahead, I saw something moving rapidly to and fro, coming closer in the faint light of my candle. It was obviously a cat playing with something, which suddenly shot past my feet and which on closer inspection proved to be a mouse, not yet badly injured.

Of course I know it's in the nature of cats to play with mice, and it can't be held against them. All the same, I don't like to watch them play with their prey, especially as I'm inclined to take the side of the mice, the weaker party. Anyone who's ever really looked at a mouse, with its velvety coat, its quivering whiskers and its amazingly lively black, beady eyes, will understand. So I came between the cat and its plaything and tried to shoo it away, hissing and flapping my hands. Annoyed, the cat launched itself furiously at me, leaving me with four parallel bleeding scratches on the back of my hand. With a quick movement that almost blew out the candle, I held the flame so close to the cat's glowing green eyes that it leaped up in alarm and darted away into the darkness of the vaulted cellars.

I turned to the mouse it had been hunting, which was now sitting trembling at my feet. It cleaned its whiskers, looked up at me and said, "I won't forget how you rescued me from that cat's fangs."

It then turned to examine the tip of its tail, which was hanging by a shred of skin, obviously severed by a playful blow of the cat's paw. The mouse bit the tip completely off—it was about the length of my little fingernail—and offered it to me as if it were something precious.

"Take good care of the tip of this sadly foreshortened tail of mine," said the mouse. "If you ever need help you have only to drop it on the ground and call me. I and my family won't let you down."

I thanked the mouse for the gift, though I couldn't imagine what kind of help such a tiny creature could provide. But having struck up this conversation with the mouse, I asked if there was any door through which one could leave the castle unseen.

"You don't like it here? I'm not surprised," said the mouse. "All you have to do is go to the end of this passage, take ten human paces along the corridor you see branching off to the left, and then you'll come to a door."

"Is it locked?" I asked.

"Yes," said the mouse, "but I know where the key is kept."

"Where can I find it, then?"

"Impatient, aren't you?" said the mouse. "It's hidden in a crack between the stones above the lintel. You can get away now if you like."

"No, I can't do that," I said. "And I don't want to, or not at the moment. I just want to feel sure I can get outside when I like. Will you show me the door?"

"I'd rather not," said the mouse. "The hole where the cats come in and out is cut in that door, and I prefer to steer clear of it."

With that the mouse said good-bye. I checked that the door was where it said. The key was in its place too, and it fitted the lock, opening the door almost noiselessly. I stood there listening to the sounds of the night for a while. When I heard a couple of cats squalling in the distance, I locked the door again and retraced my steps.

After climbing the stairs back to the ground floor, I didn't return to my room immediately, but followed the passage in the other direction. I found out that it led through all four wings of the square building and came out again in the dining hall at the far end. Halfway along I had noticed a fountain set in a niche in the wall, like the little fountains you see in monastery cloisters. Water rose in a thin jet from the jaws of a bronze lion's head and fell splashing into a shell-shaped sandstone basin. On the way back I washed my hands there, cooling the burning scratches the cat had given me. Then I went back to my room, put the candle out and lay down on my bed.

I could not sleep at first. The mingled impressions of the day kept my thoughts busy. More particularly, I couldn't make out what kept you in this castle, which seemed to me increasingly sinister, and where you yourself were treated with so little respect. What had become of my lioness? You had spoken of her as if she had nothing to do with you; you'd even said she meant me harm. All this confused but intrigued me, increasing my interest in what went on in this strange castle. But you obviously wanted me here, and that idea soothed me enough to let me fall asleep at last.

As soon as I encountered you in the corridor outside my room next morning, I asked why you had lured me into these unwelcoming walls if I must go on sleeping alone in that cold, bleak room.

You looked at me for a while in silence, and yet again I observed that stubborn set to your mouth.

"Don't you realize how badly I need you in this dreadful castle?" you said at last. "How else am I to bear it, with the surly servants, who only obey me because they must and mock me as soon as my back's turned?"

"Then let's escape together!" I said. "I know a way to get out of the castle unseen."

But you shook your head, and your lips were set in an imperious line that again was new to me as you said, "Escape's no answer to my problem. I must stay here and wait for the lord of the castle. That's my last word."

I couldn't understand it. What business of mine was the lord of this castle? I tried to make you change your mind at breakfast, and I tried even harder afterward as I rode with you through the still misty meadows above the village, past an oak that had been struck by lightning, its split branches reaching to the sky. "We have only to spur our horses on and leave the whole wretched business behind us," I urged, but you seemed to be bound to that wretched castle with an invisible chain. The harder I tried to persuade you, the more firmly you insisted that we must turn back, and finally you wrenched your horse's head around and galloped back to the castle ahead of me, over grassy meadows strewn with tiny white star-shaped flowers like daisies. As we dismounted in the courtyard the groom grinned at me, just as if he knew about my vain attempts to persuade you to escape.

I went on arguing all day, and finally I threatened to leave if you wouldn't let me sleep with you in your big four-poster bed. Although I realized you were afraid the servants might spy on us, you finally agreed in obvious desperation, but said I mustn't come to your room until night, when everyone was asleep and there was no one about in the passages and halls. And whatever I did, you said, I must keep very, very quiet.

That evening I left the door of my room open a crack so that I could hear what went on outside as I lay on my hard bed puzzling about your connection with the absent lord of the castle, which was a mystery to me. My study of folktales suggested that he might not resemble a human being at all; he could be a monster who had you in his power. The obvious conclusion was that you might intend to release this monster from his spell, but I pushed that thought aside, preferring to construct the imaginary figure of a dreadful enemy. Then I would have every right to stand up to him and free you from your compulsive attachment.

Finally all was quiet outside. I waited a little longer, then lit my candle and crept along the corridor and up the spiral staircase to your room.

"I'm glad you've brought a light," you said. "I'm so frightened every night, lying awake in the dark here, with the place as quiet as if there wasn't another living soul in it."

The curtains of the four-poster were pulled back, and you were lying among the pillows. I was surprised when you told me to put the candlestick down on the little table by the bed and leave the candle burning, for I thought of the night when I had defied your wishes, switched on the light and thus driven you away in such a terrifying manner.

You watched me as I undressed and lay down beside you, and I saw fear in your eyes. You embraced me, clinging to me hard, as if desperate, and as I caressed you, your face, in its growing agitation, seemed less and less familiar to me. I felt your body pressing close to mine, while at the same time, with increasing horror, I saw your own features dissolve and reassemble into a face I didn't know at all, except for those few characteristics that had never struck me before I met you here at the castle. In the flickering candlelight I stared at the face close to mine and realized suddenly that I was lying beside a woman who was a total stranger to me. All the time, ever since she emerged from the twilight as suddenly as if she had come from nowhere, she hadn't been you but someone else, and I had let her deceive me about her true identity.

It took me a little while to pull myself together enough to ask the woman who she was.

I never got an answer, for at that moment we suddenly heard the trampling of feet as people ran along the corridor outside. Keys rattled, doors were flung open and slammed shut again, a trumpet call rang through the night.

"The lord of the castle!" cried the woman, low-voiced, with a strange mixture of joy and fear in her eyes. "He mustn't find you here! Quick! Get yourself to safety!"

"What about you?" I asked.

She hardly seemed to understand what I meant. "But he's the one I've been waiting for," she said. "Hurry!"

Already getting my clothes on, I reached for the light.

"Leave the candle here!" whispered the woman. "Its light will give you away."

When the steps outside the door had faded, I hurried out of the room, ran down the spiral staircase and was making for my room, but servants with hurricane lanterns were coming down the corridor toward me. I turned at once, running away from them into the dark, but some of them had already recognized me. "There he goes, there's the stranger she picked up outside!" someone shouted, and they called after me to stop. "What are you doing out here in the middle of the night? Have you come down the staircase from her room? Just wait, we'll catch you!"

By the time they uttered this threat I had reached the top

of the cellar stairs and was making my way into the cool darkness. I was soon at the bottom of the stairs, but once down there I couldn't get my bearings immediately. It was a little while before I had worked my way along the narrow passage to the place where the door ought to be. Finally I managed to locate it by touch, and I was feeling for the hiding place of the key as my pursuers reached the top of the stairs, loudly arguing as to whether I had run on along the passage or gone down into the cellars. "He can't get away up here," someone said. "Let's search the cellars first! We can silence him quietly down there."

Before they could get down the stairs with their lanterns and find me, I fished the tip of the mouse's tail out of my breast pocket. "Now, mouse, bring your family and help me!" I whispered, and dropped the velvety little object on the ground.

I had not acted a moment too soon. I could already hear men clattering down the stairs, and I still hadn't found the key. But the mice were on their way. The tiny, furry animals were scurrying everywhere at my feet. I could feel them streaming toward the stairs. Next moment I heard the men shouting, cursing and yelling with pain as they all tumbled down the stairs; the flight had two sharp bends in it. Then I had the key in my hand at last, opened the door and ran for it before any of the hopelessly entangled men could struggle free of each other and catch me. "Thank you, mice!" I called before I plunged into the darkness.

Once out of the castle, I ran swiftly over the grassy meadow outside to the vineyards, climbed the fence and tried to pick my way down the slope between the vines in the pitch dark. I kept getting entangled in the nets spread over the vines, like the little bird I had freed. Again and again I heard men's voices calling from the castle as they searched for me, and saw their lanterns swaying back and forth. Once I heard an imperious voice calling, "Bring him to me dead or alive!" By that time I had reached the other end of the vineyard. I gave the village a wide berth, for I saw a troop of horsemen from the castle trotting through it with torches.

As the sky gradually grew lighter I was skirting a pond. The branches of a willow leaning over it dipped into the faintly shining surface of its water. I went on through the last of the cornfields, and then the wide steppes lay ahead again, without tree or bush. I would find no cover out on that plain, where everything was visible for miles. Yet I had to go that way or I could never hope to find the object of my quest again. The horizon widened as the light grew stronger, and at last I could see my old landmark, the tower I was bound for, in the distance. It seemed to be awaiting me like an old acquaintance, and the mere sight of it gave me a sense of security—a premature sense of security, as it turned out.

I heard the sound of horses' hooves before I saw the riders come galloping out of the village and through the fields and meadows. They momentarily reined in their horses, probably coming upon my tracks in the grassland, for next moment they were off again, yelling and shouting, making straight toward me and approaching at alarming speed.

There was no point in running away, and unarmed as I was I couldn't defend myself against the horsemen if they attacked me. I thought it very doubtful that the little bird would be able to help, but it was worth trying. The horsemen were already so close that I could see their faces, and the ground was shaking under their horses' hooves as I blew the little brown feather into the air, calling, "Help me now if you can, little brown bird!"

Instantly, great flocks of little birds rose everywhere from the fields and meadows, and assembled into a single swirling cloud of brown feathers. Soon the troop of horsemen was entirely lost from sight. I heard the whinnying of the horses and the curses of the men, but I could make out nothing until the cloud lifted again. Then I saw the horses racing away, riderless, while some of the men tried to follow, limping. Others lay on the ground, obviously unable to get up.

"Thank you, little birds!" I cried, and I made haste to continue on my way toward the tower before any of the riders could catch their horses again.

I had gone some way when, sure enough, a horseman did appear behind me. I looked around in vain for a bush from which I could break myself a cudgel, or a hollow in the ground where I could take cover. There was no hope for me this time. I was sure of that. I stood looking at the horseman, who was galloping swiftly up to me. To judge by his fine clothes and the gleam of gold on his weapons, he was a commander at least, if not the lord of the castle himself.

Oddly enough, I liked him. He sat his horse easily as he rode the last few paces; his face was sad rather than angry when he reined his horse in beside me and looked down at me.

"Why did you worm your way into my castle and the bed of the woman who loves me?" he asked. "I shall have to take you back with me now, and it will not go well with you when I have you in the castle."

I did not reply. I didn't want to give away the woman I had thought was you.

"Very well," said the rider after a moment. "I am going to tie you up now and you can run along behind my horse until your tongue is hanging out. And once we're back, you'll talk."

He spoke without haste, almost casually. But when he took a leather strap from his bag and prepared to dismount, I suddenly heard an angry roar. This time it was music in my ears. The lioness came bounding through the rustling grass and stationed herself between me and the rider, growling.

He stayed put on his horse—it was shying and he had trouble controlling it. "Well, well! You have a powerful friend to defend you," he said. "I don't think I'll try conclusions with her. But never venture into my lands again!" And with that he turned his horse and rode calmly away.

So ended this strange story, leaving me in a state of considerable confusion once again. My experiences in the castle reminded me of something, though I couldn't say what. Furthermore, I felt as if whatever they reminded me of was just as unpleasant as they were. I felt the elusive memory as a vague sense of oppression, and I wanted to be rid of it as soon as possible. So eventually I stopped puzzling over it and looked at the lioness, who was watching the horseman go and raking the ground restlessly with her forepaws. She seemed to me more aggressive than before, and I couldn't help thinking of what that woman had said about her when I still thought she was you. Did this beautiful animal really mean me harm? The woman had probably said so only to dismiss the lioness from my mind, yet a shadow of doubt lingered there.

Meanwhile we had resumed our journey. The track we were following brought us to a gentle rise in the ground, giving a good view of the tower and the mountain range behind it. The tower looked closer again, standing out clear and sharp against the blue backdrop of the mountains.

I tried talking to the lioness as we walked on over the grassland toward the tower, hoping to get some idea of how she felt about me. I spoke as I would have spoken to a dog I was training. But I was never sure if she kept close because of my repeated commands to stay at heel or if she did it of her own accord. The length of our strides struck me as well adjusted anyway.

All the same, I went on trying to tame my companion, or rather trying to impose my will on her. I had no means of actually forcing her to obey my orders or I might well have used them. I would stop suddenly; if she walked on, I called sharply when she had gone a few paces to make her stop as well. She usually did, but not in a submissively obedient way at all. Indeed, the manner in which she turned to look at me expressed something more like helpful friendliness, as if I'd called for help. At such moments it was only too easy for her gentle gaze to undermine my self-confidence, but for that very reason I persisted with my efforts.

I was unaware of their full implications at the time. Had I

forgotten whom the lioness's golden skin concealed? Had doubts of her good will taken root in my mind? I can't really remember now. But, in any case, I acted as if I had to bind the lovely creature to my will rather than try to fathom her secret, the secret of your metamorphosis. Why had you hidden in the lioness? Or had the metamorphosis occurred without your own volition? Was it entirely my own doing? Did a kind of fear reaction cause your body to cover itself with fur, growing paws armed with claws to defend itself against my intrusive gaze?

One question in particular occupied my mind. Do you remember the time you spent walking through the grass with me in the shape of the lioness? Was your consciousness there in her, though mute, or was she all animal, so that her attitude toward me can be explained only as a reaction to some lingering memory of our relationship? What did you feel as I kept trying to force my will on you? Did you feel anything at all or were you helplessly spellbound in the animal, incapable of human feelings, reverting to animal behavior patterns? If so, did that mean that you depended on the usual spell-breaking procedure of fairy tales? I understood nothing at all about you during our journey to the tower.

We came perceptibly closer to the squat, round building that day. Though still very distant, it was a striking landmark as the diffuse light began to fade yet again and absolute darkness fell. This time the vanishing of the light didn't alarm me as much as before; after all, it had come back to illuminate this grass-grown world.

However, my companion became restless again. She pressed close to me and tried to push me over, growling, until she had me lying on the ground. I was glad now I had kept my part of the chestnut, for the lioness's ferocity instantly showed me that I had merely been suppressing my fear of her by pretending to be her master. Now she was finally on top of me, baring her fangs as if to bury them in my throat.

I hastily fished the bit of chestnut kernel out of the bag, broke it in half again and pretended to put my own piece in my mouth. Then, chewing, I held the lioness's half out to her and slipped the last morsel back into the bag. "Feeding beasts of prey" was the image that shot through my mind as I did so. Of course that was an entirely inadequate way to describe the situation, but I record it here to show you how far I was in my terror from understanding the eating-together ritual. Incidentally, such ritual meals are obviously the only kind of eating that takes place out on that grassy plain. While I was walking there I myself ate nothing, and yet I never felt hungry.

The lioness failed to notice my trick again, or at least she pretended not to notice it—that is, if she was capable of such behavior. Anyway, she lay down beside me, purring peacefully, and seemed to fall asleep at once. I heard nothing but her quiet breathing as I lay awake, wondering what I would do when I had fed her the very last crumb of the chestnut next time we stopped to rest. Could I control her boisterousness empty-handed when your sister's gifts were all gone?

It was pitch dark when I was woken by a booming, crashing sound that shook the ground beneath me. I immediately realized that the lioness had left my side. A bestial stench of rotten meat and even worse hung in the air, nauseating me so much that if I'd had anything to speak of in my stomach I would have vomited. Next moment a long drawn-out howl brought me to my feet. Then, much farther away than the terrifying sounds had led me to expect, I saw bright red flames shoot up above the steppes, setting fire to the dry grass. And then, for a brief moment, the creature that had caused all these horrors showed in the somber light of the rapidly spreading fire: a monstrous dragon, prowling over the grassy plain like a chain of hills come to life. Its skull, which seemed to have almost no room for a brain, consisted mainly of a pair of gaping jaws set with countless rows of sharp, sawlike teeth, from which tongues of fire kept shooting out to singe the grass. Then the monster was hidden by a wavering wall of surging crimson smoke.

It was such an incredible sight that I stood there as if frozen. I had once seen a dragon in a film. Even there the appearance of a wrinkled rubber monster worked by electricity had been alarming enough, but it was as nothing compared to what I'd just seen marching over the grassland: the incarnation of deadly, incalculable power. The sight of it made me weak at the knees. I stood there almost too long, staring at the smoke that welled up from the flames, before realizing that the wind was driving the fire toward me. Then, at last, my legs obeyed me again and I ran blindly, ran for my life, gulping breaths of the stinking, smoky air, ran coughing and weeping from the inferno rolling over the plain behind me in a broad, blazing wall of fire.

Ordinary units of time can't express the length of my flight from the flames. When darkness gradually gave way to a gloomy, smoke-dimmed light, I saw countless creatures scurrying through the dry grass with me, mostly mice and a few hamsters, but some weasels too, and even foxes, perhaps surprised by the fire while they were out hunting by night and now sparing not a glance for the prey animals chasing along beside them.

With the coming of light, my hope of escaping the fast-approaching flames also rose. I saw a town not so very far away on top of a steep hill. Parts of the hillside dropped sheer to the plain. The houses of the town were crowded close together and surrounded by a strong wall. Then I came to a paved road where the going was easier; moreover, it seemed to lead to the town. There were freshly plowed fields to right and left of the road. The fire would have nothing to feed on here, so at last I was able to slow to a walk. Still breathless and gasping, my heart beating in my throat, I made for the hill and then, as my breath came more easily, went up the road to the little town.

Inside the walls the place was in mourning. I could see

that as soon as I was walking down the narrow streets between the tall, close-packed houses. The few men and women I met were dressed in dark colors, most of them in black, and they seemed so gloomy and lost in sad thoughts that they either failed to notice my greeting or looked alarmed when I addressed them. Even the children had forgotten how to laugh, and were as sad and serious as their elders.

I found an inn standing in a sizable square in the middle of the town. Its sign told me it was called THE SPOTTED DOG. I went in, sat at a table in the empty taproom and asked the landlord, who was standing idly behind the bar, to bring me something to eat.

"You can have a bit of black bread and some sour wine," he said. "That's all I can offer."

"Why so little?" I asked.

"We're under siege," he said. "Didn't you notice anything? You must be a stranger here, for you're certainly not one of us. I know everyone in town."

"What should I have noticed?" I asked, but I already guessed his meaning.

"The tracks," he said, as if unwilling to name the creature that had made them.

"Of the dragon?" I said. "I could hardly miss him. I only just escaped the fire he lit out on the plain. Does he come here too?"

"Not if we feed him," said the landlord.

"What with?"

"Everything we need to live on ourselves. And on top of that, a young girl once a week. He had one yesterday. Soon there'll be no girls left in town at all; they don't grow up fast enough to keep pace."

"So then what?"

"Then I suppose we all go to hell together," said the landlord.

At this point a girl came into the taproom, and I saw the landlord look at her and turn deathly pale at the thought of his own words.

"My daughter," he said, and told her to bring me the bread and a cup of wine. "We have plenty of that," he added. "The creature doesn't like wine."

The girl fetched both from behind the bar and brought them to my table. When she had put the plate of bread and the full wine cup down in front of me and wished me good health, she lingered, a query in her face as she looked at me. I was not displeased by her attention, for she was a pretty sight in her simple smock. I particularly liked her eyes, turned on me so questioningly. So I held her gaze and let it linger on me, rather enjoying the feelings it aroused.

"Why did you come to this town?" asked the girl. "Are you a champion who will fight the dragon?"

"Do I look like it?" I said, trying to conceal the alarm her question caused me. The mere idea of going out to meet that living mountain of malevolence made my hand tremble as I raised the wine cup to my mouth.

"All right," said the girl. "I was only asking. There's nothing to be ashamed of. We're all afraid here."

I stayed in the town for the time being. At least there was temporary security here, while anywhere outside the walls I risked crossing the dragon's path. The landlord gave me a room to sleep in up in the attic of the tall, thick-walled house, and I spent my days walking the crooked streets or sitting in the taproom, sometimes with the landlord's daughter to keep me company. There was not a lot to do. Now and then a man would come in and drink until he fell senseless under the table, whereupon the landlord would send his daughter to the drunk's family so that they could fetch him home. No arguments or reproaches were involved; everyone understood that a man in this town might feel the need to get drunk. Sometimes I accompanied the girl on these expeditions, and we talked.

A week after my arrival, as we were out on one such

errand, she told me she was living from week to week, since the lots that were cast to decide who was thrown to the monster could fall on her at any time. "I have another six days now," she said. "The lot fell on someone else yesterday. I knew her very well. We were cousins; her family lives only two doors away."

She spoke as calmly as if she were mentioning some perfectly commonplace thing such as a girl's engagement.

"Have they taken her out already?" I asked.

"Yes. It's always done at once, the same day."

"I didn't notice," I said, feeling oddly guilty, not for the girl's death but for not noticing it.

"I know," said the girl. "You're staying here with us, but it's as if our wretchedness had nothing to do with you. You seem to me like someone from another world, where fear isn't part of everyone's daily life. Perhaps that's what I like about you."

When I stopped and looked at her, I saw the fear at the back of her eyes. She had stopped trying to hide it. I took her in my arms and kissed her, and when she got her breath back she said, "Let's live these six days to the full!" After that she came up to my attic room every night, and I quite forgot she had spoken as if she really had only these few days to live.

As we lay together up in my room, I too sometimes forgot the threat over us, and I even draped a cloth over the window, with its view over the town walls to the plain below where the dragon sometimes passed on his fiery way. And though a somber red glow and a flicker of fire could still be made out in the middle of the night, even through the cloth over the window, I turned away so as not to see it.

I don't know if I helped the girl, in those nights, to forget her fear of the seventh day. Very likely I was only persuading myself I could. She must surely have felt that fear all the same, not least as the driving force behind our embraces.

On the morning of the seventh day the lot fell on the landlord's daughter. We were sitting in the taproom together when a messenger from the town hall brought the news, saying they would come for her that afternoon. The landlord jumped to his feet and flung the glass from which he had just been drinking his sour wine at the wall, where it smashed. "Curse the creature!" he roared. "Isn't there a man anywhere to tackle it?"

I knew he had no idea himself how anyone could tackle the monster, but I still felt his question as a reproach. He hadn't failed to realize what was going on in his house at night; he had even turned an indulgent eye, not wishing to deny his daughter a little brief happiness under so deadly a threat. But now he was staring at me as if it was my business to save his daughter from the dragon.

"Don't look at him like that," said the girl, laying her hand on his arm. "There's nothing he can do, and you know it."

She was so composed that her father looked at her, shaking his head, and then took her in his arms. "Aren't you afraid, then?" he asked.

"Oh yes," she said. "I've been afraid ever since they began casting lots for the girls. And I felt sure it would fall on me this time. But what's the use of weeping and wailing?" She hugged her father close and then, glancing at me, she asked him, "Let me be alone with him for a little while."

This time we went up to my room together in broad daylight. I was going to pull her down on the bed, but she shook her head and said, "We can't hide from what's about to happen now. Come over to the window and let's look at each other again, just for a little while."

And so we did, long and hard. Her face had never seemed to me as lovely as then, when she was hiding nothing, neither her fear nor her love for me, and I didn't know if that love was any help or just made everything worse. But I saw myself as her lover in the mirror of her face, and I stopped thinking of my inability to help her.

As we stood at the window, glancing down now and then at the spreading country beneath the hill where the town stood, I saw two horsemen trotting up the road from the plain, both of them in shining armor and carrying long spears. The taller of the two wore a bright red surcoat over his coat of mail, and a plume of the same color on his helmet.

"A knight!" said the girl. "I wonder what he wants here?"

"To fight the dragon," I said; you'd hardly expect anything else of a knight in the circumstances. I saw the girl's face change as hope dawned in it and I ought to have been glad. But at the same time I envied the strong mail-clad man who, she thought, was brave enough to fight the dragon, and who might indeed vanquish him.

When the two horsemen had ridden up the hill, they reached the gate and disappeared from view behind the town walls. "Let's go down and hear what the knight's going to do," said the girl.

A crowd of people had already gathered in the square. They watched in silence as the two armed men came trotting along the street and reined in their horses outside the town hall, which stood opposite the inn on the other side of the square.

The knight rose slightly in his stirrups. "Good people," he called, "I have heard that your town is plagued by a dragon who not only devours your goods and chattels but demands a maiden once a week. When is the monster's next victim to be given to him?"

"Today!" cried all the people at once. "Today, this very afternoon!" And many of them applauded the knight's courage, calling down blessings on him. One man, who had rushed out of the door of the town hall a moment before and was particularly eager to help, gave a precise description of the place outside the town where the offering was always made; all the formalities had been properly organized by the town council. Then he pointed to the landlord's daughter, who was standing outside the inn beside me, and cried, "And there's the poor girl who's to be sacrificed to the monster today!"

On hearing that, the knight handed his enormously long spear to the other horseman, who must have been his squire, dismounted and came over the square toward us, clinking with steel. And when he stood before us, I recognized him: he was the man who had pursued me to the last when I escaped from the castle, and whom I'd taken for its lord.

He gave me a disdainful look, as if wondering why I had crossed his path again, but he didn't say so. Indeed, he proceeded to act as if I weren't there at all, and so far as saving the girl was concerned, he may well have been right. He looked kindly at the landlord's daughter and told her she was to have no fear: he knew a lot about slaying dragons and would soon put an end to the monster. However, he couldn't spare her being taken to the place of sacrifice and tied to a stake or the dragon would suspect something. Then he took off his steel gauntlet, patted the girl's cheek and said, "Be brave, my child! It will soon be over."

There was more than one possible way to take that last remark. I for one felt angered by the hero's treatment of the girl, but no doubt it was routine behavior for such knights, who had run spears through the hearts of heaven knows how many dragons already.

As it was nearly noon, the girl was taken straight into the town hall, where every victim was given a carefully prepared meal before being taken out of the town gates and down to the place of sacrifice. The people thronged the square, clapping as the girl passed them without a sign of fear, shouting for joy and flinging their caps in the air as if the victory was already won.

I didn't care for these premature rejoicings, and as there was no more I could do, I went back to the inn and up to my room. I might be able to see the dragon approach the town from my window.

For a while I looked out over the empty plain. Nothing stirred; the grasslands lay motionless under that continual threat. Then, later, I saw the knight and his squire ride out, their tall spears upright and resting on their stirrups. Behind them came six of the town's soldiers, armed to the teeth and leading the girl. The group went down the hill to the plain, and, once there, they made for a sandpit where a cow and two pigs had already been tethered. Here the soldiers bound the girl to a post. They then cleared out in great haste, almost racing back to the town, while the two horsemen hid in a thicket of bushes above the sandpit. Then all was quiet again.

I remained sitting at the window for about half an hour, looking down at the sandpit and trying to imagine the feelings of the girl tied to the stake. I couldn't see her face at such a distance, but in spite of the knight's assurances I felt sure her fear would be plain to see at this moment.

And then the dragon approached. The first indication came from flocks of birds rising far away among the hills and circling agitatedly in the air. A little later I saw fiery smoke rise in a gap in those same hills, and next moment the dragon gradually pushed his way out of the valley between them, until his entire length was in view. He did not look as monstrously vast as he had seemed to me at first, by night, but he was still quite big enough to make me thankful I was here in my room, not tied to the stake down there like the girl. He made his way over fields and meadows straight to the sandpit, but as he approached the bushes where the knight was hidden, he suddenly stopped and raised his mighty head.

This was a sign that the game was beginning. The next moment I was watching a professional exhibition of dragon fighting. The squire, whom the dragon had obviously already seen or at least scented, rode out into the open above the bushes and trotted over the grass toward the dragon, his spear held upright. As soon as he saw the horseman, the monster turned with astonishing agility and thundered toward his opponent much faster than I would have thought possible. However, the whole maneuver turned out to be a calculated feint, for as soon as the dragon had drawn close to the bushes and was about to pass them, the knight broke cover, his own spear at the ready. He put his horse to the gallop, and next moment, before the monster even had time to look round at his new adversary, he was driving his weapon into the dragon's neck beneath the skull. The shaft of the spear split, jarred by the speed of the dragon, who careered on for some way before stopping. A shower of wooden splinters went flying around the knight's helmet.

Meanwhile the squire had ridden round in a semicircle and back to his master. He handed him another spear and tried once again to attract the dragon's attention to himself. He succeeded, but he had not reckoned with the wounded monster attacking so fast and so fiercely. Spouting fire from his gaping jaws, the dragon singed the squire's clothes and in an instant they were ablaze. Alarmed by the flames, the squire's horse shied and bucked, flung its rider to the ground right at the dragon's feet, and galloped frantically away.

But now the knight was coming up again. He had ridden a little way uphill, past the bushes, and now he turned his horse back toward the dragon and buried his spear in the scaly belly on the monster's other side, just behind the shoulder. This time the shaft didn't break, which was unfortunate for the knight. As the dragon, wounded again, swung violently round, the spear to which the knight was still clinging lifted him from the saddle and flung him high into the air. At last he let go of his weapon and fell, arms flailing helplessly, behind the bushes and out of my sight. The dragon had disappeared behind the thicket too. There was nothing to be seen but the two riderless horses galloping desperately over the hill, and the squire's body. Thin smoke was still curling upward from his clothes.

I watched the abandoned battlefield for some time. Apart from the prostrate figure of the squire, nothing but trodden grass and a black trail of dragon's blood showed what had just happened. Hard as I tried to make out what lay behind those bushes, I could see nothing moving. In the end I could

bear the uncertainty no longer, and I decided to go and inves-
tigate. I could at least free the girl from her uncomfortable
situation.

Obviously other people had seen the uncertain outcome
of the dragon fight too. They were now standing in the street,
faces downcast, whispering, but none of them seemed able
to pluck up the courage to go and see what had actually
happened. The town soldiers were standing at the closed
gate, and refused to open it even a crack to let me out. I
argued with them for a while, but eventually I realized that
nothing would induce them to go against their orders as long
as the dragon's fate wasn't known for certain, so I gave up
and tried to find another way to leave the town.

Just inside the town walls an alley divided them from the
houses so that you could walk all round them, as would
sometimes be necessary for their defense. Following this
alley, I went almost halfway round the town before finding
a smaller gate. It was locked, but using a stout stick as a
lever I managed to break it off its rusty hinges and open it
a little way. I slipped out into the open.

I climbed down the hill, which fell away quite steeply at
this spot, and made for the hills from which the dragon had
emerged. Standing on one of the hilltops, I could finally see
the place where the battle had disappeared from my view.
There lay the dragon, full length, motionless, and I saw the
gleam of the knight's armor beside his head. The knight was
prostrate on the ground too. After watching for some time
and seeing no movement at all, I plucked up the courage to
make my cautious way over to the battlefield, stopping frequently and glancing at the monstrous body in case it was
moving after all. On the way I managed to catch both horses
fairly easily.

When I reached the place at last, I saw that the dragon
was dead as mutton. The knight had succeeded in severing
the head almost completely from the body with his sword.
Nothing but a strip of leathery skin covered with iridescent
scales still connected it to the muscular neck. The knight lay

close to the lifeless monster, the hilt of his bloodstained sword beside his open right hand, so motionless that I thought he was dead too. The squire had perished as well, as I soon found out. He was a ghastly sight; the dragon must have trampled on him.

As soon as I had decided that there was no one left alive, I clambered down into the sandpit and cut the girl free from the stake. She was hanging from it more dead than alive, and fell into my arms as if she had no strength left in her limbs at all. I was going to fetch one of the horses from the meadow above, but she clung to me, begging me in heaven's name not to leave her alone again. After a while I managed to soothe her fears, assuring her that the dragon was dead, and she recovered enough for me to lead her to the place where I had left the horses.

Then I thought of taking the dragon's skull back with us, to show the townsfolk that the monster really was dead. Leaving the girl with one of the horses, I took the other over to the gigantic carcass. I sawed the dragon's head from his body with the knight's sword and fastened it to my saddle with a long strap, so that the horse could drag the grisly thing after him. He shied away from it at first, but he was a warhorse, used to battle, and soon realized there was no danger in the lifeless thing now. He dragged it over the grass after him.

Then I led him back to the other horse. The girl screamed when she saw what he had behind him. But by now I had mounted the second horse; I lifted her up to sit sidesaddle in front of me, and so we returned to the town.

The soldiers had obviously seen us coming from the walls. We were still on the road up to the town when the gate swung open and people came running out. Next moment they had surrounded us, congratulating the girl on her rescue, shaking my hand as if I were the one who had killed the dragon, and gazing in astonishment at the bloodstained trophy the second horse was dragging along.

The mayor came up to me and asked how the battle had gone. When I told him I'd found both the knight and his squire dead, he immediately hailed me as the savior of the town and led me and the girl, like a prince and his bride, through the gate to the square outside the town hall, where I dismounted and helped the girl down. There was a crowd of people in the square, all praising my courage in facing the monster.

At first I tried to disclaim any credit, explaining what had really happened, but no one would listen. They wanted a hero, and now that they had one, they had no intention of letting him go. It was some time before the landlord of the inn managed to make his way through the crowd to us. Weeping, he took his daughter in his arms, hugged her wordlessly and then embraced me too, almost begging me to accept his daughter's hand in marriage.

All this noise had so confused me that I hardly knew what to say. The landlord was now inviting the mayor and all the town worthies to a feast in his garden, and he asked the people to leave his daughter and me in peace. Surely they could see how exhausted we both were, he said, what with the battle and all the other terrors we'd survived.

When the three of us were finally sitting in the taproom of the inn, with the servants and a few women who had been quickly recruited to help with preparing the feast in the kitchen, I tried to remind myself how the course of the dragon fight had really gone. By now events were so mixed up in my mind that I couldn't really have said for sure who actually did kill the monster; but, contrary to what everyone claimed, I still couldn't really credit myself with the conquest, and I said so.

The landlord shook his head. "It's not the kind of thing a man forgets!" he said. "You must be able to remember who cut the dragon's head off."

When he said that, I saw myself out there by the thicket with the knight's sword in my hand, busy sawing off the massive skull. "Well, I did that," I said.

"There you are, then!" The landlord leaned back on his settle, satisfied. "That was what mattered. Those two spear

wounds they talk about wouldn't have bothered a creature
like the dragon much, not with his armored hide."

That settled it so far as he was concerned, and I was too
tired to go over it all again. The girl herself hadn't been able
to see anything but the opening phase of the battle, and
anyway she wanted to hear no more about it. She rose, saying, "I'm going to lie down for a while, to give me strength
to survive this feast."

As twilight began to fall, we sat at the long table in the inn
garden by lanternlight, the girl and I in the place of honor
between the landlord and the mayor, surrounded by the most
important people in the town. I didn't feel much like celebrat-
ing and the occasion made me vaguely uncomfortable, but I
let it all wash over me, drank a little soup, toyed with a
huge helping of roast beef and picked at the accompanying
vegetables while I wondered where the landlord had found
all this food so quickly, after claiming to have nothing in the
place but black bread and sour wine. Countless toasts were
drunk to me and the girl. I merely sipped from my glass
every time, not wanting to be under the table too soon.

It might have been better for me if I'd become totally intox-
icated early on, for I was still sober enough to understand
everything that happened at the height of the feast. The
mayor had just been singing the praises of my courageous
action yet again when the tall figure of a knight in armor
suddenly broke through the bushes at the edge of the garden.
He was holding a heavy, dripping object in his hand. Coming
up to the table, he asked what the rejoicings were for.

I had recognized the knight at once. It took the others a
little longer to realize he was still alive, and the mayor still
hadn't taken it in when he said bluntly, "Why, we're celebrat-
ing the deeds of this young hero who killed the dragon and
saved this maiden from a terrible death."

"Ah," said the knight. "Did he, indeed? Then I must have

been dreaming when I drew my sword and cut off the dragon's head before I fainted for a while. What proof has this young fellow of his valiant deeds?"

"The dragon's head, to be sure! He brought it back to town with him," said the mayor.

"A hard task," said the knight. "And where's the dragon's head now?"

"Outside my house," said the landlord. "I'm going to change the name of my inn to 'The Dragon' and hang the skull over the door in memory."

"In memory of the truth or a lie?" said the knight. "Well, we'll soon see. Perhaps someone in this merry company will be kind enough to go and see if the dragon's head has a tongue in its mouth."

One of the town councilors rose, took a lantern and left the garden to go and examine the trophy. He was soon back. "There's no tongue in the dragon's head," he said. "Perhaps dragons don't have tongues."

"That's a thought, to be sure," said the knight. "Then what's this? I cut it from the mouth of the carcass myself." And with these words he angrily flung the thing he was carrying down among the dishes on the table, so that black blood splashed the snow-white tablecloth, ruining it forever. The object looked like a large, well-hung fillet of beef, but it was undoubtedly a tongue, and it still stank of dragon.

What followed was deeply humiliating. Everyone jumped up and shouted at me—what had I been thinking of, they demanded, making myself out a dragon slayer and the savior of their town? The vagabond should be chased away at once, they cried. The knight stood calmly by, listening to the clamor of the angry citizens but saying nothing himself. He looked into my face, not even angry anymore, but slightly amused.

A little later I briefly stood beside the girl once more in the shade of the garden hedge, far from the light of the lanterns.

"Was that really what happened?" she asked.

"Yes," I said. "The people here confused me with their

shouts of joy, but I really knew what had happened all the time."

I looked at her and suddenly, in the dim light of the garden, she was no longer familiar to me. She seemed sad, and I saw bitterness in her face too at what she had just learned about me. But it wasn't the familiar face I had known. She was not afraid anymore, as anyone could see, and I suppose that was what made the difference.

I turned and ran out of the square, past the houses, along the road to the gateway, out past the walls and down to the plain. I ran on and on, as if I had to shake off something that kept catching up with me the moment I stopped to think, even for a moment, of my confusion and humiliation, and that change in the girl whose cause I didn't understand. I ran and ran until I fell to the ground exhausted somewhere out on the grassy plain, and I fell asleep at once.

When I woke, the grasslands were bathed in that diffuse brightness again. I could feel it through my closed eyelids, and when I opened my eyes and sat up I saw the lioness crouching in the grass in front of me and watching me— watching me, I thought, in no very friendly way, but with a fixed and almost greedy look in her eyes. As soon as I moved and tried to get up, she began growling. Her growl didn't sound playful at all, but angry, and it warned me I had better be careful. So I stayed where I was for the moment, hoping to discover what she had in mind.

She waited there a few paces away from me for some time, raking her paws with their claws extended through the coarse grass, and again the movement was impatient rather than playful. Then she rose, trotted over to me and thrust her damp nose repeatedly at my left-hand trouser pocket. At first I thought she wanted me to get up and continue on our way over the grassy plain to the tower. But that wasn't it, because as soon as I made a move to sit up, she began hissing and growling at me, so angrily that I lay back again. At last I realized she was after the last crumb of chestnut I'd been keeping safe. As soon as I put my hand into my pocket, the lioness left me alone, sat down in the grass in front of me and looked expectant.

As I had so little to offer her, I tried to compensate by making a big performance of the ritual. I began by fishing around in my pocket at great length, and in fact it did take me quite a while to find the remaining bit of chestnut, crumbled almost to nothing by now. I hid it in my closed fist, which I brought out of my pocket very slowly, to lend a little suspense to the proceedings. I made a complicated business of the imaginary division of the piece of chestnut, which had reached the stage where it couldn't really be divided any more, keeping the actual object of my labors hidden from the lioness the whole time and thus considerably increasing her impatience. It was only when I saw that she looked likely to attack me in her greed if I delayed the symbolic meal any longer that I pretended to put a piece of chestnut in my own mouth, while I offered the lioness the tiny remains on the palm of my hand.

She licked the scrap of chestnut up with her rough tongue so fast that she can hardly have had time to notice how little of her favorite food was left until she swallowed the gift, and found there was hardly any of it to go down her throat. She shook her head, disappointed, growled at me and then turned away to trot off toward the tower, which was already clearly intersecting the line of the horizon.

There was no question of any games of obedience or attempts at lion taming this time. The lioness didn't even seem to go along with my attempts to entice her back to my side. She padded morosely through the rustling grass a dozen or so paces away from me, or ran ahead without looking back at me as she used to.

But when I stopped after we had walked a long way, because my feet hurt and I wanted to sit down and rest, she immediately came close, trying to keep me going by growling and hissing at me. I felt I'd had enough of her growling, and I shouted at her to go to hell and leave me alone. For a moment she looked as if she would leap at my throat. Then she stopped just in front of me, gazing into my face with her dark eyes for a while. Suddenly she raised her head, roaring, turned and bounded away. For some time I could still see her head and her back rising and falling in the tall grass. Finally, I lost sight of her, and then I was all alone in the wide, gray plain.

I could have rested as long as I liked now, but I no longer wanted to. Automatically I set one foot in front of the other, trudging on over the uneven ground, which was strewn with grass-grown hummocks here and there, and wondering what had made the lioness so bad-tempered. She was probably tired of being fobbed off with smaller and smaller crumbs of chestnut, or perhaps she had seen through my deception. But I doubted if that was all. The friendliness she had shown me earlier had given way to a growing estrangement, and I seriously asked myself if she knew about the amorous adventures I'd been involved in since she and I began traveling together. I hadn't exactly come out of them as any conquering hero; in fact, I'd only just got away, or, to be honest, run away, in time to save my skin. And then I had yelled at the lioness and told her to go to hell. It was my own fault she'd left me, but I realized that too late.

As I walked on, deep in thought, I had been glancing at the tower from time to time so as not to lose my bearings. Now, when I looked up once again, it had vanished from sight. A dark, towering bank of clouds was spreading on the horizon, approaching with uncanny speed. The first cold gusts of wind were already sweeping over the steppes, driving bright, silvery showers over the grass ahead of them. The first big drops splashed into my face, and they were only the beginning of a driving rainstorm through which I trudged on, head bent. I was soon wet through.

Later, the rain slackened, but thick mists rose, enveloping the whole landscape so that I could see only a few paces ahead of me. More than likely I had lost my way long ago, but I didn't feel inclined to stand still in my wet clothes, let alone sit in the dripping grass and catch a cold, or worse.

After some time I noticed that the ground was no longer as level as before. I went a little way uphill and then along the foot of a slope where a few fruit trees grew. Later I came to a path and followed it, hoping it would lead to a human dwelling some time or other.

I knocked at the door of the first house in the village. As far as I could tell through the thick mists, it was a handsome place, no doubt the property of a prosperous farmer. I had to wait some time before steps approached and the door was opened by a girl in a simple smock, whom I took for a maidservant. She asked what I wanted.

"Can I come in for a while and get warm?" I said. "By a stove, perhaps, where I could dry my clothes. I hope you have a fire going."

"Yes," said the girl. "I lit the fire when the storm came up." But she still didn't stand aside for me.

"Good!" I said. "Will you let me in, then?"

"Just a moment," she said. She disappeared into the dim recesses of the hall and came straight back with a floorcloth, which she spread in front of my feet. "Wipe your shoes on that first," she said, "and shake the water out of your clothes, and then you can come in."

A tidy-minded maidservant, I thought. And quite right too, since she was the one who had to clean up the dirt other people brought into the house. So I wiped my shoes, which were dirty from the muddy path, shook myself like a wet dog, and then entered the house, watched closely by the girl.

"Who's that at the door?" called a woman from the main living room.

The girl shrank from the sharpness of her tone. "A

stranger," she called back. "He's wet to the skin and wants to sit by our stove."

"What do you know about his skin?" snapped the woman, coming to the doorway of the living room.

The girl flinched back against the wall under her stern gaze. "I don't know anything about it," she stammered. "How would I?"

"Less chattering, miss!" said the woman crossly. "Take that bucket and fetch water from the well so this stranger can wash!" And her angry manner changed abruptly to a kind of amiability as soon as the girl was out of her sight and she had turned to me. "Welcome to my house!" she said. "I do hope Marie wasn't impertinent or actually rude to you."

I made haste to assure her that the maidservant had been courtesy itself. I was surprised at the woman's mocking laughter when I described the girl in those terms.

"Maidservant?" said she. "If Marie were a servant, then at least I could throw the clumsy creature out of the house. But I'm afraid she's my stepdaughter, my husband's child. You have to put up with these things if you marry a widower." And she laughed as if she meant to tell me she didn't have much joy of her husband either.

At last she let me into the living room. "It'll be some time before Marie gets that water heated," she told me, apologetically, and added that meanwhile I could sit in the inglenook.

There was a gray-bearded man there already. He rose to make room for me as the woman finished speaking. I liked his kindly face, though it bore the unmistakable marks of grief. I begged him not to rise, for he seemed frail, and there was plenty of room on the settle that ran around three sides of the tiled stove. The old man turned out to be the woman's husband, whose obliging daughter, Marie, had come with the marriage.

As I sat on the settle, resting my stiff back against the warm tiles, the woman joined me and tried to find out, in an elaborately indirect yet extremely obvious manner, where I came from and if I was, as she put it, "a gentleman." It wasn't hard for me to pretend not to understand her meaning, so she failed to get the information she wanted, and obviously didn't quite like to ask me straight out. Judging by my strange clothes, she said, I must be the son of some eminent family, and although I neither confirmed nor denied the statement, which was more of a question, that was clearly the conclusion to which she finally came.

After a while Marie entered the room and said the water was hot now, and I could wash in the kitchen if I liked. She stood by me as I did so, wiping every splash of water off the floor with a cloth.

"Don't you have a housemaid to do that?" I asked.

She shook her head. "Why bother, when I'm here?"

Later, when it was dark outside, we sat at supper in the living room. By "we" I mean the woman, her husband and I. Marie brought in the meal and served it with such careful attention that whatever you were looking for, it was ready to hand instantly. All the same, the girl could do nothing to please her stepmother. First she had cut the woman's bread too thin, and then too thick; if the stepmother asked for ham, then as soon as Marie handed it to her, she wanted cheese instead, and the cider Marie had brought up from the cellar wasn't cool enough to suit her, although the outside of the jug was misted with condensation. In short, she harassed her step-daughter at every turn.

While we were still eating I heard a carriage drive up outside. Next moment the door was flung open and a girl whirled into the room, laughing.

"Marushka!" cried the farmer's wife. "There you are at last! Let's look at you!"

Marushka was dressed up in party clothes, hung about with all manner of trinkets, and with her flushed cheeks and her eyes flashing with laughter she was the liveliest thing you ever saw. She pirouetted in front of her mother, making her red skirt swirl around her legs.

"There, this is *my* daughter," the farmer's wife told me. "She's no wet blanket like Marie! Marie takes after her father."

The farmer raised his head, displeased, and asked his younger daughter where she'd been so long that she was late home for supper.

The girl's mother answered for her. "She's been out dancing, you know that as well as I do. Let her have her fun! She's only young once."

At that her husband looked down at his plate gloomily and said no more.

As I was passing the kitchen doorway later, I saw Marie eating thick potato soup from a single pot with the household servants. I was surprised, but then I thought, well, it was none of my business, and walked on.

That was how I came to know the two stepsisters. The weather got even worse over the next day or so, and the farmer's wife urged me to stay at the farm for the time being. I thought nothing of it then, but since she took me for a well-to-do young man no doubt she had reasons of her own for the invitation. She certainly encouraged me to go dancing with Marushka the next day, and I was perfectly ready to oblige: it gave me some daily entertainment.

During the day I saw Marie always hurrying around the house doing all kinds of work, while Marushka rose late, left her things lying wherever she liked, and let her stepsister serve her. But she was cheerful and high-spirited, and I liked her for that.

When I brought Marushka home in the evening a few days later and we sat down to supper, I was surprised to see one of the maidservants waiting at table. "Where's Marie?" I asked.

"I don't know," said the farmer's wife. "I sent her out on

an errand and she's not back yet." Her tone was casual, but I could tell she didn't like my question.

"Where did you send her?" asked the farmer. "Surely not just into the village or she'd have been back long ago." This time, you could see, he was not going to be put off with excuses. He had every reason to ask, too, for it had snowed that day and the weather was very cold.

"Where did I send her?" asked the farmer's wife. "Why, into the forest to pick sloes. They're best after a frost. I want to make the sloe brandy you like so much. It's all for your own good."

"Into the forest?" The farmer had jumped up and was staring at her. "Do you know what you're saying? She could freeze to death in this weather. She may be out all night if she's lost her way. I'm going to look for her."

"Can I come with you?" I asked, not liking to let the old man go alone, but he said, "You stay here. You don't know your way around our woods, and if you get lost I'll only have to look for you too."

He put on a warm jacket and a woolen cap, and trudged out into the driving snow with a lighted lantern.

When he had slammed the door shut behind him, the woman said, "There's not much he can do in this weather." And it sounded as if she wasn't sorry. "Oh, the trouble that stupid girl gives us!"

Hours later the farmer came back alone. I was already in bed and heard him knocking the snow off his boots outside. When he was inside the house, he spoke to his wife, not troubling to lower his voice. He hadn't found Marie, he said; the snow had covered up her tracks. The woman tried to soothe him, but he went on reproaching her.

The household was in low spirits for the next few days. Marie didn't come home the next morning or for several days after that. The farmer's wife said the clumsy, lazy creature had probably run away because she had such a strict eye kept on her at home, but the farmer became gloomier and gloomier as he came back from his unsuccessful searches of the forest, imagining his daughter lying frozen to death somewhere in the snow.

I didn't feel like dancing now, and pretended to have a cold when Marushka asked me to go out with her. She didn't want to stay at home. "It gives me the blues, sitting here!" she said. "All because of that boring Marie, who can't think of anything but tidying up and cleaning."

So it went on until on the afternoon of the fourth day, when Marushka had just gone out dancing, the jingle of bells was heard approaching, and a sleigh ornamented with gold and drawn by three horses drove up. When it stopped outside the house, everyone ran out of doors, even the servants, and watched in astonishment as a well-dressed young man climbed out. He had a golden circlet round his hunting cap, so he was obviously a prince. He was as like as a twin brother to the man who had seen me off twice already in the course of my long quest. Indeed, he was probably the very same man, for he cast me an ironic glance, as if of recognition, before giving his hand to a most beautiful young woman and helping her out of the sleigh. She wore a cloak lined with ermine and a beaver cap with a golden brooch in it. Not until she stood before us did I recognize Marie. She flung her arms around her father, who had tears running down his bearded cheeks.

"Thank heaven you're back safe and sound!" he cried over and over again, asking the couple into the house. When he took the cloak from his daughter's shoulders, everyone could see that she was covered with golden necklaces that had gold coins hanging from them.

The farmer's wife was already busy about the house, chasing the servants from kitchen to cellar and from cellar to henhouse, where three capons had their necks wrung, and then there was such roasting and simmering in the kitchen that the fragrance wafted all over the house.

Finally, everyone sat down to table, except Marushka, who wasn't back from dancing yet to hear the tale her half-sister had to tell.

Marie really had lost her way in the woods, she said. Sloes grew only on the edge of clearings, and as she couldn't find any she went farther and farther into the depths of the forest. When she was very tired, she sank into a snowdrift and almost fell asleep there, but then she saw a light among the trees not far away. She went toward it and came to a tumbledown old cottage with a little stable behind it. An old man with a wild beard opened the door to her knock, and asked in a very unfriendly way what she wanted, saying this was no inn.

She begged him pitifully to let her come in and warm herself a little. At last he agreed, saying she could stay the night if she liked, if she would do the housework just as she did at home. Then he left her.

After she had warmed herself by the stove for a while, she went out to the stable to see what needed doing there. The cow was standing by an empty manger. Marie scratched the cow's forehead between the horns, and then picked up hay from the floor and gave it to her. A few chickens were running around too, and she called them and gave them some corn. Then she went into the kitchen, made the old man's supper and set it in front of him. She ate the leavings, just as she did at home. Then she shook his bedclothes out and made his bed, and he lay down to sleep after showing her a straw mattress in a corner of the bedroom. She lay down there and slept well.

And so it went on for three days; she had to stay, for there was such a storm raging that you could hardly venture outside the door. On the third night, however, the old man complained so bitterly of cold that she lay down in bed with him to warm him.

"Did you indeed, you good-for-nothing slut?" cried the farmer's wife.

But Marie said quietly, "In all innocence, dear mother, in all innocence."

Then the woman fell silent, and Marie went on with her tale. After the third night the old man told her she could go home now, for the storm was dying down and the sun would soon come out from behind the clouds. He showed her which way to go and then took her to the door. But as she was standing there in the doorway, she suddenly heard a ringing noise, and all the golden necklaces and coins fell on her from above, quite frightening her at first. The old man simply growled that she had better be off home now, and shut the door behind her.

No sooner had she gone a little way along the path he had pointed out than the sleigh came racing up behind her with its jingling bells. The young gentleman stopped, put his fur cloak around her shoulders and the beautiful cap on her head, and then asked where he could take her. "So here I am," Marie concluded.

Her stepmother spoke to her more kindly than ever before, served her at table and admired her golden jewelry, but you could read the envy in her eyes. And when, after the meal, the prince asked the father for his elder daughter's hand, the stepmother could hardly conceal her fury, although she kept protesting, "It's too great an honor, too great an honor!"

Having received the father's consent, the prince said he would go home now to prepare for the wedding. "I'll be back to fetch you in a few days' time," he told Marie, kissing her good-bye. The mother wanted to detain him longer, no doubt wishing to introduce him to her own daughter, but Marushka still wasn't back from dancing.

The next day, however, having taken counsel with herself overnight, the farmer's wife had made her plan. She scolded her dance-crazed daughter. "Why were you so late home yesterday?" she asked. "If the prince had seen you, he might well have changed his mind and courted you instead. Now you'll have to carry your sister's train instead of wearing the bridal veil yourself."

Marushka shrugged her shoulders. "What would I want with that prince?" she said. "I'm perfectly happy with the farmers' boys I know."

But the mother wouldn't let it rest and in the end, with all the eloquence at her command, she persuaded Marushka to go to the cottage in the forest like Marie before her and get the old man's golden blessing. Marushka showed little enthusiasm, but when her mother threatened to forbid her to go dancing she finally agreed.

Before sending her daughter into the forest, the mother gave her a warm cloak and a thick woolen cap to wear, although the weather was warmer now. Kindhearted as she was, Marie told her half-sister which way to go, so far as she remembered it, and she was going to add some more good advice, but Marushka waved an airy hand and said she was sure she could deal with the old man.

No one was much concerned when she didn't come home, particularly as the weather was sunny and there wasn't much danger of anything happening to her. Life on the farm went its usual way, except that the father wouldn't allow Marie to do menial work now. So she usually sat in the living room sewing her trousseau.

One day, when I happened to be alone with her there, I asked how she had been able to endure her stepmother's tyranny so long. She smiled and brought out from the neck of her dress a locket that she wore on a ribbon round her neck. Opening it, she showed me the picture inside. "My mother," she said. "When I was sad or angry, I talked to her and she comforted me."

The little picture showed a dark-haired woman looking into the observer's eyes as if about to speak. She wore a hat on her luxuriant hair that gave her a dashing look. I could well imagine her encouraging someone. I was still looking at the picture when the farmer's wife came into the room. Marie quickly closed the locket and tucked it back into the neck of her dress.

"I'm worried about Marushka," Marie said. "I hope she's doing everything as the old man likes it."

"How can you doubt it?" said the farmer's wife. "I'm sure my daughter knows the way to behave."

On the fourth day Marushka came home, but she wasn't covered with gold. She was in rags and tatters from walking through the dense forest, she was covered all over with sticky black pitch, and her face was smeared with tears. Her mother clasped her hands above her head in horror when she saw this picture of misery.

"Whatever have you been up to, you poor unlucky child?" she cried. "Didn't you find the old man's cottage?"

Marushka could not reply. Only when she had tried in vain to wash the pitch out of her hair and off her forehead and cheeks, and was sitting in the living room with her face partly scrubbed red and partly streaked black, did she tell her tale, hesitantly and still in tears. Yes, she had found the cottage, and asked the old man to let her in and give her a bed for the night. He had been grumpy, to be sure, but he let her in and said she could do his housework just as she did at home, and so she did.

She had never had to tend cattle on the farm, so she didn't even go into the stable, and she'd never cooked or made the beds either. So she did a little dance for the old man and tried to amuse him by cracking a few jokes, but he didn't seem to care for them. He was a real old sourpuss, she said, and she had nothing to eat the whole time but bread and water instead of proper meals, she had to sleep on a prickly straw mattress in the old man's room, and on the third night he even asked her to get in bed with him. So then she'd given him a piece of her mind, the old goat!

The next morning he sent her away. Of course she stood in the doorway waiting for the shower of gold, but a bucket of pitch was tipped over her instead. And now she was home, and she was never going to let herself in for anything like that again!

I felt sorry for her as she sat there weeping. Now and then, as I listened to her story, I felt as if it had all been happening to me, and although she didn't look nearly as pretty as before, I was much inclined to take her part against the blameless paragon, Marie, whose almost unbearable virtue had won her first the gold and then a prince into the bargain. But Marushka's mother was very angry that her plan had failed.

"And it's all this young vagabond's fault," she hissed. "Turning your head, taking you off dancing every day! Well, that's all over!" she went on, turning to me. "You can take yourself off to wherever you came from, you idle layabout!"

She showed me the door, and before I knew it I was out of the house. I was just in time, however, to see the prince arrive in his sleigh to fetch his bride. It was annoying that whenever something went wrong for me, this spotless hero had to cross my path like some unattainable, towering super-ego, and the casual but dismissive wave he gave me before entering the house did nothing to improve my temper.

I wasn't wanted here anymore, that was obvious. So I set off, going back down to the monotonous grayish plain I could see through a gap in the hills of this farming countryside.

Some time later, my shoes dusty, I was making my way over the grasslands again toward the tower, although I was less and less sure what I really hoped to find there. After a while I saw the lioness on a gentle rise in the steppes far ahead. She was looking round for me. She didn't wait for me to catch up, but kept trotting on whenever I came too close to her.

It looked to me as if we were approaching the tower much faster than before, but that was probably mainly because of the noticeable change in perspective at this point, which made the tower look as if it were growing slowly taller until gradually it rose above the wooded mountain range that sank into the background behind it. Finally its mighty, rounded bulk reached to the sky, dominating the entire view.

Now at last I was seeing the tower from the angle I knew, and soon it seemed to me even bigger, for I had never been so close to it before. It was built of regular, squared stones and rose directly from the rocky ground. There were rows of windows in the walls, set one above the other in seven stories, and at the bottom a gateway stood open beneath a round arch, seeming to invite me into the building.

But I never reached it. I had stopped to look at the great building for a moment or so, and just as I was taking my first few steps toward the gateway, the light began to fade and the gates started closing. I ran the rest of the way, but it was no use. When I reached my journey's end at last, the gates slammed shut with a crash, and there was something so final about the echoing thunder of the sound that although I began shaking the gate with all my might—in vain, of course—and drumming my fists against it in an attempt to gain entrance, I was sure in advance that my efforts were useless.

In those few moments I realized, with a single sudden flash of understanding, that I had done everything wrong. Fearing for my own safety, I had not shared my last gift with the lioness, but used it as if I were giving a wild animal a tranquilizer. I hadn't dared to rely on *your* being hidden in the lioness, even though I'd witnessed your metamorphosis at the closest possible quarters; I had put my own safety before breaking the spell on you, and so I had failed in my quest.

When I turned, I saw the lioness crouching before me, ready to spring. I seemed to see blind fury in her eyes, though now I think her glance showed something more like grief. The next moment she was standing above me, growling and snarling, and I felt the points of her sharp teeth on my bare neck.

Only much later, remembering this attack, did I realize that she didn't even scratch my skin. At the time, however, I saw my imminent violent death before my eyes and my heart fluttered like a captive bird. It fluttered and fluttered; I felt myself shrinking in my fear, becoming smaller and smaller, very fast, until I escaped the lioness's paws, fluttering and beating my wings, a tiny bird the size of a sparrow climbing to the blue-gray, rapidly darkening sky. From this high vantage point I once again saw the tower as the center of a relatively small island, with the waves of the wide lake, already dark with night, lapping lazily against its shores.

Of my state after this metamorphosis I remember only my feelings and a few images, such as the one I've just described. In particular, I remember the panic terror that increased the beat of my tiny bird's heart to the racing speed of a whirring machine, sending me up into the sky in the rapidly fading light, quite contrary to the normal behavior patterns of a small diurnal bird. And then I recollect my view of the island drifting past beneath me, the tower blurred now in the formless, spreading dark, and the pattern of streaks on the rippling waves of the lake's black surface, reflecting the very last of the light, and finally, after an endless fluttering flight in terror, the gradual approach of the dark mass of bushes on the bank, toward which I let myself drop, exhausted.

I landed in the thickets of brambles, and as soon as my feet touched the ground my brief existence as a bird was over. Forced into the thorny growth, I had my human limbs again, and I tried laboriously to use them to free myself from the tangled undergrowth. When I looked up after unhooking the last tentacle of the brambles from my shirt, I saw a marble statue facing me in the rank, luxuriant grass: a naked female figure. The moon, visible again at last in the night sky, cast cold light on her breasts and gently rounded hips. Only the face of the statue lay in shadow and could not be seen.

I might have left it at that, but I wanted to see the woman's face. She reminded me of the faceless torso whose sudden emergence from the bushes by night I've described at the beginning of my story. I thought this might be my chance to see the ravaged features of that face, and so I might discover the point and purpose of my quest, which had brought me little joy so far.

She had a face; I could see that clearly as I approached. It emerged suddenly from the darkness, flooded in the pale moonlight—a face that looked strangely alive and was very familiar to me, for I saw my own face looking at me.

After the first moment of terror as I felt for that face, to assure myself that the phenomenon was real, the secret of the statue revealed itself as something of an anticlimax: I had fallen for the trick of one of the grotesque marble sculptures in the gardens of the Palladian villa. The prince who once owned it had set up a statue of Venus here with a mirror let into the oval of the head instead of a face. No doubt he had used the classically formed statue to let the beautiful women he brought to this garden identify briefly with the goddess of love herself. But in making this discovery I realized I had received an answer too. Had I not been looking at myself the whole time, during my journey to find the lioness and my travels with her? I'd been thinking of my own situation, duped by my own fears, instead of looking in you for aspects I didn't know, aspects of you still strange to me despite the night we spent together.

At the time, as I stood there before the statue of Venus with her looking-glass face, I had some inkling of the vast distance between two people who are as close to each other as you and I.

PART
THREE

I WON'T GO INTO DETAIL about how I got out of the wilderness garden of strange statues and asked my way (more with gestures and inarticulate sounds than with words) to a bus stop on a line that would take me to the nearest railway station. It was the most dismal part of my entire journey. The poverty of the dilapidated cottages among the vineyards now struck me so forcibly that I couldn't cover it up with romanticism any more. The ancient, badly sprung bus was full to bursting with people carrying all kinds of burdens, dead and alive. They were sweating, talking loudly to one another and gesticulating vehemently. Their exhalations almost took my breath away, while dust thrown up from the road outside settled on the fruit trees.

The passenger train on the local line to Verona wasn't much more comfortable either. A mustached farmer sitting beside me assumed from my melancholy expression that I was physically unwell and offered me a sip from a bottle he had with him. The grappa, warm from its journey, was so strong and pungent that it nearly knocked me out.

In Verona, heaving a sigh of relief, I managed to board the express to Munich. Once there, I thought fleetingly of going back to your flat, but the idea that you might already have been reported missing, and were still wandering the steppes of that sunless land of dream or fairy tale in the form of a lioness, deterred me from doing any such thing. So I caught the last train home. On the way, with increasing uneasiness, I worked out just how much time I had left to prepare my course for the coming winter term.

You can imagine my feelings at this point about the subject I'd announced for it. Masculine Aspects in the Animal Bridegroom Tale Type, indeed! Was I planning to inform my students that I had boldly ventured into our field of discussion in person and could therefore speak from experience? I might have mentioned, for instance, the distressing fact that the male protagonist may be prevented from breaking the spell on his animal bride by a desire to dominate, or by panicking in the face of the unknown. I could have added that in such a situation several failures may be expected unless the animal bride, her handicap notwithstanding, lends a hand herself.

No, I rather thought I wouldn't embark on any such emotionally risky experiment. As usual, when an academic problem looked like touching me too closely, I tried to distance it by investigating the structures behind it. That may sound like a displacement activity, but I've sometimes found it helpful in dealing with personal difficulties too.

So I drew up various schemes whereby the students taking my course could examine certain folktales with special reference to their male protagonists, I copied a number of texts of such tales from rare editions, and I compiled a list of the secondary literature that I thought would be useful in discussing the subject. I finished preparing my course the evening before the first lecture.

While I was preparing it, and even more so later on in discussion with my students, I found myself in a curious dilemma: on the one hand, I viewed my own experience of a quest from more and more of a distance, as if I hadn't really been on one myself, but had only read or simply heard about such things and imagined being involved. Sometimes I couldn't keep my own quest separate from the texts we were trying to interpret. On the other hand, I kept being struck by a sentence or sometimes a single word with such force that I winced, and glanced around the lecture room to see if anyone had noticed that we'd just been talking about me. Sometimes I wondered if it was possible for the events of the land of the island and the tower, which now seemed to me so much a realm of the imagination, to break abruptly into that other reality where I was a lecturer in a university town, intruding into my daily life there, disturbing and alarming me.

I was constantly alternating, therefore, between a sense of distance and a sense of being personally affected, and I clung with all my might to my hastily devised structural scheme in case I suddenly foundered in my own confused feelings in front of the whole class of students.

It was a peculiar sort of course. Once, when the discussion looked like becoming bogged down in dry-as-dust theory, some imp of mischief made me of all people say, "Ladies and gentlemen, you mustn't discuss these things in such abstract terms, as if they had nothing to do with you! Look at it a little more personally. Haven't you ever been in love?" But my students were so attuned to structural aspects and the methodology of textual linguistics (which was partly my own doing, after all) that they looked at me in some embarrassment, as if I expected them to tell me dirty stories. One, a rather stout, bespectacled, rosy-cheeked young man, asked me very seriously whether I thought it methodologically legitimate to apply such considerations to a work in this field, relevant as they might be to studies in depth psychology, as, for instance, in Freud.

What could I say to that? I agreed with him, of course, and defended my provocative remark by saying I simply wanted to point out that folktale texts, too, have some relevance to real life, upon which I was commenting only in case the fact had escaped my students.

That may give you some idea of the way I kept running my ship aground in order to refloat it laboriously. I won't bore you with any more details about my course, except to say I found it hard to fulfill my professional duties anything like adequately, and I did scarcely anything else worth mentioning. I was living in a state of total confusion. It wasn't just confusion of my feelings, but of the views I'd adopted in the course of my professional life.

I lay awake at night in my little book-lined bachelor flat trying to read, then fell asleep over my book and woke later, with a start, to find my light still on, or I was woken by discordant late-night music from a radio I'd forgotten to turn off. My heart would be fluttering, alarmed like the terrified bird in whose shape I escaped the lioness's paws, and I wondered if that flight had been my salvation or my final mistake.

No doubt a rational person would ask at this point why I didn't simply pick up the phone and call you. I knew your name, your address and the museum where you worked; Directory Inquiries would have made no bones about giving me your number. And yet I didn't try it, partly for reasons such as had prevented me going to your flat when I arrived back in Munich, and for fear no one would pick up the phone, or if someone did, a stranger's voice would tell me that for some reason or other you weren't available.

Over and beyond that, I couldn't rid myself of the notion that if I tried any such thing I'd be breaking the rules of a game that must be played out to the end if it was to reach a satisfactory conclusion. I'd failed in one test, which was bad enough. If I now acted as if that hadn't happened, I felt, I would lose the game for good. Or no, not just me; I had at least got that far in my thinking. We'd both have lost the game in which there could be only two losers or two winners.

Sometimes, when I couldn't sleep, I was obsessed by the idea that you were lying awake too, waiting in vain for me to call, but I still didn't reach for the phone; I clung to the hope that you would be irrational enough to understand my silence. And it was cheering when the other speakers on my course pointed out that of all the masculine protagonists of fairy tales, the fools, idlers and layabouts were the ones who generally came out on top in the end. I could readily see myself in that sort of part, though by now I'd discovered that it isn't always easy to play the fool and enjoy it.

Then, at some time in November I received a communication from the organizers of the conference where we first met: would I be available to give a paper at the next such conference, to be held at the same place in the Easter vacation? My previous lecture, the letter continued, had given rise to such lively discussion that they expected another paper from me would be equally stimulating. I quote that just to amuse you: it shows what an impression a thoroughly confused person can still make on a serious-minded audience.

I was taken aback and spent some time considering my answer. I knew at once that I must be at the conference; it seemed logical that my quest could conclude only in the place where it began. So I agreed to attend, but asked to be excused giving a paper because of my workload at the university. I would be happy to take part in discussions, I said, but I didn't see myself finding the time during the winter term to prepare a lecture on a new subject.

That winter will linger in my memory as one of damp, cold, sticky snow with the dirt of the streets mixed into it. I don't like winter as a season anyway. I hate the cold, and I'm no fonder of damp, dull, cloudy weather. I begin to revive when I feel the sun on my skin in spring, but in winter I feel like creeping into a dark, downy cave and hibernating like a bear. However, I had all sorts of irksome duties that meant I couldn't do that. I had an introductory course to take as well as the one described above, and there were practical exercises in textual interpretation to be set for first-year students, not to mention tutorials on essays, departmental committee meetings and any number of further engagements, all obliging me to leave my book-lined retreat and venture out into the horrible weather.

I wouldn't have minded this any worse than usual if I hadn't been in a permanent state of uneasiness about my wholly unresolved relationship with you. I was tormented by a sense of being caught up in a case still pending, and unable to do anything to speed it up.

That sounds like legal terminology, and it's a very inadequate description of my feelings at the time, although accurate in that from my viewpoint everything *was* still pending. I'd won you and immediately lost you again; I knew your address, but not where to look for you; I'd set out on a quest, and in my mind I was still on it while simultaneously operating as a university lecturer. But these observations are all about me, which indicates what bothered me most: I hadn't the faintest idea what position *you* occupied in the game. Were you in charge of it, playing it with me, or were you subject to its rules just as I was?

Even that question misses the crucial point and doesn't convey the essence of my uneasiness or that sense of being in a state of suspension I mentioned. I'll try—I must try—to put it more clearly without employing the usual meaningless clichés. The main reason why I was suspended between fear and hope was this: though I knew hardly anything about you, I'd still met you, and you had affected me—my body? my mind? my soul? all three at once, no doubt—in such a way that I'd feel miserably incomplete without you in future. And once I had become aware of that, I finally began to suspect that it was your very strangeness I needed.

So I pursued you in my mind as I lay awake in my own little cave by night. In the daytime, however, the island with its tower receded farther and farther into the realms of imagination, and it grieved me to find that, caught up in ordinary everyday life, I was gradually losing my ability to see the story of the lioness and myself as something that really happened, for with it went my hope of ever seeing you again.

It's a pity that a mind busily at work doesn't do more to blot out everyday annoyances such as bad weather. But it really was a particularly hard winter. In early February the temperature scarcely rose above freezing, so that the snow in town didn't melt but was trodden into a discolored slush that seeped into one's shoes, leaving one with cold, wet socks.

Around this time, when the city was in the grip of hectic Carnival gaiety, I was trudging home through the unpleasant slush one evening and saw a party of people in fancy dress coming toward me, laughing and talking. I was about to cross the road, not wanting to get drawn into the crowd in my morose mood. But one figure detached itself from the group: obviously a woman, wearing a mask and a close-fitting costume that covered her from head to foot. In the light of the street lamps it had a silky, golden glow. Running, she came up to me, put an arm around my shoulders and looked into my face as if she were going to kiss me, which wouldn't have been anything out of the ordinary at Carnival time.

My heart stopped as I looked into her eyes, the eyes of a lioness. Any mask can hide its wearer's true identity from an observer, and this was such a good mask, or at least it seemed so real in that split second of surprise, that I felt transported back to the time of my travels with the lioness. I was abruptly overwhelmed by the joy of recognition, and by fear too.

"Wait and see," said the lioness, in a deep woman's voice that could indeed have been yours. "Wait and see, you won't escape me!" And she pressed her catlike muzzle to my mouth. I felt soft, warm lips and the quick twitch of the tip of a tongue. "You won't forget me now," she said, and then she was gone, running in long strides after the others.

I still don't know what to make of that. She can't really have been you, but how else can I explain the little incident? Coincidence? What does coincidence mean, anyway? That some unknown woman, dressed up as a lioness, should take it into her head to make for me of all people in the middle of the street, and kiss me and say such things to me?

Well, people here say anything's possible at Carnival time, but then again, what does *that* mean? Could it mean someone unknowingly playing a part in a game that involves more than just the two of us? Was it coincidence that at the very

moment when the lioness ran away and I walked on, I saw
the planet Venus shining in the sky above the snowy bushes
of the dark, nocturnal park? Or that when I got home a little
later I found a letter from the conference organizers, giving
not only the program for the Easter conference but a list of
registered participants, and this time your name was on it?

I had difficulty getting through the rest of the term. In my
present state of mind I was more and more aware of the
inadequacy of our academic methods. They seemed to me to
aim deliberately wide of the mark in handling the subjects of
our texts. In fact, can we, should we, "handle" such texts at
all in that way, picking them up and breaking them into their
component parts with the aid of unsuitable tools, looking
only at the details, as if they would enable us to draw conclusions about the sense of the whole, which long ago became
unrecognizable or was entirely lost from view amid all this
academic activity?

Eager to break new academic ground, most people in my
field didn't perceive this dilemma at all while lectures were
being given and discussed. In view of my own confusion I
was glad of that, though I hoped I could point out the flaws
in such an approach at some more suitable time, when I had
solid ground under my own feet again. That happy state of
affairs, however, was a long way off. During the last of my
classes that term, therefore, when the question of the conclusions we had come to during the course suddenly presented
itself like the ghost of Hamlet's father, there was an awkward
silence, and I couldn't think of anything sensible to say to fill
it.

Eventually—and it now seems to me, rather rashly—I
promised to write up the main results of our labors in a
schematically constructed paper by the beginning of the summer term, and have it duplicated for the members of my class
by the department's secretarial staff. As I told my students
this and wished them a pleasant vacation, I was thinking of
nothing but meeting you in a few weeks' time, an idea that

made it easy for me to push my academic debacle to the back of my mind.

I did so very successfully at first—obviously I've had quite a bit of practice in the mainly subconscious workings of repression. But the closer the day came when I was to leave, the more troubled I became by my uncertainties, both professional and personal. How was I going to face you, when I'd left you still spellbound in the shape of a lioness at the gateway of the tower, put to flight by my fears of being no match for you? And how would you receive me? With distant friendliness, making any attempt to come closer to you impossible from the start? With cold contempt, even? Or would you be able to come at all if you were still under the spell, inside the lioness's skin?

A couple of times, just before the conference began, I nearly withdrew from it. But then, the night before I was to leave, I had a dream that changed my mind, although at first glance it didn't seem to have much to do with my plans. The more I thought of its imagery, however, the more it seemed to be encouraging me to venture into unknown territory. I noted down the dream itself:

I'm visiting a library somewhere abroad. It is a large academic library; I leave the reading room for an indefinite time, and on coming back I can't find the books I was working with and which I'd left arranged on the table. I turn to the librarian, quite a young man who speaks broken German; he is dark-haired, with a narrow black mustache. His explanations mean nothing to me, and his wife, who joins us, is very friendly but can't make me understand her. I think the couple is inviting me to their home. I follow them out of the relatively dark reading room, up and up, climbing many flights of stairs, and the higher we climb, the lighter it becomes.

Finally we step out of a door and into the open air. We are high up on the flat roof of a Mediterranean type of building with battlements around it, painted bright white. I see some pieces of marble lying at the foot of the parapet between two embrasures. One of them is about twenty centimeters long and seems to have a very regular shape, like a slice cut lengthwise from a melon, or the section between two meridians on a globe. I have to reach through a grating to pick it up. As I turn it over, I see that underneath the dirt the back of the marble (which turns out to be the front after all) is finely chiseled into drapery. Wiping it clean with my hand, I see that the stone is the bust of a woman, shaped rather like a ship's figurehead. A delicate head on a slender neck rises from the rich folds of the drapery. The face, about the size of a large hen's egg, is very lifelike. I am delighted with the beauty of my find, and that feeling is still with me as I wake.

When I took a taxi through the streets of the little town for the second time the next day, under a pale-blue springtime sky, I didn't even glance at the façades of the old town houses so well restored in line with the good business sense of their occupants, though last year I'd seen them as a deeply satisfying confirmation of the rightness of my own projects. Today I looked neither to right nor left, but straight ahead to my journey's end—the park, where the first green leaves were beginning to show and where I hoped to meet you.

In my mind's eye I was already walking down its gravel paths toward you, although the fact that I couldn't picture your face or figure was a serious stumbling block to my fantasies. I remembered the façade of the castle, the conference members walking up and down outside it, the trees and bushes of the park forming the background against which I'd seen you, but as soon as I tried to focus my memory on you I suffered from a selective blindness of the mind's eye that kept blotting you out of the familiar scene, making it impossible for me to picture you, as if you were a blank spot in the storehouse of my memory.

This time I had set out early enough to reach the park in the bright sunlight of early afternoon. As the taxi sped round the curve in the drive, the broken statue that had leaped out so abruptly into my field of vision before whisked past, a scarcely definable grayish object, although I was ready for it now, and indeed I was looking out for it. It resembled a pale, weathered tree stump, holding the remains of its lopped branches helplessly up to the sky.

This anticlimax was easily explained: at night the taxi's headlights had suddenly picked the statue out from the dark, formless mass of bushes, showing it to dramatic effect, while today everything was bathed indiscriminately in the steady, sober light of day. Yet I felt disappointed as the driver drew up and stopped outside the entrance—disappointed and let down, as if I'd gone to a long-awaited rendezvous only to find not the woman I loved but a seedy-looking messenger with a mocking grin, who handed me her letter calling it off.

Nothing went as I'd been imagining it for weeks. I had hoped to enjoy the first warm days of spring walking in the castle grounds with no duties weighing on me, meeting you again among the beds of daffodils and tulips, perhaps meeting you in a new way too, strolling down the garden paths with you to heaven knows where—oh, and there were all kinds of other dreams I'd cherished as well.

The spring and the sun had come up to scratch—I'd guessed right there—and the beds of tulips were certainly a glorious, colorful sight. But the optimistic mood I'd hoped for refused to set in, particularly as you were nowhere to be found: not near the reception desk, not in the dining room, where the first cups of coffee were being poured, not in the grounds. I went down the garden paths, looking for you everywhere, and past the pond, where a half dozen ducks were rocking gently in the sun, quacking at me as I passed as if they were laughing at me.

I couldn't stand it in the park for very long, so I wandered around the reception area, keeping my eyes skinned for any new arrivals. But still you didn't come, and I didn't see you in the lecture hall during the brief opening session to greet conference members or at supper afterward.

After supper I paced restlessly along the broad corridors of the castle, abstractedly looking at the oil paintings on the walls, portraits of various members of the old ducal family. Then I hung around the entrance, imagining all kinds of complicated reasons for your absence. I was in a state of considerable nervous strain by the time an older colleague hailed me. We meet quite frequently at such conferences, and are fond of each other in a vague sort of way without making any song and dance about it. When Erik suggested a drink, I thankfully seized on it: anything to divert me from my obsessive activities.

And obsessive they were: I was chasing about like an animal in a zoo, running from side to side of its cage. Erik said nothing about my behavior, but it was obvious enough that he'd noticed from the look in his bright eyes, which always seem to regard their surroundings with a trace of irony. He bore me off to the cellars and the wine bar there, opened as a place for conference members to meet in the evening, grabbed a bottle of red wine and two glasses in passing, and made a beeline for an empty table in a corner where we could talk undisturbed. Still in charge, he opened the bottle, poured the wine and raised his glass. "You'd better have a drink," he said, as if he knew exactly what I'd been through.

Then he turned his full attention to the wine, sipping it appreciatively (he had made a good choice) and waiting some time before he asked if I was expecting anyone.

"How do you mean?" I said, foolish enough to pretend surprise.

"Oh, come on!" said Erik. "Anyone can see you are!" And before I could repeat my protestations he raised a hand to ward them off and continued, "I know, I know, you don't want to talk about it. Well, there are plenty of more important things to discuss." And changing direction abruptly, he began going on about the financial situation of the universities, which meant, as he said, that the lifeblood was being systematically drained from the humanities departments. "Research and teaching, don't make me laugh! These days we have to teach students literature that high school graduates used to know by heart before they came to us. All it amounts to is cramming, and the rest of our time's taken up by administration."

He sounded like an actor improvising because he's forgotten his lines, and I wasn't sure if he was really trying to start a serious discussion of the subject or just sounding off to show me how idiotically I was behaving.

However, I wasn't about to give him the satisfaction of admitting that, so I readily entered into the conversation he'd started, bewailing the state's preference for putting its ample funds not into research in the liberal arts but into nuclear power stations now threatened with closure. Or sometimes, I said, investing in high-speed trains, which allow a few industrial tycoons to race from place to place on land at almost the speed of a jet aircraft, but send a shudder down the spine of any reasonable person at the thought of a crash between such supertrains—and when it comes to issues of noise and danger, I argued, they're just shifting the problems associated with low-flying aircraft to the railways.

In fact, I talked myself into a frenzy, because I do feel strongly on the subject. In the process, though it may sound odd, I calmed down and settled into a comfortable state of indignation, especially as Erik encouraged it, reminding me of the jobs such projects provide, which have to be weighed in the balance against the possible risk. "How much totally unnecessary junk do you think gets manufactured today just for the sake of jobs?" he said, and added, glancing at me sharply, "I mean, look at yourself, advertising such gimmicks with a fast car embroidered on your shirt pocket."

His grin made it obvious that he was trying to get a rise out of me.

"Not guilty," I retorted. "I needed a shirt this particular

dark blue, and there weren't any without some kind of motif on them. The car seemed the least obtrusive. Frankly, I know so little about it I couldn't even tell you what make of car it's meant to be."

Erik told me, and even I knew it was a top-range model. By now we'd both stopped acting and ended our game in laughter. Not that Erik and I don't take these things seriously, but we've discussed them so often that we sometimes indulge in a kind of verbal shadowboxing to remind ourselves of the realities of life.

The first bottle was empty now, and I fetched another of the same. I could see this was going to be quite a long session and I prefer not to mix my drinks in the interests of my own comfort. When our glasses were full again, I said—in a tone that made Erik look up sharply, because it indicated a complete change of subject from our little game—I said that over the past term I'd lost all confidence in my old methods of textual study.

"And about time too," said Erik, as if he'd been expecting some such collapse of my intellectual arsenal. "You can't really study anything until you realize that every basic attitude you adopt, every method you use, is going to distort the study of your subject in proportion to your absolute, and thus uncritical, acceptance of such assumptions. If you believe your own approach and your own methods are the only right way to discover the truth, you end up with absurdities, and you may not even notice it either. What's brought all this on?"

"Something that happened to me," I said. "The thing that had me hanging hopefully around the door and being so obvious about it just now."

"Ah," said Erik. "Tell me more."

You know, at that moment his ironic but not unkindly tone reminded me of the stork I met when I was a frog. Or perhaps the stork reminded me of Erik, although I wasn't aware of it at the time. I don't know quite how to define the similarity: take it however you like. But anyway, Erik has the ability to listen sympathetically to very personal revelations while preserving the kind of distance that makes it easy to talk.

So I was looking for a way to begin my story when our colleague Schachtel came up to our table and asked if he could join us. You don't know Schachtel, of course; you spend most of your time in the rather more elevated realms of art history, and don't have to crawl through the academic jungle of German studies on ground constantly undermined by ideological wrangling. Schachtel is a philologist and wants radical spelling reform, which means he not only wishes to abolish the German capital letter for nouns (with the exception of proper names, a wide concept that proves hard to define precisely, so that the issue extends almost to infinity), he's also eloquently in favor of doing away with orthographic traces of the original roots of words. He wants people to write "filosofer" instead of "philosopher," which means that the reader or writer of the word will forget its connections with the Greek *philos*, loving, and *sophos*, wise—and who knows Greek today, anyway?—and be more likely to think of *filou*, a rascal, adopted into German from French, and *softie*, borrowed from English: thus making a philosopher a rascal inclined to take a soft line—perhaps the kind of sophist who gave Socrates such trouble. You see the risks we'd be running of having a fine concept misunderstood. Or perhaps the whole idea is to induce such a misunderstanding? I can easily imagine some technocrat university administrator looking down on me as a filosofty.

Well, anyway, Schachtel carries his plans for reform before him like a banner, and it takes him only a couple of introductory remarks at the outside to get mounted on his beloved hobbyhorse. He obviously intended to join us, but Erik said quite brusquely, "Sorry, this is a serious discussion we're having," laying such malicious emphasis on the word "serious" that Schachtel marched off in a huff to find an audience for his ideas of spelling reform elsewhere.

"What's he doing here anyway?" I asked.

"Haven't you looked at your program?" said Erik. "He's

speaking on the orthography of the surviving manuscripts of the tales of the Brothers Grimm."

"Oh yes," I said. "They were against initial capitals too, of course. The fact is, I haven't looked at the program yet, only the list of conference members."

This remark gave Erik another chance to say, "Ah!" and he added, "I suppose her name was on it?"

In some ways he's very inquisitive. Well, the level in the second bottle had sunk quite low by now, and with it my willingness to talk about my peculiar fairy-tale experiences had risen. Erik is a good listener; in particular, he'll accept the most improbable circumstances so long as he feels the teller of a story is not leaving things out on purpose. He notices at once if, for some reason or other, you're falsifying your account of events just a little.

I told him, of course, about the Palladian villa and the wilderness garden with its grotesque statues (in fact, Erik had been there once himself and could still remember the details), and then, leaving out the precise circumstances—from my description, he'll have supposed it happened in the park— then I told him you had turned into a lioness.

Up to this point he had been looking away from me, mostly at his still half-full glass or at the red, strangely swirling, wavering and changing patterns that the candle on the table cast on its wooden surface through the wine in the glass. When I offered him this abbreviated version of your metamorphosis he glanced sharply at me at once, and from the ironic gleam in his eyes I knew he wasn't convinced by my account of it. He said not a word suggesting doubt of the metamorphosis itself, just as he had accepted my previous brief metamorphosis into a frog. All he said was, "What, there?" Then he recollected himself and added, "Sorry, none of my business. I can imagine how it must have been. I found that garden frightening myself. I was alone there, unfortunately." Then he fetched another bottle, poured wine, settled back into the attitude of a listener and, apart from sipping wine now and then, sat almost motionless until the end of my story, so far as it went.

When I had finished, I added, "She hasn't come. What am I to do?"

Erik thought for a moment and then said, "You'd better try again. And do whatever you think right at the bottom of your heart."

"But when?" I said. "And where?"

"Now!" he said. "Here and now."

"In the middle of the night?" I began to suspect that, as sometimes happens, Erik had suddenly reached a state of total intoxication. But he seemed almost sober as he said, "When else? Come on, you'd better get moving."

He accompanied me to the door, nodded his head vaguely in the direction of the grounds and pushed me out on the path, so that I stumbled down the three steps leading up to the door. "Go on!" he called after me. "Follow your nose!"

I tried taking that literally, as I had when the little brown frog set me on the right track, but I could catch no trace of the perfume that had led me on before. The sweet, heavy scent of the daffodils, their flowers hovering like pale stars in the darkness above the beds, drowned out any other odors my nose encountered as I walked down the gravel paths leading on into the grounds, and it still lingered long after I had gone through the bushes and under the trees in search of the duck pond.

After a while I realized I must have lost my way again. The area of the park that surrounded the pond was quite open, with only a few isolated groups of shrubs, whereas I was walking through trees growing so close that I could hardly make out the path. That will have been partly because there was no pale gravel on it now, and at this point the smell in the air suddenly changed as well, turning from the scent of daffodils to an odor of water, living water with fish in it, and the farther I groped my way along the path, which was only just discernible between the trees and bushes, the stronger that odor became. I now knew I had already crossed a secret frontier, and was in that land where time had no meaning and the laws that appear to rule and restrict our reality were suspended.

That thought and, above all, that smell made my heart beat faster, exciting me and luring me on. Though I felt myself on familiar territory, there was no telling what would happen to me this time. Erik had said I should do whatever I thought right at the bottom of my heart, which sounded very like the advice of some helpful figure of fairy tale. And he had put it tactfully, for I now knew only too well what he really meant: I mustn't let myself be intimidated yet again by those fears that had kept leading me to do things I knew at heart I didn't want to do.

The slope ahead of me fell steeply away, the trees gave way to bushes, and I was standing on the banks of the lake again. The crescent of the waxing moon stood low in the western sky and if I strained my eyes, I could make out the island by its faint light. For a moment I toyed with the thought of swimming to it; then I realized I was thinking of making all that effort simply to avoid meeting the ferryman. So I walked slowly over the beach toward his cottage and sat down for a while on the dry sand to watch the multiple wavering reflections of the crescent moon on the gently moving surface of the lake.

As I rested the ball of my hand on the ground, something sharp cut into it so keenly that I quickly withdrew it. This time it was bleeding. I sucked the cut and tied my handkerchief round it. I could still taste the sweetness of blood as I felt for the sharp edge again. What I now drew out of the sand was an intact pair of shells held together by a desiccated remnant of muscle. They opened out like a tiny book with a perfectly formed pearl about the size of a pea between its covers. It turned the light of the crescent moon to an iridescent glow. So there really were pearls to be found here, and I must make sure I kept this one. I closed the two halves of the shell over the pearl and put it in the breast pocket of my shirt, which buttoned up. Then I set off to rouse the ferryman.

But he opened the door at once, fully dressed, as if he had been waiting behind it for me.

"To the island," I said.

He nodded, came out of the door, closed it behind him and was on his way down to the landing stage. However, I held him back and asked the price.

"That can wait till we're over," he said. And then I had a foreboding that I wouldn't be able to fix the price myself after we had made the crossing.

"No," I said. "Payment in advance, on the spot."

This didn't seem to suit the ferryman at all. He stared sullenly at my face with his froglike eyes, and he did indeed demand the pearl I had just found. He even put his hand out for it. His swift greed merely confirmed my guess that I could fix the fee myself before the journey began.

"No, you're not having that," I said. I took my wallet out of my pocket and put the largest denomination of coin it contained into the ferryman's outstretched hand.

I could see he would have liked to fling the hard metal coin down on the sand, but it seemed he couldn't

"A fee is a fee," I said. "Now I want to go over."

So he pocketed the coin and shuffled down to his boat ahead of me.

During our nocturnal crossing, the crescent moon slowly sank to the horizon and finally laid a shimmering path of light over the dark surface of the lake, before dipping behind the hills on the far bank. We were close to the island harbor now.

Silently, the ferryman steered his boat in through the harbor entrance, and as he rowed toward the quay I saw the top of the cliff cut higher and higher into the sky, extinguishing the stars one by one. No sooner had I disembarked than the boat set out again, and after the ferryman had rowed a few strokes through the dark water, I could no longer hear or see it. I set out to climb to the village.

The narrow alleys and crooked flights of steps were silent as the grave. There wasn't a gleam of light to be seen. In the faint starlight the buildings looked like ruins. Or were they really ruins? The ruined walls of long-gone dwellings, now inhabited from time to time only by the frogs as they went about their mischievous business, imitating a kind of life to lead visitors astray? Not even a cat prowling by night crossed my path.

Had I let them lead me astray on my first visit? At the beginning of this story I asked you if you were Rana, the girl who sometimes seemed so like you. Now, thinking of my third visit to the island, I feel more and more doubtful. On the other hand, I can't rid myself of the idea that there really was something of you in the girl, even in the female frog I chased down the slope and into the fertile bubbling of the water. Something of you, but not your real self.

Busy with such thoughts, I looked for a road through the ghostly village, groping my way past crumbling masonry, my footsteps echoing as I passed through a maze of narrow entrances and unevenly paved alleys that would suddenly turn in the wrong direction. I knew I had to go uphill; that was the only way to the tower. But the village obstructed me with a persistence that began to be frightening.

I tried to remember which road I had taken on my last visit. It had led me straight past the houses until I came out in the open, but on this moonless night, none of the streets seemed at all familiar. The walls towered up beside me and in front of me, black, hostile and casting no shadows, merging at the top with the blackness of the sky.

I wished I had a thread to help me through this labyrinth, but no Ariadne had pressed a spool of thread into my hand, and I began to think I might run into the Minotaur's powerful arms here in the dark just around the corner without any means of defending myself against that terrible monster.

I certainly had no weapon, but then I began to wonder if I did, after all, have something I could use against the spell of this labyrinth and any ill-intentioned denizen of it. I was still carrying the shell containing the pearl the ferryman had coveted. He must have known its uses, and perhaps I could discover them too. So I took it out of my pocket and opened it out. There lay the pearl shimmering in its dark bed, looking as if it were glowing from within.

At first I could hardly take my eyes off the iridescent marvel. It sent the terrors of the night scurrying back into their dark corners. When I finally looked up, my heart had steadied again, and straight ahead of me, where I could see nothing but solid masonry before, I now made out an opening into a narrow alley that led uphill and out of the village.

As if one final attempt to divert me from my purpose must be made, I heard the croaking of frogs far off, borne to me on a night wind that suddenly rose. Perhaps the pearl also checked my interest in their nocturnal chorus. Anyway, I didn't put it back into my pocket until the sound had died away.

By now the last street was behind me and I was climbing the slope. I felt rough, short grass underfoot, though I could hardly make out the ground in the darkness. But pale, rounded objects rose from it here and there, looking almost as if they were hovering in the dark. I took them for sleeping animals at first, perhaps sheep, until I saw that they were limestone rocks worn smooth by countless storms.

Soon I reached the wall. This time I thought I knew the extent of the drop on the other side, so I climbed it very carefully, determined not to let go and fall into the black depths awaiting me until my arms were stretched full length. However, I was spared that testing fall; the dimensions here seemed to change every time I arrived. On this occasion I felt ground under my feet before my arms were fully stretched.

Ground under my feet. The phrase reminds me oddly of the course I'd just finished giving, or rather the course that had come to an end without reaching any real conclusion, or maybe had simply petered out. Up to the very last day I hadn't been able to feel ground under my feet. I now find myself rather pleased to think that at least my students couldn't go home with any cut-and-dried answers. The idea the expression conveys is that you are standing on firm, unassailable terrain in whatever is the subject of discussion and will be able to move there freely without any risk of falling into an abyss at your next step—and so far as the way our minds function in making sense of the world, that idea's an illusion anyway. Once again the ground on which I'd landed was not where I expected it.

In my discussion with Erik, he had really been doing no more than to reduce what had happened to a formula: the experience of a discrepancy between the cool calculation of theory and the heart-stopping anxieties of practice, proving that the knife of theory always cuts just wide of the real heart of the matter. Or if, by some strange chance, theory does hit the mark, it will be more likely to destroy it than lay it bare.

The familiar phrase about having ground under one's feet is rather a questionable concept, therefore, as I was to find out the moment I was the other side of the wall. Its height from the ground was now no more than my own. But before I could really get my footing, something shot out of the darkness through the tall grass and rammed its round, furry head so hard into me that the ground was immediately knocked from under my feet again and I fell full length on my back.

Even as I fell I knew who had been waiting for me here, and my fear of the fierce lioness gave way to the joy of finding her again—or finding you again in her—something I'd longed for ever since you leaped away from me in her shape. I hugged the beautiful animal as hard as I could. I felt rather than saw her standing over me; I felt her smooth, short fur against my skin and the caress of her living body as we wrestled pleasurably in the grass.

Finally I sat up and produced the shell with the pearl in it from my pocket. I thought I was about to play the part of the great magician, performing a transformation scene with spectacular stage effects. However, nothing of the kind happened, although once again the pearl glowed with a gentle light, which was reflected in the lioness's eyes as she bent her head to look at the wonderful thing and nuzzle it with her moist lips. But that was all. The time for metamorphosis hadn't come yet.

It was time for something else, however, though I didn't yet know what. But the lioness seemed to feel there was no time to lose; she wouldn't play any more games, but used her familiar methods to get me to my feet and on the move—uphill, of course, toward the tower. Now that she had seen the pearl she urged me on as eagerly as if life itself depended on my accomplishing or finishing something there. My life, her life, our life.

It was still night as we reached the tower at this fast pace, as if driving or being driven. I had been looking out for it all the time, and suddenly I recognized its outline by the way it hid the stars. It rose to the sky, black and mighty. At that moment a blaze of light illuminated the gateway from inside, as if someone had switched on a strong lamp. The gate was open.

I went toward it. The lioness stayed by my side until I stopped directly in front of the gateway, dazzled by the bright light. Then she rubbed her head against my hip once more, leaped away and disappeared into the dark.

I know now that the task awaiting me in the tower had to be done on my own, but at the time, standing alone and dazzled in the open gateway, my first feeling was that I had been abandoned. Indeed, I was angry with the lioness for deserting me in such a situation. Yet I don't even know if she was fully aware of what she was doing and acted of her own free will, or if she followed some secret command she didn't understand herself. Do *you* know the answer? I have so many questions for you that a lifetime will hardly be enough to put them, let alone answer them. What was all this like for you? That's probably a different story, and one only you can tell. Just as my story is a different story to you.

And no doubt that's why you asked how it began for us. You knew your version and wanted to hear mine. I look forward to the nights when you'll tell me your side of the story.

For instance, where were you while I was in the tower? Did you roam the grass of the steppes alone, restless and longing—longing for what? Just for a sweet chestnut kernel? What did your consciousness permit at the time? Or did you play with the little girls, the seven Pleiades, whose melodious singing speech was such music to my ears and yet conveyed no meaning to me? Or perhaps you amused yourself with the monkey who met me there, gave him a fright and chased him up one of the few trees?

But then again, the monkey may not have been where I first met him. I have an idea I encountered him again in the tower, waiting to receive me once more. When I walked through the gateway I was dazzled by the brightness after my long walk through the moonless night, and at first I could make out nothing at all. I stopped in case I ran into a glass door or some such obstacle. Someone spoke to me, in a voice that sounded masculine rather than otherwise, with a tenor register and a strange accent, although it seemed familiar to me.

"We've been expecting you," said the voice. "Well, pull yourself together and come closer! I suppose you can prove your identity this time?"

"My identity?" I repeated. Yet again, I had no idea what we were talking about. I blinked, and tried to make out the person who had addressed me. So far as I could see he was a rather short, wiry character with a dark complexion and, if my eyes didn't deceive me, a narrow black mustache. He wore a pale, ivory-colored suit and he seemed to be the receptionist. It struck me that I had seen this dweller in the tower before, and when he gave a small bow, raised his head again and bared his lips in a broad grin, a thought shot through my head: Why, it's the monkey! But properly dressed this time.

"Your identity, yes, of course," said the monkey, though

he now looked more like the librarian in my dream. "No doubt you've brought the right thing this time?"

Finally I understood. Someone else was after my pearl.

"I'm not letting the pearl out of my hands!" I said, as firmly as could be expected of a man who's just come out of the blackest of nights into a dazzling light to find himself facing a monkey who might also be a librarian.

This curious character, part man, part monkey, raised his hands in a gesture that was both defensive and placatory (the palms of his hands were brown too, and strangely wrinkled). "My dear sir!" he said. "Please! No one here wants to rob you! It will be quite enough if you show you have the precious treasure."

Well, I could do him that favor. I took the shell from my shirt pocket, opened it up like a passport this time—and displayed the iridescent little pearl. Even in this brightly lit hall it glowed with great intensity.

The man-monkey bowed at the sight of it, as if bowing to some royal personage. Then he indicated that I could put the lovely thing away again, and asked me to follow him to my room.

So I had a room allotted to me in the tower. I was surprised. When I asked my companion more about this room reservation, he said, "Anyone who comes here has a room," as if it were obvious. As he preceded me, I noticed that he limped slightly.

We climbed up, past floor after floor, first over broad, carpeted flights of stairs, then up bare stone steps in narrow stairwells to an equally narrow passage. The monkey receptionist opened a door at the end of this passage and said I should go into the room when he had switched on the light, which consisted of a strong opaque bulb with a shallow enamel lampshade.

"What you need to sustain life will be brought to you," he added, "and your body can get rid of what it doesn't need any longer in here." He pointed to a narrow door on the right-hand wall of the room. "As for the rest, you'll find material to keep you occupied."

And with this scanty information, he left me alone and locked the door behind him.

I found myself in a place that was no hotel bedroom, nor even like the rooms in conference centers, Spartan as they usually are in their furnishings. In fact, the monkey warder had shut me up in something more like a prison cell.

I stood there for some time, examining the furniture of the room. A bedstead resembling a wooden camp bed stood against the right-hand wall in between the door to the lavatory and the wall with the window in it; two coarse, gray-brown woolen blankets lay folded at the end of the bed. Beside it there was a stool made of a thick piece of plank and four squared legs crossing underneath, with a slit in the seat wide enough for a hand to lift it by. This was obviously where I was to sit, and I must put my clothes on it too, since there was no wardrobe.

However, a tool rack hung from the opposite wall at a handy height. It held a quantity of tools fitted into slots in two parallel shelves: knives and chisels of different shapes and sizes, more delicate blades for finer work. In front of this rack, on the pale, varnished wooden floorboards, stood a simple woodcarver's bench into which a piece of work could be clamped. A heavy mallet lay on top of it.

Well, this room might be more like a prison cell than anything else, but I had a well-equipped woodcarver's workshop available to make up for it. Whoever had devised the place for me must have known what would set my imagination working. It was a long time since I'd tried my hand on a piece of wood—concern for the progress of my academic career had kept me from carving—but at once I was eager to seize this opportunity. There seemed to be other craftsmen at work here too, for from time to time I heard the metallic ring of a smith's hammer working a piece of iron down in the depths of the building.

I found material for my carving on the windowsill: three

roughly shaped heads, chunks hewn from wood of a golden color with a slight grain. Judging by the indication of abundant hair, they were supposed to be female heads, but their faces were still hidden beneath the ovals of the front surfaces, where the wood had hardly been touched. The three unfinished wooden heads were not identical; each already showed remarkable individuality, although I couldn't have said exactly how they gave that impression.

When I finally took the few steps over to the window and picked up the heads one by one, that first impression was heightened, if anything. It was rather like seeing a dark shape walking down an unlit street and thinking you recognize it as someone you know, without quite being able to account for the fact; indeed, you may not even be able to put a name to the familiar figure approaching in the dark, you're just sure you had dealings with that person before, whether for good or ill.

Something or other was about to catch up with me. It came from that area of life I used to think of as my actual everyday reality, and I had been running away from it. It was coming closer—indeed, it was at the door and it wouldn't be kept out of this sparsely furnished room. If I had seen the island with its tower as a refuge where I could be safe from my own past, my failures and my guilt feelings, then I'd failed to understand where I really was all along. The images and figures of this apparently imaginary world of fairy tale would have no real meaning for me until I allowed my own reality to take shape in them. How often, even in the strange involvements of my long quest, I'd run away from situations linked to my own life in a way that still wasn't clear to me!

That feeling forced itself upon me as I looked at one of the heads in particular. I picked it up, turned it this way and that, and tried to think who could have aroused such painful sensations in me. But I still couldn't track down the buried memory whose face awaited me in the roughly shaped piece of wood. I would just have to work on it, lifting shaving after shaving of wood away until I gradually uncovered it again.

The First Portrait

I fixed the head into the carver's bench that night, but otherwise I didn't touch it. I just looked at it: a head with no face, yet it already weighed on my heart. Perhaps I should try to bring out the line of the lower jaw to the chin more clearly, I thought; it was not so much shaped yet as merely indicated by the grain of the wood, and there was a suggestion of obstinacy about its curve. I reached for a suitable knife, but when I had it in my fingers and was about to set it to the wood, I could feel I was tired from the way my hand trembled, and I let it alone.

It would be tedious for any reader, even you, if I were to describe the progress of my work on that head in the following days and weeks—I didn't count them. The frugal meals the monkey warder brought me aren't worth mentioning, although they were all that broke my days working at the carver's bench. Even at night I sought that face in confused dreams of which I could remember only fragments in the morning.

And it wouldn't mean a lot if I were to tell you which tool I used, and at what angle I applied it, in order to lift a spiral shaving of wood from the hidden face gradually beginning to reveal itself before my eyes. An account of the movements of my hands couldn't convey the tension that increasingly bound me to this piece of work, for it arose less from the process of carving the wood than from myself, my buried or suppressed memory, which I was now trying to lay bare with every stroke of my sharp blades. So I won't tell you about the wood itself and the carefully sharpened knives; I'll tell you what they brought to light in my mind while my eyes followed the tracks of the blade in the landscape of a face that was emerging ever more clearly.

As I've already mentioned, there was something stubborn about the shape of the jawbone, for all its feminine delicacy. It was the first thing that struck me about the block of wood, barely recognizable as a head, and it brought an image back to my memory: a crowd of people of different ages in a large room—I wasn't sure of its exact dimensions—some kind of lecture hall, perhaps, where someone has just finished speaking. Most of the audience have already risen from their seats and are standing in small groups, talking, while a few are still seated.

Obviously, I myself am the person who has just been speaking from the platform. My right hand is still resting on the desk, and a manuscript in my handwriting lies there. I've become involved in a conversation of which I don't, and indeed can't, remember the slightest thing, since I am looking past the people talking to me into the body of the hall, where a young woman with her back to me is talking to a bearded man whom I know slightly. Well, all I really know about him is that he organized this lecture and introduced me. I'm really looking at the woman; I didn't notice her before, although she must have been in the hall during my lecture. As she talks to the organizer, all I can see of her head is in quarter profile, little more than that stubborn set of the chin, which makes me curious to see the face I'm already beginning to picture to myself, although no more of it is visible. When she finally turns round and comes toward me, with the bearded man, her face is indeed just as I'd imagined it.

Or so it seemed to me, anyway, at that first meeting. As I worked on her portrait, however, I began to suspect I might merely have imposed my own image of her on that face. How reliable is my memory? As my hands tentatively made their way over the rough surface of the wood I tried to find the woman's true face again, or perhaps find it for the first time, and I wondered if I'd ever looked at it with the interest of a man willing to venture into unknown territory.

Some kind of introduction must have followed, presumably performed by the organizer as a matter of routine. I don't remember the unimportant things said on the occasion. The woman's face doesn't surface in my memory again until we are sitting opposite each other at a restaurant table, knives and forks in our hands. Her plate is already half empty, whereas I have hardly touched the food on mine. I've obviously succumbed to the temptation of continuing my lecture on a private basis.

Something must have been said at this point that has made me look particularly closely at the woman's face, no doubt asking a question such as: what did she mean? Yes, now I remember what we were talking about. Our subject was the fairy tale even then, of course. I hear my companion referring to a passage in my lecture where I pointed out that in a number of tales the animal bridegroom sometimes removes his animal skin, usually in bed with his bride by night. She doesn't seem to agree with my saying this could be regarded as a relic of totemism, long preserved in certain taboos. She asks whether that's all I have to say on the subject. When I begin a long explanation, bolstering up my thesis with yet more theoretical material, she interrupts me. "You strike me as a person ready to lay down the law over a meal he hasn't even tasted."

Those are her exact words, and they strike me as rather uncalled for, especially as her tone makes it clear that she isn't just referring to my almost untouched plate. But then I look into her face and wonder what she really does mean. The expression in her dark eyes is neither aggressive nor impertinent; they are looking at me in a way I find very unsettling.

At this moment our conversation winds backward, so to speak, and I find all kinds of verbal stumbling blocks in her remarks; I'd missed them earlier, passing over them in a light, conversational tone, but as I think back they keep tripping me up, in a way that seems linked with a sudden quickening of my heartbeat.

As I tried to wrest the expression of those eyes from the recalcitrant wood, that scene was so present to my mind that I was impelled to pursue the meaning of her remarks again. At the time I'd settled very quickly for a simple interpretation of the kind of meal she meant. It's easy to form an opinion that chimes with your own wishes, and why correct it later if what happens next seems to prove you right?

But now, working on the area around the eyes of the wooden head, I began to doubt if it was fair to reduce the woman's motives to a wish to enjoy that kind of meal with me. It couldn't have been so simple. What part was I really meant to play in the game in which we both became increasingly involved?

I could remember no more of that first meeting. Days later, working on the lips of the woman's head, I suddenly see them clearly in my mind's eye. I see the mouth I am trying to shape and notice the characteristically uncompromising line of its lips for the first time.

"I was expecting you," she says. I remember the occasion, my first visit to her flat. I was on my way back from a symposium on the subject of "Myths Today." The train stopped at a station and when I looked out, I saw the name of the city where she lives. On impulse, I got out and called her from the station. "Yes, do come round," she said. "I'll put the kettle on." The taxi brought me to a suburb of modern terrace houses, with children playing in the street and daisies flowering in the lawn in front of the building.

As soon as she opened the door, I went in and put down my traveling bag, we came into each other's arms and kissed. That was when she said she'd been expecting me. As if she knew in advance I'd come, and perhaps more too. Now, as she speaks, I see the uncompromising set of her lips, always to be in evidence when she says something about our relationship or what I shall come to describe later as her design for life.

But we don't speak of that yet, not that day, although I sometimes feel as we talk that I have reached a place that has been waiting a long time for me without my knowing it. We look at photographs she has taken, most of them pictures of trees, one of a willow leaning over calm water where dead leaves drift—you can almost see the tree fall into its own shimmering reflection; there's an ancient oak against a background of freshly plowed fields and a very distant horizon, holding its gnarled branches up to the sky like a man in despair.

Later, when it gets dark, we drink red wine from the same glass. A candle is burning somewhere on the floor, throwing flickering shadows on the ceiling. We talk, trying to share each other's experiences, so far as words can describe them. And since words prove increasingly inadequate, we try to replace them by touch, touching each other's hair and skin, each breathing in the other's scent, a sign of the excitement bringing us closer and closer together, the woman's face beside me, under me, over me, very close, and the closer it is, the stranger it becomes, gone somewhere very far away.

As these images came back to me, I had great trouble catching that impression of distance and imprinting it on the refractory wood without losing sight of the face altogether. But the impression was a lasting one: I had received it not just that once but on later and more deliberately arranged visits. We would try again and again to find words that meant enough to us both to bring us near a certain understanding, yet there was always, inevitably, that sudden retreat into strangeness and distance when language failed under the force of desire.

The experience didn't discourage me, however, not while I worked at the carver's bench and not at the time, when the woman was ever present in my thoughts, ideas and feelings in a way that made me almost unable to do any proper work, though I was writing my thesis, or at least I was supposed to be writing it.

Instead of equipping myself for an academic career, I suffered from my inability to grasp the system whereby the woman had designed her own world. That may sound odd, but I can find no better description for the way in which she imposed her own idea of her life on the people she met and the things that happened to her.

But then again, I may be wide of the mark in my description of her attitude. Even at the time, the perspective from which I saw it and have tried to describe it could change from one moment to the next. On such occasions I couldn't ward off the impression that outside the time frame we usually impose on reality there was really a plan made long ago, one by which she ran her life, although she hadn't arranged it of her own volition, and I was a part of that plan: myself, my meeting her at that precise point and all I thought I now meant to her. All this, so it seemed to me at the time, was part of a mysterious nexus; she herself obviously seemed to be aware of it or at least to have some notion of it, though in a way that wasn't open to rational explanation while, as far as I was concerned, her world was organized in an incomprehensible manner, and I was groping about in it like a blind man who can gradually form an idea of a space and the objects in it only by touch.

Sometimes I felt a kind of enchantment in the idea that I'd found a place in this woman's life, a place intended for me long ago, odd as the thought seemed to me at first. The loving, passionate embraces with which she welcomed me on my increasingly frequent visits may eventually have made me feel that this relationship—so exciting and satisfying from my point of view—had been arranged just for me by some mysterious power of fate, or because my individual personality structure marked me out as this woman's partner, a notion that may well have given a considerable boost to my sense of my own worth. After all, I was familiar with such themes from my studies of folklore, a fact that probably did even more to encourage my tendency to see myself as the center of my world and its point of reference.

You'll have realized, from the way I write this, that I'm trying to analyze my conduct and my feelings of that time retrospectively. In my increasingly delirious rapture I can't have been fully aware of all this while it was actually going on. I'm putting it down now to explain to myself what happened next. For that, obviously, was what had made me push the memories I now retrieved, in order to carve the woman's head, into the most inaccessible corners of my subconscious mind.

I can't say how long I sat in front of that head, doing nothing, while the events I've just described surfaced from the murky depths of my memory, in fragments that it was difficult to assemble into any coherent meaning; they asked more questions than they answered. Now and then I picked up a knife, but I dared not apply it to the wood or even scratch the surface of the unfinished head. I was afraid I might alter the expression of the face for good, interpreting it in a way that might not chime with the woman's reality, and would merely show how little I understood the language of her face.

"Is it so hard for you to understand?" she says, and I remember the vertical line now dividing her smooth, round forehead above her nose. Only now do I really see her way of pressing her lips together and the uncompromising lift of her chin, rendering her expression almost disturbing, so that I make haste to transfer these nuances from my imagination to the wooden head and so put them on record. And now I also know that this is the moment I've been hiding from ever since.

I try to visualize the effect the look of her eyes had on me as she said it. I thought I saw something almost like a rebuke in them, as if I'd come too close to a place where I was not allowed. There was a rebuke in them, then, but also a kind of affection, which made everything even worse. Much worse.

"Is it so hard to understand?" she repeats, and as she says it, I stare at the expression on her face. She has gone so very far away from me. "Is it so hard to understand that he's the center of my whole life and always will be?" She means the man of whom she has just told me, the man I never knew about before. Or didn't want to know about. For there were indications, although I've forgotten the details because I didn't want to notice them, indications of a secret center around which her life revolves.

"Of course you matter to me too," she says. *Too.* I hate that "too," as she goes on. "You're a part of my life. But it has no meaning at all without him."

What kind of words are those? I can't understand what they mean. I don't want to understand. The fear of loss wrings my heart and I say terrible things, lashing out in a blind rage.

As I sat in front of the still unfinished carving, after finally dragging that scene out into the open, I felt dull, constricting pain again. I even felt remnants of my anger, although not the fear of loss, not anymore. I had suffered that loss long ago. But at the same time I tried to remember the face at which I'd hurled my angry words. I was looking for some echo of my anger there, as if that would justify it. I found only grief.

Her expression of grief had stuck in my memory, although I had to blot it out at the time because it was more than I could understand. Only in working on the carving did I begin to guess that she had felt that grief for me. Can you imagine how it feels to look back and see yourself like a schoolchild, to all intents and purposes sighted but really blind as a bat, falling into a trap of your own? I saw myself as small and ridiculous when I realized that all this time I'd seen nothing but my own pain and the likelihood of loss, obsessed with my own desires and longings to the point where I couldn't even perceive another person's grief and desperation.

For she was indeed desperate at that moment, and I couldn't leave the desperation out of the face that was emerging more and more clearly from the wood under my knife.

So desperate did she feel about the man, a relationship which could come to nothing and yet which she couldn't end, that she told me she was going halfway across the country the next day just to sleep with him.

Her words were like a blow in my face, almost knocking me senseless, and I gave her no more chance to explain things from her point of view. I didn't want an explanation, I didn't want to understand her—or more precisely, I was afraid to understand her and so lose sight of the object of my anger.

But I had seen that expression of desperation or I couldn't write about it now. And perhaps her vulnerability made me angry too. That, however, was a realization that came to me only as my blade made its last few marks on her face, forming the expression on the face of the woman in my memory: a desperate determination to fly in the face of all accepted reason and hold to what she had decided to make the center of her life.

So now I put the carved head aside, not because I thought it was perfect, finished, complete, but because it was at a stage where I couldn't add any more to it from memory. It was back on the windowsill, looking at me daily as soon as I got out of bed and crossed the room. Sometimes I doubted whether I'd caught even an approximate likeness of what the woman's face showed of the workings of her mind, her thoughts and her questions. And there was one thing I understood more clearly every day: she had put me to a test and I'd failed it.

Naturally, the monkey who saw to my needs noticed that the head was back in its old place when he brought my food. After putting my frugal meal down on the stool, he went across the room and over to the window, which he never did in the normal way, and took a long look at my work. He held the head at an angle, stepped slightly to one side so that he could get a different view of it, changed his position again, and in general assumed all the airs of an art expert as he finally nodded his head and made a few indistinct, smacking noises of the kind usually if inadequately rendered in writing by the consonant group "tsk, tsk."

His antics annoyed me and I inquired, with some sarcasm, whether he was employed as an art critic as well as a servant in this house. Perhaps, I suggested, he also pronounced on the work of the smith whose hammering was always ringing in my ears.

"Oh, did it disturb you?" My monkey warder went a little red with embarrassment. "That was me. I work in my smithy now and then in my free time. Not professionally, it's just a hobby, though it used to be my main occupation in the old days."

"Then your qualifications don't seem to amount to much," I said. But then, after all, I asked if he had any criticisms of my work.

"Well," he said, "I can see you've taken a certain amount of trouble. I don't suppose more could have been expected of you, not over this one."

As he spoke, he moved the subject of his remarks a little way apart from the other two chunks of wood, still in their rough state, as if their proximity would disturb his examination of my work. At the same time, however, the effect was to make the work I hadn't yet done stand out more clearly in the bright rectangle of the window, and I couldn't help suspecting that this was his real intention. Before I could object in appropriate terms to his slighting comments on my carving or his attempts to patronize me, however, he had left the room and closed the door behind him.

So there I was, locked in my cell, and when I looked out at the clouds sailing over the wide sky, high above the surface of the lake that shone in the sun, I had those two heads before my eyes, their faces still hidden under the rough wood, a constant irritation to me as my thoughts tried to fly with the clouds. They were like invisible bars over the apparent opening of the window, forcing my mind back to the vague indications of personality conveyed by those rough-hewn chunks of wood.

I felt more and more clearly that this place, which seemed to exist only in the realms of imagination, and yet was as real to me as if I were sitting at home at the window of my book-lined flat and looking out at the sky, was becoming the point where two realities intersected, one of them forcing stored memories of my past into the other, which until now I had thought was imaginary. The view from the window also opened up a view of my own past, and the more I tried to ignore the rough chunks of wood restricting my field of vision, the more those erratic blocks washed up here from my past leaped to my eye, until at last I picked up one of them, the one that seemed particularly bent on bothering me, and fixed it into the carver's bench. I could observe its contours better there than on the windowsill, where not much showed against the light except for a shadowy outline hinting at no kind of internal structure.

Only then did I really begin to concentrate on that second head. It reminded me more and more strongly of the time I spent in a foreign country in my student days. On the outward journey I had inadvertently been mixed up with a civil-war type of conflict. Somewhere in the middle of the country, soldiers stopped the train in which I was traveling to its capital city and university town. They escorted all the passengers to a partly burnt-out village—for our own safety, they said—and I was put in a cottage that was still relatively intact along with three older men and two women. We literally holed up there in the small cellar, which had a musty smell of sprouting potatoes and pickled cucumbers, while the ground above shook with dull explosions and we heard the clatter of submachine gun fire filtering down to us through the closed trapdoor.

We spent weeks in that cottage, fed on bread and soup by the soldiers at irregular intervals, and supplementing our diet as best we could with the potatoes and cucumbers that we did indeed find in that damp cellar. The potatoes were half buried in an earth-covered clamp, the cucumbers swam in a barrel of brine, its staves held together by split and twisted willow withes.

None of us knew exactly what was going on outside or who was fighting whom. I had never been very interested in politics before, certainly not the politics of this particular country. I'd come to it mainly because there was a scholar well known outside his country's borders who taught at the university in the capital.

The information about the country I'd occasionally gleaned from newspapers turned out less than accurate during my stay there—either that or I was seeing its people and the way they lived from quite a different angle. And anyway, although most readers don't realize it, news of the problems of remote areas tends to be influenced by the interests of the reporters or the publishers of their reports, and they aren't always deliberately distorting the facts. It's only human nature to see mainly what we want to see and ignore what would merely disturb our own ideas of the world.

The village suffered several air raids, but our cottage was spared except for its windowpanes, which shattered when the first bombs fell. However, it could have been worse: it was the beginning of the summer term and the spring weather was warming up. Others in the village weren't so lucky.

Gradually a kind of camaraderie arose between us and the soldiers, something that's almost bound to happen when people are frightened together, all creeping into whatever holes are available and waiting, in fear and trembling, for a bomb to smash through thatch and floorboards and down to the cellar, blowing the cottage and everyone in it sky-high.

This broad understanding between us and the soldiers was all the more easily formed because none of us in that cottage had a very clear idea of the aims their leaders were pursuing in the war, while the soldiers themselves didn't seem to know or even want to know too much about it, if you were to

believe their sarcastic comments on their commanding officers' orders and proclamations as soon as those officers were
out of earshot. Eventually, the war was won by the party for
which our soldiers were fighting (in very much the same way
as they'd have tackled any other job of work) and we were
able to continue our journey to the capital.

All this came back to me as I looked at the head, but I still
hadn't pinned down the connection. It could hardly be to do
with the two women who had shared the cottage and our
fears with me; I couldn't remember what they looked like
now.

I arrived in an old city that seemed to me very large, positively labyrinthine. To all outward appearance its structure
was intact, but the fighting that had just ended had left its
mark. The tall façades of the town houses, ornamented with
baroque architraves and voluted capitals, showed their age
but were otherwise undamaged. The shop windows displayed an abundant and well-arranged selection of goods;
public buildings and churches seemed to be serving their
usual purposes as if there had been no unrest; and yet I felt
a sense of something oppressive as I walked down the narrow streets of the Old Town. It came not from the buildings
but from the people, who hesitated to venture out of their
doors, peered from their windows or scurried down the
streets beside me and ahead of me.

At first I didn't notice the large number of men in uniform
out and about in the streets; I'd become used to their constant
presence over the last few weeks. Later, I realized that some
of the people of this city avoided them. I thought nothing
much of that to start with, I simply registered the fact, as you
might notice the way oil and vinegar behave at the bottom
of a salad bowl: the oil forms circular islands, which can be
split into smaller islands or merged to make larger ones, but
it doesn't mix with the watery liquid of the vinegar. I realized
that there was a similar kind of segregation here: without
making a great fuss about it, some people were just not anxious to meet the uniformed men. I noticed the same thing

during the first few weeks of my studies: some of the university lecturers kept apart from others. But it was nothing to do with me.

One day, however, something did happen that affected me, and when I remembered my change of attitude I also realized that there was a connection between it and the roughly carved woman's head on my bench. The face began to reveal itself when I happened to look at the head from one side.

The Second Portrait

I see the girl glancing at me sideways, just for a moment, but having once caught that expression on her face, I was able to catch it more and more frequently, until the day came when I found out what it meant. As I picked up a knife and began to work on the side of the face that, as I already guessed, lay beneath the grain of the wood, the expression that had rather annoyed me at first was present to my mind again: it's as if the girl wanted to see my face without being noticed herself, for she glances away the moment I look back at her, as if caught in the act of doing something wrong. And yet she wasn't looking at me with any hostility, far from it. It seems to me she was trying to work out what to think of me. Can I trust this person? Some such verbal translation might have rendered the expression on her face that puzzled me.

And now I also know when I first saw that glance. Her cousin has just introduced us. Like me, he was inadvertently involved in the fighting and was accommodated in the cottage next to mine. Fearing the same bombs for weeks on end, often lying side by side in the mud while aircraft thundered overhead in a surprise raid, we soon became friendly, and when the fighting ended, we went on to the city together. He was going to continue his studies there too.

All that time I'd noticed that he kept his distance from the soldiers more than I did. I assumed he didn't agree with the political aims of their party. However, he never talked about it and I hadn't asked any questions, not being particularly interested in such things at the time.

I hadn't thought of those days for years, but now the scene was so clear in my mind's eye that I could carve the line of the girl's brow on the wooden head. We are sitting in a café, with cups and glasses of water on the round marble tabletop, and I have been saying I got on fairly well with the soldiers who made me leave the train and took me to the village. I've just remarked, not without a certain assumed nonchalance, "It was quite fun when the bombs weren't actually falling."

That glance follows at once. As if I were being assessed. By what criteria? What for? I don't know. I feel rather awkward anyway in this city, with the two young people who are at home here, and show it.

I feel awkward, but also enchanted by the way they treat each other and me. And enchanted because I've never had much to do with girls yet and I tend to be shy in their company. I am having all kinds of unfamiliar experiences here— unfamiliar, new and exciting. For the time being these feelings and experiences drown out the quiet discordancies I occasionally register, almost below the limits of audibility. I take no notice of them and remember them only later.

This girl's opinion of me as a person matters to me far more than her views on her country's politics. I know now that my "friendly" soldiers—although supported by part of the population—originally came to the country as usurpers, closely followed by political functionaries who ruthlessly intended to stamp out any resistance as soon as they encountered it.

For the moment my memory held the image of that face from our first meeting, as I've just described it. It meant I could work on the outer contours of the head, which kept me busy for the next few days. However, I was careful not to add too much detail. What does a face really tell you at a first meeting, especially when such caution has to be observed at that meeting as in the circumstances I mentioned? I shaved the wood away very carefully, doing a little less every day, until one morning I sat there looking at the incomplete, still expressionless face and knew I would get no further like this. The monkey art critic would never approve of such superficial work.

What had really happened then, I wondered, which made it so hard for me to recall the events that followed and the feelings that determined my decisions? I still had the picture of my first meeting with the girl before my mind's eye, like a still from a film, although a film shot in a setting that, to me, held something of the fascination of the unfamiliar and exotic. And sometimes it held the fascination of forbidden fruit as well.

I am standing in front of a bookcase, trying to decipher the titles and authors' names on the backs of the books it contains. Most of them are new to me. One odd-looking title, consisting of just four capital letters, catches my eye. I take the book off the shelf and open it. It's a novel by an American author with whose work I'm not familiar.

"You can borrow it if you like," says the girl, standing behind me and looking over my shoulder. "But don't leave it lying around."

"Why not?"

"Politically undesirable," she says. "You could get into trouble. And not just you."

"Who else?"

"It has my name inside it."

That's when I feel it, the fascination of forbidden fruit. I turn and look at the girl's face. I see that searching expression in it again, and this time she doesn't bother to hide it.

So I gain time to observe the face closely. She's looking at

me searchingly, yes, no doubt about that. But there's more
to be seen in her expression. It may be that she isn't sure if
she can trust me yet, but I also get the impression she wants
to preserve me from something—what it is I don't yet know—
and that lends a singular tension to her face. Contradictions
or emotions at variance with each other come together there
in a manner that gives it beauty. She looks so beautiful to
me now that I want to take her in my arms.

This visual memory at last got my work on the portrait going
again, just as the sight of the girl's face had got the relationship between us going. I'd liked her as soon as I met her,
but that was hardly surprising after all the weeks I'd spent
in the combat area in horrible conditions, dirty, hungry and
frightened. Once out of it, I'd plunged into the vast, labyrinthine city as if into a dream; it seemed so unreal to me at
first not to be living from day to day anymore, not to be
startled awake at night by explosions, to have no one firing
at me from fighter planes. I walked the streets aimlessly and
unafraid, like a man in a dream, looking at the shop windows.

The girl was the first person of the opposite sex to show
me friendship in this foreign city. I was bound to like her; I
couldn't help it. But that evening in her room, standing by
her bookshelves, I saw, for the first time, more than just the
friendly expression on the smooth surface of her face. I realized that her liking for me was shadowed by fear, a feeling
that touched me so much that I overcame my inhibitions.
Next moment I was quite surprised to find my clumsy attempts to embrace her meeting no resistance.

After that, I walked the crooked old streets of the city in a
different manner, not like a foreigner with no real business
there but like a person who had been accepted and was
beginning to feel at home, rather as if the whole city had
embraced me at the same time as the girl. I found myself
tenderly stroking the ancient gray stones of a nobleman's

palace, or raising my hat politely as I passed one of the many
baroque churches. Candlelight twinkled at me from their
open doors. I had seen the people of the city raise their hats
like that and I copied them, although I didn't yet understand
the gesture's deeper meaning. I imitated them because I
wanted to look like one of them.

It was no news to me that the new masters of the city
did not like to see such evidence of friendly feelings toward
churches, and it struck me that many passersby raised their
hats in a particularly demonstrative manner for that very reason, but I still imitated them, even though the curious gesture
of courtesy might have been read as defiance—indeed, I may
have done it just because I knew that.

"You must know now," the girl tells me. I see her face in
profile, in the light of a candle burning in a wooden, rustic
Balkan candlestick on the little table where we sit. A carafe
of dark yellow wine stands on the stained tablecloth, and
two half-full glasses, with cutlery beside them.

This afternoon she's done something she very seldom does:
telephoned the flat where I rent a room and asked to speak
to me. I was working, immersed in a difficult passage of
Wolfram von Eschenbach's *Parzifal,* when my landlady called
me to the phone. "A lady for you," she said, with the knowing smile she keeps for such occasions hovering around her
mouth.

The girl's voice sounded agitated as she said, without pre-
amble, that she had to talk to me. Soon. This evening, if
possible. Could I make it?

I suddenly had an uncomfortable sinking in the pit of my
stomach. I felt as if something were going on that ought to
worry me. But when I put a question to that effect, her answer was evasive. "Not on the phone," she said. "Can you
be at the Dalmatian at eight-thirty?"

I guessed at trouble ahead and my mind briefly returned

to my studies of *Parzifal*, only to be reminded how that holy fool and knight errant used to act when a damsel was in distress.

Two hours later, making my way through the already twilit streets, I still hadn't shaken off my vague sense of menace, and I glanced around now and then as if someone were following me and had to be shaken off. I felt as if all the people in the streets were on their way to their own hiding places, to go about some secret business there. They were hurrying, as if to reach safety; they reminded me of the cockroaches in the cottage, which used to swarm around the wooden floorboards by night, rustling, and disappearing down the nearest crack if you put a light on.

Eventually, I too broke into something that was almost a run and arrived at the Dalmatian Café before the appointed time. I found a small table in a corner where we could talk undisturbed, and ordered a carafe of the dry, golden-yellow wine. When the waiter brought it, I saw the girl standing in the doorway, looking for me. I waved and she came straight across the room past the other tables, so that the waiter could fill both our glasses at once. Now she is sitting opposite me, we have both drunk a little of the dry wine, and then she makes that remark.

"*What* must I know now?" I ask. And at this point I can make out the look of fear in her face quite clearly, but I don't know what kind of fear it is. Fear of something strange and dangerous, approaching inexorably from outside? Or fear of losing me as a result of something I don't know about yet?

Her fear begins to communicate itself to me. I feel it growing, and before it can overwhelm me and make my voice waver I ask her to stop dropping hints and put me out of my misery. "If it's something I must know, then I'd rather know straight away," I say, trying to keep my voice level.

As I say that, I look at the girl, not just to lend force to my request but to see the expression on her face, the obvious conflict in it between her wish to keep a cautious distance from me out of fear, and a loving wish to come closer in the hope that she can trust me. The visible signs of that conflict impress themselves on me so deeply that I now find I can uncover them in my buried memories and carve their traces on the wooden head with my knife.

The wish to trust me finally wins and the girl produces a variation on her first remark. "I must tell you now, so you know what you're letting yourself in for with me."

I feel my heart suddenly beat faster at learning, in this way, that she envisages the possibility of our relationship developing and binding us even more closely together. In my mind that strong heartbeat completely drowns out the other possibility of difficulty or danger, although that too was written clear enough.

So now I learn that she belongs to one of those families persecuted by the new rulers with all the force of their inhumane laws, and that she and her relations have escaped so far only because they're all living here in the city with forged identity papers. She has told me all this quietly, and so fast that I can still sense the effort it must have cost her. She talked and talked, quickly and quietly, almost repeating herself several times, then suddenly breaking off in mid-sentence.

Now she is just looking at me, and I see her unmoving face again. I still see it now as I shave wood away with my knife.

At first I didn't know what to say. In those few minutes I understood a good deal which I'd only guessed at before, and I also understood the danger of which she spoke. But all of that was as nothing compared to my excitement at the sight of the sincerity in her face. She wasn't trying to conceal anything from me now, neither her fear nor her love.

Overcome by my own feelings, I felt like standing up and taking her in my arms in front of everyone. But no doubt it was wiser not to attract attention. I can never find fine words for such moments, so in the end I said, almost casually, that she mustn't worry, her revelations hadn't changed anything between us, and now why didn't we have some goulash and bread rolls?

After eating our meal, we walked down the nocturnal streets for hours on end, until there were very few other people out and about. Never before had we been able to talk as intimately and frankly as on that walk past tall, dark buildings. Finally I took her home, and as we still couldn't tear ourselves away from each other at her door an hour later, she took me up to her parents' flat, where everyone was asleep, and into her own room. We undressed in the dark and lay side by side in her bed, like two frightened children, until the waves of desire broke over us.

I hadn't been able to see her face in the dark, so now I sat in front of the wooden head again, trying to work out what marks such an experience might have made on it. The experience was a new one for both of us, those strange sensations of skin against skin exploding like fireballs, wildly and blindly felt, unchecked by any kind of visual involvement. It was still dark when I crept out of the flat.

I remember looking for traces of the night in her face next day, when I fetched her from work in the evening. Something in it must be different, I thought, yet I could see hardly anything except a touch of weariness about her eyes. But that wouldn't last. Had I wanted to see her changed, changed by me? Had I hoped to see traces of the desire I'd aroused in her? Am I the kind of person who's interested only in the marks he leaves on the world, fascinated by reflections of his own face? At that time I understood nothing, nothing at all, of the terrible dimensions of her fears.

After the day when she opened herself up to me in so many ways, however, my ear was quicker than before to hear undertones in the conversations I heard in the street, in shops, in lectures or in the tram. Even before that day I'd noticed, if not with such close interest, the muted hostility to be detected in the words and actions of many people in the city. Now it seemed to be everywhere. Indeed, it's quite likely that such signs of protest and discontent did increase or were more openly expressed during those weeks. You could hear people saying, more and more frequently, that the new rulers were nowhere near as firmly in control as their proclamations and official news bulletins tried to make it seem.

Soon we heard that troops had already crossed the border to liberate the country and its capital—official government reports spoke of withdrawal maneuvers going as planned. And then, one day, the soldiers who had stopped me on my journey and later marched into the city in triumph were out in force in the streets of the suburbs again, but this time in the disarray of an army on the run and gradually disintegrating. Sometimes, with the fury of the losers, they meted out violent punishment to a civilian onlooker for his mocking laughter. It was better to keep off the streets.

I find it hard to describe the mood among the girl's family and friends accurately, especially as I felt later that even then they didn't speak freely in front of me. I may really have seemed to them a Parzifal-like innocent, aware of the exciting, adventurous aspect of the situation, but with little idea of its attendant dangers and still less of what had made the people on both sides fight for this country and its capital city.

There was already concealed triumph in the eyes of the girl and her friends when we heard talk of the possible imminent defeat of the occupying troops, but they seemed subdued too, like patients facing a dangerous operation and unsure of its outcome.

"I wish it was all over," the girl whispers. We're lying beside each other on her bed and this time the light on the bedside table is on, so I can see her face close to me, lit from the side with heavy, sharply marked shadows, as in a woodcut.

I think about that remark for a moment. Then I ask, "All what?" Although she spoke softly, what she said sounds to me so sweeping, as if she were speaking of the condition of her personal world or indeed of the world itself, that it frightens me. Well, she may have meant that too: she may have wished the bloody battles were over, the oppression, the constant watchfulness, the fear lying in wait every morning as soon as you opened your eyes. But what else did she mean? That living under a threat were over, and the way we cling together at night in order to forget? Or that life itself were over, a life leading only from one kind of oppression to another?

She doesn't give me an answer. I look for it in the dark clefts of the face beside me, seeing a bitter line about her mouth that I never noticed before, the marks left by grief or I know not what, and I dare not ask.

The sight of her face at close quarters, recovered in this way, enabled me to do some more work on the head, making it a little more like the image my memory was so slow to release. I tried to express the shadow cast over that face by danger, so as not to forget it, since it wasn't to be seen there later.

It wasn't to be seen there later—but I become aware of that only in writing the words down. I must remember what led to it.

There was chaos in the city at first. While the retreating soldiers were hastily moving out through some of the suburbs, leaving a few deserters strung up from street lights or trees in the parks, the tanks of the new conquerors were lumbering toward the center from the other side of the city, and the advancing infantry acted as if the entire population, without exception, had been on the side of the forces they had just driven out. There were certainly plenty of people who were, but I now knew those who had looked forward, if with some trepidation, to being liberated.

It didn't feel much like liberation at first. I remember the piercing screams of raped women, the rattle of machine guns, the incomprehensible, guttural barking of orders. Those who hadn't dared to leave home before now huddled in the farthest corners of the cellars. The operation was in full swing—painful and mortally dangerous, though it might save life in the end—and the dazed state in which I witnessed these things wasn't a general anesthetic but left memories behind, memories that fell into my consciousness like a rockfall once they had been knocked free.

However, conditions in the city didn't last as I've described them for too long. One day I suddenly realized that things were peaceful, at least by comparison with all the time I'd spent in this city to date. The ruins remained for some time, but the sight of them merely emphasized the feeling of being able to walk without fear through the streets where gangs of men were already beginning to clear the rubble.

"So now it's all over," says the girl. We have been walking together through the streets, stopping for a while because a fatigue party with picks was clearing the remains of a toppled wall ahead of us. I look at the girl's face, perhaps hoping to discover what she means this time. I look at it in search of her familiar features, but there's something missing, something I've always found in that beloved face before. I couldn't make out what it was at the time. Today, trying to recall that moment, I begin to suspect that I could no longer see the marks left by constant danger on her face, marks so indissolubly part of it in my mind that I no longer recognize it as the face I loved.

From then on we had difficulty in communicating. Perhaps it was because the end of that constant danger meant—for us or just for me?—the loss of a level of communication on which our language was in tune. I felt, with increasing frequency, that I was talking to empty air, and I suddenly found some of the girl's remarks disconcerting. The more I felt like that, the more clearly I saw myself as a stranger in the city, even in the girl's arms.

For a little while I'd thought I belonged there, but it turned out I was only a visitor after all: a visitor who had indeed been exposed to the same difficulties and dangers as the other inhabitants of the city, by the very nature of the situation, but who was now clearly separate from them again. Even the way I talked showed I was an outsider.

If I still wanted to stay, I would be expected to adapt, or anyway that's how it seemed to me. The city really did feel like a labyrinth now, and I would never find my way out of it if I didn't get out at this point. Or did the girl, in my mind, actually become the strange and menacing being who lurked in the maze, ready to swallow me up body and soul? I don't know how accurate I'm being here, or if such remembered impressions are really an adequate reflection of the situation in which I found myself. Perhaps I was simply following Parzifal's example; he was in the habit of leaving damsels as soon as he'd rescued them from danger, even when the happy consummation of a marriage was to follow the rescue. More likely I'm just inventing excuses for packing my bags and leaving without saying a final good-bye.

"So now it's really all over," says the girl. And now she really does mean everything there ever was between us. I needn't puzzle over her remark this time: the answer can be read only too clearly in her face. The fear has gone from it, the marks left by the threat of danger have gone too, but I leave them in my portrait, for they now seem to me almost the only familiar thing about that wooden likeness. I can see a trace of grief, grief she doesn't want to show me. And a great deal of bitterness.

She has followed me to the city where I lived and studied for some time after this episode. We are facing each other at a round marble-topped table in a café again, just as we did at the beginning. This time she's the stranger, or at least she seems to feel herself a stranger in this unfamiliar setting.

I look at her face so long and so hard that now I can add that last look of bitterness to the portrait. It sinks into the flesh of my subconscious like a barbed hook, ready to show me now, as my blade carves that bitter line beside her mouth, that it's still there inside me. No, as it finally turned out, I wasn't to be trusted.

I looked at her face for a long time, then, and when I could find nothing in it that seemed familiar anymore, I said, "Over. It's really all over."

I could find nothing else in my memory to help me complete that second head, although the surface of the face still seemed roughened by perturbations that troubled me now—had indeed troubled me then, and finally drove me to leave. I found a tin of wax in my rack of tools, below the rows of blades, and I hoped it would help me to smooth out the features of the portrait. But when I had waxed the wood and polished it with a soft cloth, I found the effect rather alarming. The contradictory elements in the girl's face stood out even more obviously, particularly that bitterness, which felt like a reproach. Something I'd tried to indicate with almost timorous caution, cutting away the thinnest shavings of wood, now accused me only too clearly. Was it just my own inconsistent behavior I'd projected on the girl's face? I didn't know, and I didn't feel able to free my memories from my own subjective perception of them.

As a critic of my wood-carving abilities, the monkey seemed to agree with me. I'd put the head back on the window-

sill when he entered the room, carrying my not very appetiz-
ing meal like the head waiter in a first-class restaurant (it
consisted of an unattractive gray mush made of a mixture of
coarse-ground grain, with a little chopped parsley on top as
the highlight). When he had put down the earthenware bowl,
he struck the pose of experienced art expert again, casting
me occasional glances in which I thought I saw something
like surprise. "More like a self-portrait, really," he said at last.
When I was about to speak up in defense of my work, he
added, "I don't mean that as criticism. What did you know
about women then?" And he bared his yellow teeth, grinning
impudently. But when, making an effort to inject some irony
into my tone, I asked whether he was going to mark my
work "Unsatisfactory" this time, he shook his head and said,
solemn as a judge, "Self-knowledge is acceptable too."

It was extremely irritating to see this dressed-up monkey
putting on the airs of a moral authority. But before I could
repay his arrogance in the same coin, he added, "Satisfactory,
perfectly satisfactory!" nodded condescendingly to me and
left the room, limping.

I could have thrown the third chunk of wood after him,
the one I hadn't touched yet, but I decided not to lower
myself to do it after all. Over the next few days that third
roughly shaped head stood beside the other two portraits,
turning a blind, unidentifiable face toward me, like the face
of the broken statue of Venus with which this story began.
And my memory of the goddess's battered face seems to have
led me very far astray, for at first I could connect it only with
you.

When we met by the statue in the park and I tried to hide
behind my cynicism, you'd already found out more about me
than I dared admit to myself. You probably even realized that
my retreat into biological theories about the dictates of our
hormones and so forth was simply a flight from experiences
of the kind that those two portraits brought out into the open.
A comfortable excuse for my own inadequacy. Someone must
have treated me badly, you said at the time, which was a

very considerate way of putting it: I ask myself now who exactly treated whom badly.

For a while I did wonder if I was supposed to be providing the monkey with a portrait of you, but somehow I couldn't see your face in that chunk of wood. The reason was probably not so much that it wasn't right for the wood as that I realized for the first time just how little I knew about you. I couldn't form any detailed picture of your face, so how, in the circumstances, could I even try to carve its likeness? The chunk of wood stood there on the windowsill, dumb and sightless, giving nothing away.

This went on until one day my monkey warder, seeing me sitting idle on my bed again, lost patience. He put my bowl down on the stool so roughly that the potato soup in it slopped over, went to the window, picked up the silent head and turned it round at an angle of ninety degrees, so that I would have seen its right profile if it had one. Tilting his head, he then took three steps back, regarded his work with satisfaction from that distance, gave me another encouraging glance, and finally, when I shrugged my shoulders helplessly, he left the room shaking his head over my dim-wittedness.

At first the face hidden in the wood that had been roughly split by hatchet blows seemed no more accessible to me after the monkey's manipulation than before it, and I eventually went to bed, after spending the whole afternoon looking at the head from every possible angle, trying to lure the face out.

When I woke the next morning, the first thing I saw was its black outline against the bright sky, looking as if it had been cut out with scissors. And now, still half asleep, I thought I saw something like the hint of a profile, a profile that did seem familiar. But it still took me a long time to remember where I had seen it.

At first all I knew was that the face had been important to me for quite a long time, and I tried to conjure up as vivid a picture as possible of everyone of the opposite sex who had ever played any part in my life: fellow students at university, dancing-class partners, schoolgirls, aunts, cousins, neighbors' daughters. But the profile at which the wood hinted didn't fit any of the faces I could dredge up from my memory; it fitted no living person I could remember. And yet the image of the face I sought stood out ever more sharply and clearly in my mind, dark against a reddish background, a face that had obviously always been there, although it didn't seem to belong to any living being.

Any *living* being—when I repeated the phrase, emphasizing the second word, I suddenly saw the picture before me as if one last veil had been pulled aside. That day I fixed the chunk of wood into the carver's bench.

The Third Portrait

I can see the picture now, a woman's head in right profile, drawn in charcoal on wine-red card. It hangs above and to the left of my father's desk, and it's been familiar to me as long as I can remember.

I am standing beside my father. He is sitting at his desk, writing on a sheet of paper in his tiny hand. He uses his thin black fountain pen with the gold nib, the pen I'm not allowed to touch. I am so small I can only just see over the top of the desk. While my father writes I watch him, not daring to disturb him. When he puts the pen down and lifts his head, he may look up at the picture hanging on the wall to the left of his desk. He often does.

Since first noticing that, I often go to my father's desk, even when he isn't sitting there working. I stand there, looking up at the picture. It shows the head of a woman looking to the right. I like the woman. Even though she's just a picture, her face seems very much alive, as if she were just about to say something to someone in her line of vision. That someone must have been standing there when the drawing was done, and she's looking at the person in the way you look at someone you love. Perhaps I am particularly fond of the woman because she looks like that, with large eyes opened wide.

I've often wondered who the woman in the picture is, but I don't know anyone who looks like that. Her dark hair is pinned up in the nape of her neck, like my mother's, but my mother's hair is smooth, a little thin and very neat, while the drawing of the woman's hair makes it look as if she had trouble keeping it up. The coils of hair on her neck suggest that if the comb holding it in place were taken out, it would flow down over her shoulders, heavy and abundant. A few untamed locks curl boldly on her forehead. No, it can't be a picture of my mother, or any of the aunts who sometimes come visiting.

I once plucked up the courage to ask my father about the woman in the picture.

"That's Liesl," he said, giving no further explanation. I realized it would be no use asking any more questions.

I now saw the picture so clearly that I began transferring the contours of the profile to the chunk of wood: the straight brow beneath the unruly curls, the strong nose, the full lips, slightly opened as if about to speak, the rounded chin. And at the same time, over the distance between me and the years of my childhood and youth, I remembered what part I had allotted to that picture in my childhood world.

Since the way the woman in the picture wore her hair reminded me of my mother's hairstyle, I thought she must be a mother too, though a very different one: a mother who would hug me tight when I was banished from my own mother's love for some reason or other, usually my own fault, and was therefore in particular need of comfort. While my real mother preserved a painfully cool distance at such times, suffering in silence, I took refuge with that other mother. I willingly (though silently) confessed my misdeeds to her, and then I immediately felt safe in her heart-warming embrace.

Moreover, I felt sure my father felt something similar when he interrupted his writing to glance at the picture. I don't know exactly what explanation I gave myself about his relationship with the other mother; perhaps I imagined him asking her advice when he couldn't get on with his writing, or just checking on her presence in order to immerse himself in that warm sense of well-being I had myself when I went to her for comfort. Anyway, I thought I felt something like a tacit understanding between us when I stood beside him at his desk and we both conducted our silent conversations with the other mother.

I never discussed the picture with my brother, who was a good two years older than me, and I suppose that initially my mother didn't take much notice of what I was doing by my father's desk, although she did tell me I wasn't to touch anything, and I most certainly wasn't to take anything off the faded green leather of the desktop.

The question of my father's relationship with the other mother didn't enter into my childish mind at all at first. No doubt, as children do, I was going by my own feelings for the picture and thought it only natural for other people to feel the same. Only definite knowledge of the background of such a relationship may shake such emotional certainties.

It is a summer's day. My parents, my brother and I are visiting my grandparents. I remember the flat, low-lying countryside and the meadows of tall grass and flowers. Grandfather sometimes picks a wild flower, shows it to me and tells me its name, looking lovingly at it through the gold-rimmed pince-nez perched on his narrow nose. Later we pass bushes and a few spreading poplars, before the path leads us on through ripening cornfields. My brother and I are walking in front now; behind us, in varying groups, come my grandparents, my parents and a family friend just back from several years in South America. I can still hear his high, rather squeaky voice as he says, "Oh yes, I'm quite a Chilean now." I turn and inspect his face for Indian features, but it isn't even tanned.

I have never seen this man before and, despite his pallor, I think him interesting, not just because he comes from South America and must have seen amazing things there, but because he has a funny pointed beard. I've only ever seen one like it in church, in a picture dark with age showing a pastor in a black gown and an ornate ruff.

As I walk ahead with my brother, we can't help hearing parts of the grown-ups' conversation. I am hoping to hear interesting stories, even tales of adventure, so I pay particular attention to what the bearded Chilean says. He has just been talking about immensely high mountain ranges with snow-covered peaks. I can't imagine them at all, not in a southern country. Then he asks my father all of a sudden, "The bigger boy is your first wife's, isn't he?"

It was thus that my brother and I discovered we didn't have the same mother. We both stopped, turned and stared at the Chilean in such astonishment that despite his volubility he began to stammer, realizing that we hadn't known about the first wife before. My father, who didn't particularly seem to like the man anyway, was having obvious difficulty in suppressing his annoyance.

That evening, when we were on our own again, my father told us that my brother's mother had died soon after he was born, and he had married my mother a year later. He hadn't meant to tell us until later, he said, in case my brother thought the mother he had now might not love him just as much as she loved her own child. When he said that, my mother took my brother in her arms and hugged him, as if to comfort him for a loss he'd never felt before.

Up to this point I thought the whole thing was rather exciting, but I didn't feel personally involved. The events we were discussing happened far too long ago for me to fit them into my own scheme of things. But then my father said we'd both always known his first wife from the picture above his desk, to the left of it, and he looked up at the charcoal drawing on the red background, the picture of my other mother.

This last piece of information went right to my heart. My other mother was his first wife! So did she belong to my brother now? Just to him? I decided not to give her up. If my brother was going to stake a claim to my own mother's love now, then I'd continue to draw on the love of the other mother. I'd really always known she was the *first wife,* while my brother hadn't guessed a thing. Looking at the picture, I felt a longing for the embrace of that first wife, the one who came first, before any other women I knew. It was like a pain that couldn't be assuaged.

After that I became a watcher, carefully observing everything that went on in the family. What did my father feel when he looked up at his first wife's picture? Did he feel the same longing for her embrace, a longing that couldn't be assuaged? Were we just talking about a series—first wife, then second wife? Or were they ranked in order of merit? Was I worth less than my brother because I was only the second wife's son? Second wives' children aren't usually much good in fairy tales: the first wife's child gets the shower of gold, the second wife's child the shower of pitch. And experience seemed to confirm my fears when I thought of the different degrees of approval with which our parents and family regarded my brother and me.

My brother was a tidy child and used to clear his things away conscientiously. He wasn't irritatingly fussy about it: he just liked his own part of the world to be neat, easily viewed at a glance, while my own mind would jump suddenly from one subject to another and I simply dropped everything to do with the first idea, leaving it where it was when I last wanted it.

Unfortunately, I couldn't convince other people that I knew exactly where to look for what I'd dropped when I wanted it again. (Well, I usually knew, anyway.) Neither my parents nor the cleaning lady nor even my brother showed any understanding of the chaotic structure of my room; so although

I felt perfectly comfortable in my own little world, my sense of inferiority grew with time. I was the second wife's son, wasn't I?

I fled all the more desperately to the other mother. She might not be looking straight at me, but her glance was always loving, never clouded, while my own mother, upset by my untidiness, only too often had a disapproving look in her eyes.

It's hard to carve a three-dimensional head from a profile drawing. I had soon reached a stage in my work where the line over the forehead and nose to the slightly opened lips and the beautifully rounded chin was recognizable, firmly imprinted on my memory as it was from so much staring at the picture, but I still had no idea what the face looked like from the front until the little photograph came back into my mind.

I am sitting on the floor by my father's desk, looking through an album of old, yellowing photographs. A woman I know looks at me out of a small picture that may once, long ago, have been stuck in a passport. She wears a broad-brimmed hat, almost like a *vivandière's*, set jauntily on the hair that spills out from beneath it. A few unruly locks have come loose and are playing around her ears as if she had just come in, windblown, from a walk across the autumn fields.

"Yes, that's Liesl," says my father when I look inquiringly up at him. I see the sorrow in his face.

For the first time I realize how much my brother resembles her: dark eyebrows curving gently toward the top of the nose, the straight nose itself, the full lips—he gets them all from her. As the envy rises in me, I feel the first wife's glance resting on me. This time she looks straight into my eyes, firmly and frankly, with the loving expression that's on her face when she looks to her right in the drawing, perhaps at my father. He may have been sitting there when the artist drew her, looking into her eyes as I look now. Her glance seems to me loving but serious, as if she knew I wouldn't see it until she looked out at me from the kingdom of death. It is a long time before I can take my eyes off that glance, and meanwhile I forget my envy. It can't withstand the look in her eyes.

So my father's first wife continued to be my comforter, my secret love, and I could be sure of *her* unswerving love when I needed it. And I needed it often, whenever I felt I had been neglected, misunderstood or condemned. For my mother was reserved in her expressions of affection. Later, I often wondered why I can recall hardly any hugs or even affectionate gestures. I am sure she can't really have been as cool and unforthcoming as she usually seemed to me in my childhood. She may have kept a strict watch on her own behavior to me, so as not to let my brother feel she might love me more than her stepson. And it's possible that spontaneous expressions of her love were inhibited by the constant presence of the first wife, kept alive by the picture, not only claiming my father's love but also attracting the devotion of the child she herself had borne as his second wife.

It's difficult, almost impossible, to stand up to the beloved dead whose images shine ever brighter in the minds of those who knew them in life, even the minds of those born later, who never met them. Dead people can't make any more mistakes, and if you remember them as loving, or you go by an unchanging picture that clearly shows their love, they can never disappoint you. It wasn't until much later that I began to guess something I saw more and more clearly now in the tower: how hard it must have been for my mother to live in the shadow of the beautiful picture of the dead first wife.

Busy with these thoughts, I was able to go on with the portrait. I had a model not just in my memory of the little photograph, but in the resemblance between the face seen full front and my brother's face, which I could still remember very well, although he went missing in Italy in mysterious circumstances while my parents were still alive.

It may be that since we lost him, his features have come to seem even more like his mother's, so that to some extent they merge in my memory, but the fact that my idea of the first woman in my life is so closely bound up with my brother must contribute a great deal to its significance. So I let their superimposed images guide me as I carved the delicate brows, the shape and set of the cheekbones, and tried to give the face that loving, serious expression that only the faces of the dead can wear in so steadfast a way.

When I was smoothing out the last irregularities in the portrait, I wondered whether my early devotion to the unchanging look of love on the dead woman's face might have kept me from pursuing the ever-changing nature of the living. The picture of the dead woman knew no moodiness, no ill humor: it was fixed for all time in a moment of love, which the artist may well have freed from the dross of ordinary reality. Could it be that, whether consciously or unconsciously, I had judged every woman I met later by the standards of that picture?

I put the third head back on the windowsill the same day. I couldn't add to the work I had done on it; everything I knew about my father's first wife came from those two pictures, and I wasn't even sure whether my memory might not have changed them long ago into monuments to my adoration. The marks of that adoration might well be the most characteristic feature of the portrait. I stood in front of it and looked at it. Once more the woman's beauty overwhelmed me, and the thought that she had now been dead for longer than I had been alive brought tears to my eyes.

Only when the portrait was back in its old place did I see that it was a little like you too. I can't really say if there is any resemblance between you and my father's first wife; perhaps I unconsciously projected traces of your features onto the dead woman's face because I was always looking for yours at this time, and I could no longer find it in the inaccessible chambers of my memory. Perhaps it's as well I have no very distinct picture of you; it means I'm always ready for the surprise of seeing you in a new and different light at every meeting.

I awaited my artistically inclined warder's verdict the next day like a schoolboy who isn't sure what kind of mess he may have made of his essay. When the monkey finally appeared with a steaming soup bowl around noon, he seemed to me more monkeylike than ever. After giving me my food, he limped with his knock-kneed gait over to the window, picked up the third head from the sill in his brown, wrinkled hands and held it in front of him. His outstretched, hairy forearms stuck too far out of the sleeves of his jacket. He tilted and turned my work to left and right, obviously to examine its three-dimensional effect in half-profile, then put it on the windowsill again and stepped a little way back to conclude his expert examination.

"So that's what you've been dragging around with you all this time," he said. "Amazing how the picture you constructed as a child has lasted!"

"Didn't she look like that, then—the first wife?" I asked, feeling disappointment rise in me at the notion that my idea had been so far from the reality.

The monkey's wide mouth twisted mockingly. "Ah well, you humans—which of you really knows what another person looks like?" he asked. "You hardly know yourselves."

"I hope you at least know you're a monkey," I said, angered by the moralist's irritating pedantry. But I didn't succeed in provoking him.

"I'm not so sure of that," he said, without any noticeable emotion, and as I looked at him standing there in front of me I wasn't so sure either. Suddenly he seemed to have shed every simian quality; he was more like the librarian in my dream again. He might not be particularly tall, but he stood perfectly upright in my room, and there was no mistaking the fact that his light linen suit fitted him perfectly as he made me a small bow, not at all clumsy or apelike, and told me I had completed my work to the satisfaction of the house and could go where I liked at any time. "However," he added, "you would deprive yourself of a special pleasure if you didn't first accept my invitation to come up to the roof terrace with me. The view of the island and the lake is particularly fine today."

And now everything seemed to be happening as it had in my dream. The librarian's wife was waiting for us in the corridor outside my door. He introduced me to her with such practiced courtesy that I thought it right to sketch a kiss on her hand, and then we all climbed two stories farther up, over creaking flights of wooden stairs. I remembered that in my dream I had hardly been able to communicate with the couple whom I must consider my hosts, and was surprised to find that I now understood every word they said, although I was aware that they were still speaking some foreign language with a southern sound to it; I couldn't have identified it beyond that.

The stairs finally ended on a landing outside a wooden door, and when the librarian opened it we stepped out into bright sunshine. The top of the stairwell was in the very center of the circular terrace, which was surrounded by whitewashed battlements of a swallowtail pattern. I followed the couple over crunching gravel to the edge of the roof. There was indeed a magnificent view from up here. The first thing to catch the eye was the wide expanse of the lake, shimmering with light and surrounded by gently rolling hills in the blue distance. A taller mountain range, barely visible in the haze, rose behind them.

As I looked at the view that gradually opened out, I was startled by a shadow passing overhead with flapping wing beats. Looking up, I saw a stork flying low above me, borne up on its great wings. It had risen from the broad, untidy nest built on the little roof that sheltered the top of the stairs. The female still sat on the nest, but she was flexing her wings, about to take off too and go down to decimate the chorus of frogs in the shallows on the banks of the lake. So threatening did the shadows of the great birds still seem to me that I involuntarily ducked.

At that moment I felt my hostess lay a hand on my arm, as if to point something out to me. In the dim light of the passages and the stairs, I had seen her face only vaguely, and up here on the roof she had gone ahead of me. With eyes only for the shimmering surface of the lake, I hadn't taken much notice of my companion. But now that I stood beside her, looking into her face, a beauty that seemed almost imperishable in its agelessness took my breath away. Her regular features radiated an immense vitality, although they were covered by a fine network of countless tiny lines, like those on the face of a very old woman.

As she stood there erect beside me on the battlements, her pale robe flowing out behind her, pressed close to her body by the wind, she resembled in that, and in every feature of her vital face, the little marble idol I had picked up from the debris in my dream. She was like the statue of a queen still powerful despite great age, even like a goddess looking down on her world. My eyes followed the direction of her pointing hand, which she had reached out in command or blessing or just to show me something, and then I saw the lioness down on the grass among the reddish rocks. I cannot say if my hostess had summoned her or if the lioness had come to the tower of her own accord. I hadn't seen her coming either: she was just suddenly standing down there in all her beauty and her power, looking up at me.

"Have you never called her by her name?" asked the lady of the tower, and only as I was about to reply did I realize that in fact I'd never tried it. She beckoned to the lioness, inviting her to come up and join us on the roof of the tower. My heart thudded as I watched the tawny-coated animal reach the gateway in a few bounds and leap through it. A little later she emerged at the top of the stairs and trotted over to us.

"And now it's time for you to try the power of your pearl," said the lady of the tower.

The lioness looked at me with her dark eyes, and for the first time I had no doubt whatsoever that she was looking at me out of your own eyes. Now I only had to solve the problem of finding a suitable way to give her the glowing jewel. She helped me by putting her forepaws on the parapet of the battlements where it was about waist-high, and raising herself on her back legs so that our heads were at about the same level. I was glad: now we could gaze into each other's eyes without either of us having to look up or down.

The librarian, or perhaps the smith, who still limped but otherwise looked nothing like a monkey now, had already withdrawn tactfully to the top of the stairs, as if he didn't wish to intrude on the intimacy of what was about to take place. Arranging it was obviously his wife's business. The lady of the tower stayed with us, but I felt rather than observed her presence now. I saw nothing but the lioness's face as I brought the shell out of my pocket, opened it and took out the pearl. For a moment I hesitated, not sure what to do with it. Then I pressed it into the thick fur above the lioness's eyes and called her by your name.

I expected to see you standing in front of me next moment. But I'd failed with that trick once already, and it didn't produce the desired result this time either, although I actually did think I saw you, but more as one suddenly sees the likeness of a beloved person in the mind's eye, as if that long-lost face had been lit by a flash of lightning and the visual image lingers on. That was how I seemed to see you.

At the same moment it suddenly turned dark, as if someone had switched off the illumination of the wide view over the lake like a light. I just had time to see the circular terrace on which I stood duplicate itself in a curious way. My two hosts rose upward on the shimmering blue disc that separated from the level where I myself was standing. That disc and everything on it, including the two figures now standing there rigid and motionless, became translucent and spun away into the impenetrable blackness, dwindling rapidly until it was only a distant point of light, and then it disappeared.

I stood there as if dazzled, still hearing the sound of my voice speaking your name. The sound rose to a mighty roar, a bronze ringing of the syllables of your name that shook the darkness, not just the impalpable darkness around me but the ground on which my feet still stood. Up to this point it had been solid, but now it began to quake and sway under the force of that resonant sound. I tried to cling to the wall that had surrounded the roof just in front of me, but there was no wall left for me to grasp, and then the ground under my feet gave way too and I fell, along with the disintegrating masonry, down and down in a fall as interminable as if the tower, the island, and everything growing and living there were being drawn into the lake by a monstrous whirlpool. I fell and fell, down into the dark. In the end I felt like someone falling from the immeasurable heights of another world to an earth that will not receive him gently.

I didn't land as hard as I had feared, but I was still jarred, as if I'd slipped on a scree slope and been brought up abruptly against sharp-edged rocks. Swearing under my breath, I scrambled up and tried to get my bearings. It was so dark that my eyes could see nothing but blackness. Moreover, it had begun to rain.

The first thing was to extricate myself from this pile of rubble, I decided, groping my way cautiously forward in what seemed to be a downhill direction. But my second step landed me up to my ankles in water, and some ducks, splashing and quacking, flew noisily up from the water just in front of me.

I panicked at finding water so unexpectedly close, for I was genuinely afraid the island had sunk into the lake, leaving only the ruins of the tower still above the surface. I stood there for some time, paralyzed with fear and waiting for the water level to rise slowly higher up my legs. Frogs began croaking quite close, as if they were making one last attempt to induce me to join their slippery company and save myself from drowning in this flood.

However, the water level stayed put, which reassured me enough to start exploring my immediate surroundings. Both my feet were in the shallows as I felt my way around, and I eventually concluded that apart from a heap of sizeable stones barely half a meter high, there was nothing around me at all except water.

I decided that I'd better stay on this tiny island in the middle of the vast lake and keep my eyes skinned for a boat to pick me up and take me ashore. But then the darkness was broken by two lights, quite close together and moving rapidly toward me. I heard the sound of an engine, and the car headlights shone through a few trees and bushes, showing myriads of raindrops sparkling in their beam. As the taxi passed me on the nearby drive, its headlights rested briefly on the surface of the little pond where I stood on the stones of the ducks' island, and I finally realized where I was.

My shoes and socks were so wet that I didn't even bother to take them off. I waded to the bank just as I was, through water that came up to my knees in places. In the process I disturbed a few frogs, which shot off, swimming rapidly away from this strange water creature coming ashore by night. My wet trouser legs slapped around my calves as I walked along the gravel path through the park.

Then the statue came into view again among the bushes. I couldn't help crossing the turf to look at it. I imagined that this time the broken goddess would have your face and look at me with your eyes. It seemed to me only logical: she'd shown me her shattered face at that first meeting, and the second time—although that was in a different place and she was in another form—she showed me the reflection of my own face. So she always showed me what I was looking for, and this time, I thought, after all the tests I'd undergone and to some extent had passed, I really was in search of you.

Which just goes to show you the sort of person I am again. I have to put everything into the kind of order that satisfies my sense of logic. First, second, third—my imaginative powers obviously don't get much farther, even when I've emerged with drenched trouser legs from a pond into which I fell from the unimaginable height or distance of a world far removed from all logical calculations. Do I find learning so hard that even at such times I'll erect mental barriers, trying to preserve myself from any surprises within their apparent safety?

When I looked at the torso, wet with rain, of course nothing had changed; it was as battered and mutilated as ever, and its shattered countenance bore no likeness to any human face. It told me nothing. The statue kept silent, and even before it was damaged I dare say it showed nothing but an abstraction devised by the human imagination and at odds with human reality.

So there I finally stood in front of that statue again, just as I did at the beginning of our story, and once again I wondered why it had been treated so violently. Perhaps someone really did want to bring the goddess down to his own level. Perhaps man has to injure divinity in order to recognize himself in it. Or perhaps divinity allows men to injure it so that the image will teach them to love others in its flaws. Maybe there was some point in exhibiting such a damaged sculpture after all.

At least I no longer felt the sight was too much for me. I turned away and crossed the grass to the path, taking no notice of the light rain, and went on toward the voices I could hear ahead. I was caught in the beam of the taxi's headlights as it drove back away from the castle. When it passed me, I tried to see if the driver was the one I'd asked to stop here by the statue, but no: there was a woman at the wheel. Her profile, visible for a split second, struck me as familiar. I watched the car until the red taillights had disappeared beyond the bushes at the curve in the drive, and then went on through the gentle rain in no particular hurry. Soon I saw the pale façade of the castle between the dark tree trunks. There were still lights in a few windows, and a few conference members were standing on the roofed forecourt of the entrance talking to each other. It looked as if I'd been gone only a few minutes.

Then I met you in the entrance hall. You were waiting at the reception desk, with your case on the floor beside you.

"Where have *you* sprung from?" you asked, looking at my sopping wet trouser legs.

"Another world, and straight through the duck pond," I said.

You smiled and gave me your hand. "Do you always have to make things so complicated?" you said. "A taxi's more comfortable, particularly in weather like this."

I still couldn't grasp the fact that you were there at last. "Why are you so late?" I asked.

Instead of answering, you put back the hood of your coat from your hair, and the first thing I saw was the pearl-sized, iridescent raindrop hanging from the tangled curls above your forehead like a strange jewel. Then I looked in wonder at your hair, untidy from the hood, at the scratched mosquito bite on your chin, at your nose, reddened by an incipient cold—but I didn't see just those superficial features, I saw the hopes and fears hidden in the depths of your brown eyes, the scars of the wounds suffered by the person who is you, the injuries of which I knew nothing yet. And looking at you like that, I saw all your marvelous imperfections, the many imperfections that make people in general and you in particular need love as much as you merit it, and so make you unique. Only then did I understand the wrong I would have done you in wishing to see your face as that of the perfect goddess. And I understood the wrong I'd have done myself too.

You didn't answer my question; you looked at me as if I must surely know why you hadn't been able to arrive earlier. I looked back at you, and it was as if I were seeing you for the first time. I realized how much a stranger you still are to me, even more of a stranger than the lioness on the steppes beneath the tower. Your face was a wild, trackless forest in which I would probably get lost, but that wasn't going to stop me. It seemed that only now was I really beginning my quest, and now it would depend on whether I could ignore the risks to myself.

I have no idea how long we stood there, looking into each other's eyes. At some point I realized we weren't alone, although most of the witnesses of our meeting were glancing tactfully aside, as if they hadn't noticed what was going on between us. All except for Erik, who had just come up from the wine bar and into the hall, and had no such conventional inhibitions. Erik stood in the doorway, looked at us quite openly, and grinned.

If you and/or a friend would like to receive the *ROC Advance*, a bimonthly newsletter featuring all the newest and hottest ROC books and authors, on a complimentary basis, please fill out this form and return it to:

ROC Books/Penguin USA
375 Hudson Street
New York, NY 10014

Your Address
Name _____
Street _____ Apt. # _____
City _____ State _____ Zip _____

Friend's Address
Name _____
Street _____ Apt. # _____
City _____ State _____ Zip _____